The Wings of Victory by Fred M White

Fred Merrick White was born in 1859 in West Bromwich in the Midlands of England to Joseph White and Helen Merrick who had married the previous year.

Joseph was a solicitor's managing clerk, who by the time the family moved to Hereford a few years later, had become a solicitor's article clerk.

Little is known of White's early years but what is known is that he followed in his father's footsteps and worked as a solicitor's clerk in Hereford. His father by now had also become a solicitor and times seemed quite prosperous for the family.

However in the late 1880's something went badly wrong for his father and he was imprisoned.

White had by now decided that writing was a more preferable career for him than the law. By 1891 Fred M. White, now 31 years old, was working full-time as a journalist and author, earning enough to support himself and his mother, Helen. By this time Fred's younger brother, Joseph A. White, had left home and working as a glass-blower.

In 1892, White married Clara Jane Smith. The wedding took place at King's Norton, Worcestershire, and the couple went on to have two children; Sydney Eric White (1893) and Ormond John White (1895).

As the century closed Fred's father had been released from prison and was living as a "retired solicitor", together with Helen, in Worthington in West Sussex.

By the time of the 1911 census, Fred M. White, now 52 years old, and his wife Clara were living at Uckfield, a town in the Wealden district of East Sussex. As the ominous shadows of the First World War gathered White had established himself as a popular and extremely prolific author. Indeed whether it was novels or short stories they flowed from his pen with a startling speed and many of them were initially serialized in the popular weekly and monthly magazines. His clever use of science to create imaginative and highly adventurous story lines was a particular talent of his.

During the First World War, both of his sons served as junior officers in The Royal Inniskilling Fusiliers.

The titanic struggle of the First World War and his sons' war-time experiences in it greatly influenced this phase of his writing. His novel The Seed of Empire (1916), describes early trench warfare in great and gritty detail. He went on to describe how the social changes after the war created many problems for returning soldiers as they attempted to fit back into a now peaceful society.

Fred and Clara spent their twilight years in Barnstaple in Devon, an area which also provided the backdrop for his novels The Mystery Of Crocksands, The Riddle Of The Rail, and The Shadow Of The Dead Hand.

Fred Merrick White died in Barnstaple in 1935.

Index of Contents

CHAPTER I

Once Lanton Place had been one of the historic landmarks in mid-Devon. What remains of it to-day is a mere shell, practically a ruin half-smothered in ivy and other parasites, and apparently hiding itself away in the wooded country as if half ashamed of the change that time has brought it.

At one time it had been, to all practical purposes, a castle, a long low line of noble buildings overlooking the Dart and dominating that part of the country. But that had been in the day when the Dorns were a great clan and the head of the family went into the field in front of a thousand or two of his own vassals and tenantry. The name is writ largely enough in the history of Devon.

To-day, however, it is another story. To-day Lanton Place consists of half a dozen rooms, mere shells hidden away behind thick ramparts of stone covered with ivy and clinging plants that served to hide the desolation of the place behind a mask of living greenery. For twenty years ago a disastrous fire had levelled most of Lanton Place to the ground, which was no bad thing in one way, for the fortunes of the family were as decayed as the building itself, and Major Dorn and his wife and daughter were more or less content to hide their diminished heads in what remained of a great historic house.

It had been the old story, told over and over again both in fiction and in fact. Two generations of reckless Dorns had wrecked the fortunes of the family and brought themselves to the verge of ruin. One farm after another had been mortgaged to meet dissipation and extravagance, and on the top of that had come a ruinous lawsuit which left Major Manby Dorn with practically nothing on which to live. But for the fact that the property was in Chancery he would not have been there at all. In his cynical moments he described himself as a caretaker, and that, literally, was exactly what he was. Some day an enterprising purchaser would come along and buy up the dilapidated estate with its weed-covered farms, which were a crying disgrace to the county, and turn it into smiling land again. Meanwhile Dorn clung there in his few rooms, which were still furnished with some taste, until the hour arrived when the Court would give him notice to leave. And, in the meantime, he contemplated the remains of the family story, the faded carpets and tapestry, and the few old pictures, with a certain melancholy pride and a bitterness that was but skin deep.

For he cared little or nothing for the family, of even his own reputation, so long as he had the wherewithal to pander to his own vices and dissipations. He was the last of his race on the male side, and there were plenty of people in the neighbourhood who declared that this was a good thing. For, sooth to say, Dorn was not popular. He was vicious and dissipated, absolutely and entirely selfish, a soured and disappointed man without a single redeeming feature. He was always well dressed, always beautifully turned out, and from time to time he managed, by some means known to himself, to obtain the funds necessary for an occasional jaunt to London.

What he did there neither his wife nor daughter knew, and, indeed, he would not have told them had they asked him. There were times, on the other hand, when he was practically penniless—times when he had not the necessary sixpence left for a cigar. And there were times, on the other hand, when cigars were plentiful enough and Dorn lived on the fat of the land—that is, so far as he was personally concerned. He had his own snug little sitting-room, where he kept his cases of cigarettes and his cases of wine, which he indulged all too freely. And these were the times when he expanded and became quite amiable to his wife and daughter, who, on the whole, preferred him in his darker moods. For that smooth manner and polished politeness of his almost covered a sneer or a sarcasm that at one time had brought the tears to Sylvia Dorn's eyes, but now she had grown out of that and outwardly she was hard enough.

A gloomy, desolate place on the whole, a place suggesting crime and misery, with its weed-grown paths and ragged lawns and overgrown shrubbery rambling up to the edge of the house. There were people in the neighbourhood, farm labourers and the like, who whispered of the strange things that took place there, behind the screen of green that nobody ever penetrated. They said that Mrs. Dorn was mad, that her husband's constant cruelty had driven her out of her mind, and that in all sorts of weathers she could be seen creeping furtively about the blackened ruins always searching for something with a rake in her hand. And perhaps there was some foundation for these dark legends, for an old servant of the family, now happily married, had spoken to intimates of the night when Lanton Place was burnt down, and how, on that dreadful evening, Dorn, in a fit of drunken passion, had thrown a lighted lamp at his wife. All this was legend of course, though plenty of people in the neighbourhood were prepared to believe it, and in this instance it happened to be true. It was true, too, that from then on Mrs. Dorn had never spoken a sensible word. Now and again some adventurous youth or sanguine poacher, approaching too near the house had seen that slim, sad-looking figure in black searching about in the charred ruins, like some poor woman hunting fuel in a wood. And the daring one had crept away, feeling just a little nervous and superstitious and rather afraid of encountering that pathetic vision there amongst the ruins.

So far, that was true enough. There must have been something more on that fateful night than tradition spoke of, some terrible shock that had robbed a beautiful woman in the prime of life of her reason.

There were plenty of people in the neighbourhood, of course, who could remember the time when Dorn had brought his wife home, a beautiful, sparkling, fascinating creature who had been a noted figure on the stage, both in London and Paris. Lots of people knew that Mrs. Dorn was half French, and in those early days, when things were more prosperous, and before the great crash came, she had been a popular figure in the neighbourhood. But for years now no local resident had called at Lanton Place. There were lots of people who were immensely sorry for Mrs. Dorn, and quite as many who would have held out their hand in friendship to Sylvia. But the girl had always kept them at arm's length; she was proud enough in her way, and though, like most girls, she longed for friendship, she shrank naturally from anything that savoured of pity or sympathy.

Sylvia was about twenty now, tall and slim like her mother, and inheriting her proud spirit and vivacious beauty. She had waited patiently enough for the time to come when she could turn her back upon that dreary spot and earn her own living, and for the last six months she had been touring the country with a theatrical company. But misfortune had dogged the venture from the first, so that, reluctant as she was, she had been glad enough to come back home again till fortune should smile once more.

She was wondering about the dismal grounds that fine summer morning, a morning so fine that even Lanton Place seemed almost attractive. She came presently by a well-worn track at the back of the house past a thick belt of laurels to the blackened spot where the main portion of the house had stood. Her eyes dimmed slightly as she saw that sombre figure in black raking over the dead ashes, as she had seen her mother doing many a hundred times. And then the look in her eyes changed to one of contempt and loathing as she saw her father coming in her direction from the far side of what once had been a lawn.

Dorn was smiling to himself as if something had pleased him. There was a cigar in his mouth, his well-cut suit of grey flannels bore the unmistakable mark of Bond-street. He was handsome, distinguished enough, despite the weakness of his eyes and the shakiness of his lips, unmistakable signs of the kind of life he lived. But still, he was a fine figure of a man, looking every inch the country gentleman, with an air that there was no mistaking. And as Sylvia looked at him and then at the pathetic figure groping there amongst the ashes, her lip curled scornfully.

"Ah, a nice morning, Sylvia," Dorn said, raising his hat gallantly. He always prided himself that no misfortune could ever make him forget that he was a gentleman. "A most delightful morning, my dear. Any news? Anything from those people in London?"

"I have had a letter," Sylvia said coldly. "A letter from the man I told you about."

"Ah, the man with the funny name?"

"Mr. Maxwell Frick, yes. He thinks, from my description, that Lanton Place would be ideal for the purposes of cinema photography. The firm that has engaged him are making a great picture, or rather a great drama, with Dartmoor for a background, and these people want a picturesque place like ours that suggests desolation and misery."

"Well, upon my word, they couldn't have selected a better spot," Dorn said cynically. "This might be a haunted house where a murder was committed. But the point is, Sylvia, what are these people prepared to pay—"

"I don't know," Sylvia said impatiently. "Mr. Frick is coming down here in a day or two, and you can make all arrangements with him. They won't want to use the interior of the house—at least, not very often—and they will erect their own studios here in the grounds. If it is any satisfaction, I believe that the firm is quite a wealthy one."

Dorn turned aside, humming carelessly. Then his eyes turned upon his wife, and they narrowed and his thin lips were pressed together ominously. There was anger on his face as he spoke, but his words were smooth enough.

"Don't you think, my dear," he said, "that you have done enough—er—gardening for one morning?"

Mrs. Dorn looked up with a vacant expression on that still beautiful face of hers. She held up one blackened hand as if for silence.

"Sealed lips," she whispered. "Sealed lips. But this I have found. Only this."

CHAPTER II

THE COMPLETE LETTER-WRITER

As Mary Dorn spoke, a scrap of paper fluttered from her fingers. It was apparently part of a charred letter or envelope, and had no doubt been there, protected from the rain by a fragment of charred wood, all these years. Dorn glanced at it carelessly enough, much as one regards some gaudy flowering weed which a child has gathered from a neighbouring hedgeside under the impression that she has found a treasure. It was only a tiny scrap of paper with the ink faded, a scrap of paper that had been evidently torn from an envelope. There were only two words "street" and "London, E.C."

"Ah, you are in luck this morning, my dear," Dorn said. "And now having done so much, don't you think it about time that you went in and looked after the lunch? Sylvia, I want you for a moment or two."

"What is it?" Sylvia asked defiantly.

She would have turned and followed her mother slowly into the house if her father had not detained her. She had only been back home a day or two, but she guessed what he wanted.

"I'd like you to help me," he said. "There is an important letter that ought to be written."

"What, already?" Sylvia demanded. "I can't do it, I won't. I told you before I went away that I would have nothing more to do with that sort of thing. Of course, you know where it will end eventually."

Once more Dorn's eyes narrowed, and once more his thin lips were pressed together.

"My dear child," he said, smoothly enough, "you must allow me to be the better judge of that. Besides, unnecessary as it may seem, we have to live. And when I tell you that I am down to my last five shillings you will see how pressing the situation is. As a certain philosopher once observed, 'there are people who have plenty of money and no brains, and other people who have plenty of brains and no money.' Therefore, by a natural evolution, the brains attract the money. You wouldn't have your mother starving, I suppose?"

"Oh, I quite understand your natural solicitude for my mother," Sylvia said bitterly. "You are—"

"There, that will do," Dorn said ominously. "You forget who you are talking to."

"As, I wish to Heaven I could."

Dorn's manner changed suddenly. He approached Sylvia and grasped her roughly by the arm.

"Enough of that," he said. "Now go and do as I tell you. I can't compel you, of course. . . ."

"No, but you can hit my mother through me," Sylvia retorted. "It would not be the first time. Oh, you make me tingle from head to foot with shame. And you have brought it all on yourself. You were not so badly off when you came into the property. And my mother had money too—more than enough for all of us. Why, her diamonds—"

"Are all a myth, my child, all a myth. I don't believe there were any diamonds. And if they did exist they were probably stage paste. At any rate, I have never seen them, though your mother did say something about them one time when we were on our honeymoon."

"I believe in them, all the same," Sylvia said. "My mother was incapable of telling a lie. I believe she is hunting for them now."

"Oh, pooh! That's a girl's romantic fancy. Let's be practical. I must have fifty pounds this week, and I can see a way of getting it. Don't be a fool. It's only a few lines I want you to write to a man who has more money than he knows what to do with. And you've done it before."

"Ah, yes, when I didn't understand," Sylvia said. "I blush for shame when I think of the scores of begging letters I have written on your behalf. Oh, it is bad enough to borrow money in any case, horrible to write to strangers and ask them for assistance. I understand now. Those letters I wrote were deliberate frauds, lies written to kind-hearted people. Oh, can't you see how criminal it is?"

"Ah, that's a nasty word," Dorn said soothingly. "A very nasty word, Sylvia. And perhaps, occasionally, I have overstepped the—er—bound of truth. But what can I do? We are practically penniless, and your mother—"

"Oh, I implore you not to bring my mother into it. If she were in a mental condition to know what is going on, she would shrink from it in horror."

"But, confound it, we can't starve."

"Why should we starve? I am capable of getting my own living, and therefore—"

"Oh, are you?" Dorn sneered. "Then what are you doing at home again? You started out bravely enough. You shook the ashes of the old home from your feet in the traditional theatrical way, but you came back, my dear child, you came back, as I, a man of the world, knew you would, and here we are, to come down to a practical basis, down to our last shilling. Why, by the end of the week, we shall actually be short of bread. And you know we couldn't get credit here for a pair of shoe-laces. How am I going to tell your mother that? Come, don't be silly, Sylvia. I won't ask you again."

Sylvia stood there, hesitating. It was all hopelessly wicked, indeed criminal, and her whole soul revolted against it. But she knew only too well, if she refused, that her mother would be made to suffer. Not openly or brutally, of course, but with those refined and polished little cruelties of which her father was a past master. She followed him meekly enough into the house presently, and sat down in the library to write the letter. It was the one room in the house where all the comforts and luxuries were gathered together, a room where Dorn spent most of his time working out his schemes.

He stood up now, a fine figure of an English gentleman, smiling and debonnaire, with a choice cigar in his mouth, whilst he dictated the letter that might have brought a blush of shame to the cheek of a harder rascal than himself. The address was a fictitious one, an address somewhere in London that Sylvia had used on many a revolting occasion before.

"Dear Sir (it ran)—

"May I venture, a mere stranger to you, in deep distress, to approach you on a matter that is exceedingly dear to an anxious mother's heart.

"I am the wife, or I should say the widow, of a man who once was a distinguished soldier. My name will convey nothing to you, and I will say nothing of my dear husband's services to his country; indeed, rather than drag his honoured name into it and have his record shown, even to a kind-hearted gentleman like yourself, I would rather that you ignored my plea altogether.

"But I must approach you, not on behalf of myself, but in the interests of my only daughter. For years now I have lived at a little quiet cottage in the country, where I have managed to keep body and soul together with the aid of my needle. My own friends I cannot approach; there are reasons why I shrink from doing so.

"I have managed to bring up my daughter and educate her in the station to which she was born. It has been a hard and weary struggle, but, thank Heaven, I have managed it. And now the dear child is twenty-one. She has been on the stage for the last year or more, and competent judges tell me that she is likely to go very far in her profession. She has just a magnificent offer from America, which will also enable her to help me considerably. But she has to get to America and purchase a wardrobe. This we find cannot be done for less than—"

Dorn paused, and seemed to be turning over something in his mind. Then he went on dictating.

"Um! yes—a hundred pounds. Cannot be done for less than a hundred pounds."

"Now you, sir, are a rich man, and, moreover, have a reputation for a kind heart and overflowing sympathy. And to you I appeal. This sum, which is a fortune to us, is nothing to you. But to myself and my daughter it means everything. She is a most charming and delightful girl, exceedingly popular with everybody, and is wrapped up heart and soul in her profession. She has to refuse this offer for the need of the money I mention, then indeed she will he heartbroken. And that is why I have adopted the desperate step of writing to you and imploring your assistance. Nobody but a mother could have done it. I have dragged myself to my desk like a body in pain. I have forced myself to write these words to you, and I cannot say any more. Out of your plenty, will you help us?

"Yours most gratefully,

"HENRIETTA MARVIN."

"Yes, I think that will do," Dorn said. "It is not too gushing, but just gushing enough. I can quite imagine a fool of a woman writing a letter like that."

"What's the address?" Sylvia asked coldly, as she took an envelope from the case.

"John Bevill, Esq., Baron's Court, near Tavistock," Dorn said. "I think that will do very well. Oh, one moment. A postscript to that letter. Quite an inspiration. Now, write as follows:—

P.S. "Since writing the above, I have thought it as well to enclose a photograph of my daughter. I have enough confidence in you to do this, and besides, I want you to see what the dear girl is like. You will return it, I know."

There, that's a touch of real genius."

Dorn stopped and smiled as he took the letter from Sylvia's hand. He glanced it over carefully, then proceeded to place it in the envelope.

"And whose photograph are you going to send?" Sylvia asked. "Where are you going to get it from? If—"

She started suddenly to her feet as a dreadful thought crossed her mind. Then she hastened up the stairs to her bedroom and flew to the mantelpiece, where an hour ago a photograph of herself in theatrical costume had been standing.

The photograph was no longer there.

CHAPTER III

AGAINST LONG ODDS

It needed no great discernment on Sylvia's part to see what had happened. One glance at the empty frame on the mantelpiece confirmed her worst suspicions. Beyond the shadow of a doubt her father had entered the bedroom and taken away the photograph for the express purpose of sending it to his intended victim. It was a cunning scheme altogether, and not the least cunning part of it was the way in which Dorn had lured her on to write the letter, even to the very postscript, so that she should not see the trap. And here she had walked blindly into it, she had rendered herself liable to a criminal charge.

She had seen quite enough of the world lately to know that. Surely her father must have been desperately placed before he would run a risk like this? In all the years that Sylvia had been his unwilling tool in his course of mean crime he had never placed his own hand on paper. Always he has written as if he had been a woman in distress, and invariably Sylvia had been his medium. But this was a different matter altogether. She had not the least idea what type of man this John Bevill was, but if he made inquiries and used that photograph, then there was just a chance that she might have to stand in the dock, and face a prosecution. The mere thought of it was terrible.

And here she was, at the very outset of what might be a promising career, face to face with the possibility of ruin and disgrace. She had not gone very far on the stage, it was true, the tour in the north had been a disastrous failure, but she had made one or two useful friends, poor ones, perhaps, but useful from a business standing. There was Maxwell Frick, for instance, a seasoned old comedian who bore all his misfortunes with a smiling face and who always fell on his feet. It was he who had introduced her to the Western Production Company, for whom she had done certain cinema work which had given satisfaction and had elicited the promise of further employment later on. It was this work that had led up to Sylvia having her photograph taken in connection with it, and it was this photograph which had been the cause of all the trouble.

So Sylvia had come home at the end of a fortnight's engagement with a promise for something better and more regular in the near future. For instance, the Western Company fully intended to establish themselves somewhere in Devonshire, and Sylvia's description of her own home had appealed to Maxwell Frick who seemed to think that the neighbourhood would suit admirably. On behalf of the Company he was coming down in a few days to make arrangements. It seemed to Sylvia as if she had found a really good opening at last.

But all this had been blown to the winds by that dastardly act on her father's part. The mischief was done now past all recall. She knew only too well that no tears or protestations on her part would induce Dorn to change his mind. He would only laugh at her; he would only tell her not to be a fool, and remind her in his flippant way that necessity knew no law.

Well, her mind was made up. She would not remain there to be made the victim of further conspiracy. She would go back to London, where, no doubt, the amiable Frick would find her at least with employment good enough to keep body and soul together until her services were required.

But how to get to London? That was the difficulty. Sylvia had only a matter of a few shillings in her pocket, not enough to take her farther than Salisbury. And even then she had made no provision for keeping herself on the way. But, all the same, she was resolved to go. She was doing no good there, and her presence in the house was calculated to do her mother more harm than good. She would walk the rest of the way from Salisbury and trust to Providence when she got to London.

Was it possible, she wondered, to see this John Bevill at Baron's Court before the begging letter containing her photograph reached him? She could walk to Tavistock in an hour or two, and from thence take train to Exeter. Possibly she might invent some plausible excuse on the way for getting her photograph back; she might even adopt some desperate expedient for getting hold of the letter. At any rate, it was worth trying.

She crept carefully down the stairs a little later on, cautiously avoiding her father, and made her way out into the grounds, where she knew she would find her mother somewhere. She walked along the narrow track in the grass which had been worn bare by Mrs. Dorn's footsteps in going backwards and forwards to the ruins. And there the unfortunate woman was, as usual, raking over the blackened ashes with a patience that had something pathetic about it. She looked up with uncomprehending eyes as Sylvia approached her.

"I am going away, mother," the girl said, much as if she were speaking to a child. "Do you understand, I am going away? I shall probably be back in a week or two, but I can't stay now."

"That will be plenty of time," Mrs. Dorn said in that strange monotone of cheers. "I hope to be finished by then. I may find it any time."

It was quite useless to ask her what she was seeking for, and so Sylvia turned aside with the pity in her heart that brought tears into her eyes. Some day the whole thing would become plain, but that time was not yet. And so it had gone on all these years, and so it might go on till the end. And what that end was, Sylvia did not dare to ask.

She struck off quite boldly and resolutely enough across the fields in the direction of Tavistock. Practically all she had in the world she carried in her handbag, which contained that slender purse of hers and its precious contents. She was not in the least cast down, not in the least daunted at the task that lay before her. At any rate, she was turning her back upon the so-called home that she hated and loathed more than any spot on earth. It was no use her staying there, either. If her presence there would have done her mother the slightest good in the world, she might have forgotten her outraged feelings and remained. As it was she was best away.

It was still quite early in the afternoon when she arrived at Tavistock and inquired the whereabouts of Baron's Court. It was a big house, she was told, on the main road, just on the outskirts of the town. She came at length to a pair of handsome iron gates, beyond which she could see a wide-spreading park, and the outline of a great house in the distance. Evidently the residence of a rich man, and Sylvia smiled a little scornfully as she realised her father's worldly wisdom in writing that fateful letter. She would have passed through the gates, but they were locked, and therefore she had to knock at the lodge and ask for admission.

The rosy-cheeked woman that came to the door shook her head.

"I'm afraid I can't let you in, miss," she said. "You see, no one passes this way unless they come here on business. I have strict orders to keep the gates locked because of the animals."

"Indeed?" Sylvia smiled vaguely. "Do you mean the deer?"

"No, miss. Mr. Bevill is a great man with animals. He has spent his time with them all over the world. He knows more about them than anyone. We have got all sorts of creatures in the park there. You will notice there is a high wall all round, and indeed, miss, it's wanted sometimes."

"But I want to see Mr. Bevill," she said.

"I am afraid you can't, miss," the woman said respectfully enough. "You see, he isn't here. He went away a day or two ago on some important business—"

"Perhaps you can give me his address?" Sylvia asked.

The woman shook her head.

"No, I can't do that either, miss," she said. "You see, my master's a very peculiar gentleman. He's got this beautiful place here, and two thirds of the time he never comes near it. He's always lending it to some gentleman or another, and indeed we've got two or three of them staying here now. But you see, Mr. Bevill, he's so wrapped up in a book he's writing that he can't think of anything else. He's off now in some quiet little bungalow of his somewhere writing—"

"But you can tell me where he is?" Sylvia said hopefully.

"Really and truly I can't miss. Nobody knows where the place is. We forward his letters to an address in London—some bank I think it is—and that's all I know about it. But I can't allow any stranger to come inside."

The woman was very civil, but quite firm, so that Sylvia was forced to turn away with a feeling that she had wasted her time. But, at any rate, she had gained something. She had learnt a good deal about the eccentric owner of Baron's Court, and, moreover, she knew now that the fateful letter containing her photograph would not reach its destination for a day or two. Her first impulse was to turn into some shop and obtain the materials to write a letter to him in which she could explain the situation. But, on the other hand, she had a certain duty to her father, callous and criminal as he was. She could not go out of her way to injure him and place him within the reach of the law. No, she could not do that. She made her way quietly along the road in the direction of Tavistock; she reached the station at length, and took a ticket as far as Salisbury.

She was proceeding in the direction of her platform when a voice behind suddenly hailed her. She turned and looked into the smiling, rosy face of a man who might have been any age between fifty and seventy. He was fresh and clean-shaven, with a humorous mouth and a pair of twinkling blue eyes that would in the most adverse circumstances have looked life cheerfully in the face.

"Why, it's Miss Dorn!" the stranger cried.

"Maxwell Frick!" Sylvia exclaimed. "Whatever are you doing here?"

The fat, rosy little man threw back his head and laughed heartily.

"I don't know," he said. "I came down in these parts on a little matter of business. And here I am, stranded, without a penny in the world."

CHAPTER IV

THE BUNGALOW

Sylvia smiled back again. It was impossible to feel depressed in the presence of Maxwell Frick. Here was a man who had been connected with the theatrical profession all his life, a sound and experienced comedian without a vice save his own incomparable optimism, and yet a man who never contrived to remain in a show, as he called it, for more than a month at the outside. He was known in the profession from one end of England to the other; he was popular, and yet most of his time he spent in a desperate struggle to live. A little more businesslike aptitude and he might long ago have had a theatre of his own.

And yet here he was, shabby and smiling, stranded on the platform of a local station miles away from everywhere, and treating the whole matter as if it were the finest joke in the world.

"How did it happen?" Sylvia asked.

"Well, it's like this," Frick explained. "I came down here on business for the Western Company, and before I started I clean forgot to give them my address. And I forgot to draw any money, either. I only realised I had nothing when I walked to the station just now. I was going to see you."

"Really? Why didn't you write?"

"Oh, I don't know. I suppose I forgot all about it. You know my way. I was coming to look at that old house of yours. They told me in London that if my report was all right they would send the secretary down here to try and make all the necessary arrangements with Major Dorn. But where are you off to? Where are you going?"

Sylvia hesitated, but only for a moment. She would like to have taken this friend into her confidence, but she could not; it was not possible just now to make a confidant of any one. Whatever happened, she must go through the next day or two alone. But, at any rate, Frick might help her at the other end. Therefore she would keep her counsel.

"I am going to London," she said carefully. "I shall be back again when you have made your arrangements. But that may be some little time, and there are reasons, Mr. Frick, pressing reasons, why I must find something to do."

Frick nodded his grey head sympathetically.

"Ah, I understand," he said. "You want a shop for a week or two. Well, I think I can manage that."

As he spoke he fished a dingy card from his pocket and scribbled an address upon it.

"You call there," he said. "And it will be all right. It won't be much, not more than two quid a week at the outside, but Coventry Martin will do that much for me. He hasn't forgotten the days when we were in the Cambridge Dramatic Club together. He will help you all right. And now, about this business of yours. Is your father of the same mind?"

"I think so," Sylvia said. "I discussed the matter with him and he seemed to be favourable. Oh, I must be candid with you. We are so desperately poor that we cannot turn our back upon money, however small it is. I am sure you will find it all right. Lanton Place is an ideal spot for your purpose, and, as I know the country so well, I shall be able to help you. And as soon as ever your arrangements are made, let me know. I shall be only too glad to come back again, only too glad to feel that I am earning my living."

"Oh, I shouldn't worry about that if I were you," the optimistic Frick smiled. "With your face and figure, my dear, you are bound to get on. Lor' bless you, directly our company gets going, you will be drawing your hundred quid a week and forgetting all about poor old Frick."

"I shall never do that," Sylvia smiled. "I shall never forget how good and kind you have been to me. What should we have done up north if it hadn't been for you? How should we have contrived to get back to London again?"

"Oh, that's all right," Frick said. "It's all in the day's work. Why, bless you, I shouldn't know what to do with myself if things went prosperously for over a month."

With which characteristic remark Frick saw Sylvia to her carriage and went his way smiling. Salisbury came at due length, and then gravely and resolutely Sylvia set her face towards London. She walked on till the darkness fell, after which she contrived to obtain a night's shelter in a tiny cottage on the far side of the Plain, and a simple breakfast at the outlay of a shilling. Then all the next day she trudged through Hampshire, until evening found her on the borders of the New Forest, and here she supped on a loaf of bread and a jug of milk picked up literally by the wayside, and that night she slept by the side of a haystack under the summer stars.

It was something in the way of a desperate adventure, but Sylvia was not frightened or in the least cast down. She knew that every step on the way was taking her nearer to London, and once there she had every faith in the introduction that Frick had given her. And even if that failed, she knew that there were one or two humble members of the company she had been with who, poor as they were, would be quite willing to share a dingy lodging with her. She calculated by the time she reached London she would have just four shillings left. And if that was gone then, her situation would be desperate indeed. But that was the thought that she put resolutely out of her mind.

About midday following she contrived, when in the heart of the New Forest, to enlist the sympathies of a kindly old dame, who gave her a substantial meal and the opportunities of a thorough wash, so that when she turned out on to the road again she felt almost as fresh as she had done when she left home. It was very quiet and lonely there in the heart of that beautiful country, and as she went along she was conscious, for the first time, of a certain uneasiness. It had turned very warm and sultry, and overhead the clouds began to gather in an ominous manner. And this was a contingency that Sylvia had not reckoned on. Whatever happened she must not get wet, and so far as she could see, there was every chance of her being drenched to the skin in the course of the next hour.

She pushed on rapidly till the heavy drops began to fall and the thunder growled ominously overhead. Then there was a vivid flash of lightning, followed by a crash, and then the rain came down in earnest.

Sylvia dodged under the trees, making swiftly for a little cart-shed thatched with heather that she could see in the distance. She was thankful enough to gain this shelter, and there, safe at last, for the next two hours she stood there looking at the blurred landscape through a curtain of drenching rain. And so it went on till night began to fall, and when it cleared up at length Sylvia found herself absolutely alone, without the least idea where she was or in what direction to turn.

Well, if the worst came to the worst, she must spend that night in the solitude of that lonely hut. Everything was absolutely drenched; the big drops were shaken from the trees, which were moaning of the wind that had got up, and, moreover, the floor of the hut was running with water. It was impossible to stay there unless she stood up all night, and equally impossible to find shelter within a mile or two so far as she knew. There was only one thing for it, and that was to get away from the trees into the open and find some cart-track along which she could make her way.

It was comparatively early yet, barely ten o'clock, and Sylvia was feeling her courage coming back to her again. She was not too tired to walk for another mile or two, nor did she despair of finding shelter somewhere. And so far as she could see presently when she reached a comparatively high piece of ground there was not a light visible in the whole world. Still, she held doggedly on with that fine courage of hers until away in the distance, on the edge of the moorland it seemed to her, she could see the twinkle of a friendly light. But the light was a great deal further off than she thought for, and by the time she reached it her limbs were trembling under her and she was feeling faint from want of food.

The light appeared to shine from the windows of a large bungalow that was fenced in from the road and backed by a fringe of high woods. This was no farmhouse, no labourer's cottage, Sylvia could see, even in the dark. She would have passed by and sought shelter elsewhere, but there was no light to be seen anywhere, and presently she took her courage in both hands and walked up the pathway.

But though she knocked and knocked again there was no reply, though from both sides of the rustic porch a light shone out. It was very strange, all so very still and ominous in that desolate spot so far from civilisation that Sylvia began to fear that she had stumbled upon some tragedy. Just for a moment she fought with a wild desire to fly back along the path into the friendly shelter of the night, then she got herself in hand again and tried the handle of the door.

It yielded to her touch at once. She crept inside and looked about her cautiously. She saw a big hall sitting-room, a room paved with flags with a large ingle-nook in one corner. It was a cosy, comfortable room, luxuriously furnished with fine old stuff; there were good pictures on the walls, and the floor was covered with skins of various animals. Opposite the door was a big roll-top desk littered with manuscripts and proofs, and on the desk a silver lamp. There were big lamps, too, on the side-tables, and in the centre of the room a dainty supper had been set out on an old oak table.

And yet, strangely enough, there was no sign of human life anywhere. It was all very mysterious and just a little awe-inspiring. As Sylvia stood there, her eyes roamed round the place, taking in everything from the luxurious meal on the table to a little pile of letters laid on one of the plates. With a spirit of pardonable curiosity Sylvia picked up the letters and turned them over in her hand. The second letter fluttered from her fingers and dropped on the floor.

Not before she had seen the address. It was the envelope in her own handwriting directed to John Bevill, Esq., at Baron's Court, and obviously forwarded on.

CHAPTER V

ON THE THORNS

Manby Dorn had taken no heed of Sylvia's characteristic outbreak when she had discovered the trick he had played upon her. He had seen her like that before. Many a time she had written those letters of his either in sulky silence or with a wild outburst of passion, and once, indeed, she had actually threatened him with a riding whip. But nothing had come of it, and in a day or two the usual cold and distant relationship between father and daughter had been restored.

Sylvia knew him for what he was, a fact that did not disturb him in the least. Indeed, why should it, when all the world had put a proper valuation on him and treated him accordingly? There were, of course, plenty of people in the immediate neighbourhood of his own class who had known him from boyhood, and there had been a time when young Manby Dorn had been welcomed everywhere. But that time had long ceased. Men of his own class met him and passed him as if he had been a stranger; there was not a woman within miles who would have spoken to him. Not that he cared; he was long past that. So long as he could have his creature comforts and retain a certain measure of credit with his tailor, nothing mattered. And the last thing in the world he thought of was to give any consideration to the feelings of his wife and child.

Therefore he folded his letter and posted it in his own cynical way. He would see Sylvia at lunch, no doubt, then the incident would be forgotten. But there was no Sylvia at lunch, and no sign of her anywhere in the house. This was rather unusual, and Dorn began to have his misgivings. For Sylvia had never behaved in this way before. She had been cold and contemptuous or blazingly indignant. And now, apparently, she had vanished, bent upon some scheme of her own. That she had little or no money he knew very well. That she had left the house and was seen walking down the road with a bag in her hand, going in the direction of Tavistock, he discovered later on from a road-member by the wayside.

It was useless to ask Mrs. Dorn anything, of course. She did not know what had become of Sylvia, and she did not seem to care. That confused mind of hers had long been past comprehension of anything.

When Sylvia was with her she seemed glad enough for the presence of her daughter, but once the girl was out of her sight she might have had no identity at all.

"Here, wake up," Dorn said. "What's become of Sylvia? Where's the girl gone?"

Mrs. Dorn shook her head slowly. No gleam of intelligence crept into those dark eyes of hers, those eyes that would have been as beautiful as any in the world had there been but one spark of expression in them.

"I don't know," she said. "Sylvia, who is Sylvia? And where has she gone? I don't know. I shall find it some day; I shall find it before I die. And then she will be happy and comfortable, and I shall die in peace."

Dorn turned away hopelessly. All this was so much beating in the air. And it had been going on more years than he cared to count. It was always the same. Whether he treated his wife cruelly or indifferently, or with an outbreak of passion, she met it in that absent way of hers; it formed a wall so thick than even all his cunning could not get behind it. And so it had been ever since that fateful night when, in a moment of drunken passion, he had hurled that lamp at her, and Lanton Place had been burnt to the ground. It never occurred to him that this tragedy had been the culmination of three years of torture and tyranny, and that the fine, sensitive mind of his wife had gone down before it. It never occurred to him that his neglect and sinful extravagance had led to this deplorable condition of things. It never occurred to him, when he was away from home spending his own money and hers, that he was leading up to a painful tragedy. All he knew now was that he had come to the end of his tether, and that he was saddled with a mad wife and a daughter who hated and despised him. And, indeed, things were very critical. He was at the limit of his resources. He could not think of even one of those little criminal schemes of his which had hitherto been successful. If this man Bevill failed him now, then within a few hours the Dorns would be on the verge of starvation. It was a black and bitter outlook, rendered all the more depressing by Sylvia's sudden disappearance.

Where was she? Where was she gone? Dorn asked himself over and over again during the next day or so. It had been so unlike Sylvia to go off like this. And Tavistock was not very far off. Had she revolted at length? Had she made up her mind that at last she would expose him? Was it her intention to call upon John Bevill and throw herself upon his mercy?

But no, she would never do that; she would never forget that he was her father, and that any confession of hers would place him in the reach of the police, whom he knew had been only too anxious to lay him by the heels for many years. There was comfort in the thought that Sylvia would not so far forget herself. And yet, why had she gone? Why had she disappeared in this strange fashion without saying a word to anyone?

Over this problem Dorn brooded for the best part of two days. He even roused himself so far as to walk into Tavistock and make a few inquiries. It was quite a relief to learn that Mr. Bevill was not at Baron's Court for the moment, so that if Sylvia had called there to see him she would most certainly have been disappointed. And beside, Dorn was not the sort of man to address that begging letter to Baron's Court without first having ascertained something about the man he was addressing. And it was characteristic of Dorn, too, that he cared absolutely nothing what happened to Sylvia so long as she did not betray him. He could have heard without a single regret that she had been found dead at the bottom of the Dart. He was thinking of himself always.

At any rate, it was good to discover that Bevill was away from home, that nobody knew where he was or when he was likely to return. So Dorn, neat and immaculate as usual, plodded his way homeward, relieved in his mind to a certain extent and, at the same time, deeply annoyed because he had failed with those blandishments of his to elicit a further meed of credit from a local wine merchant. There was absolutely nothing to drink in the house, his last cigar was between his lips, and the prospect was dreary enough. There was a certain amount of food which he partook of later on, seated moodily at the table opposite the wife, who never spoke to him now and, indeed, never spoke to anyone unless in reply to a direct question. It was like sitting at a table with a corpse, some dread skeleton opposite him that reminded him vaguely of the past. He was glad to get it all over presently and shut himself in the library.

And there he sat till the light faded and the stars crept out, one by one; sat there moodily with an empty pipe in his mouth, and an empty glass by his side. He heard the one old servant fasten up the front door, he heard his wife creeping restlessly up to her bedroom. Then he opened the window and stepped out into the still night.

"Heavens, what a life!" he murmured to himself. "What an existence! Where is it going to end? Where—"

He pulled up suddenly, conscious of a solitary figure standing there against the background of the ragged shrubbery. It seemed to him that the figure carried something in its hand.

"What are you doing here?" Dorn demanded.

"It's all right, sir," the man said civilly enough. "I didn't want to disturb you or anybody in the house. I am one of the warders from the convict prison."

As the man spoke he turned, and in the dim starlight Dorn could see that he carried a rifle in his hand. The sheen of his peaked cap was visible in the gloom.

"Is that so?" Dorn asked. "One of those poor devils managed to get away I suppose?"

"Yes, sir," the warder said. "Yesterday afternoon. There are a dozen of us out altogether and we have tracked him as far as here. We are bound to have him before morning. This isn't a bad hiding-place of yours, sir."

"Oh, you are about right there," Dorn said bitterly. "It's an absolute wilderness. But we've got no outbuildings he can secrete himself in. Have you been all through the shrubbery? Plenty of cover there."

"There are two other men with me, sir," the warder explained. "And we've been all over the place. Don't let us disturb you, sir. You can go back into the house with an easy mind."

"I'm not quite so sure of that," Dorn said. "I am practically alone here without a weapon, and the man you are looking after is pretty sure to be desperate. By the way, has he managed to change his clothes?"

"I don't think he has, sir—at least he was in prison clothes when he was seen by a workman a couple of hours ago. You had better go back to the house, sir, I think."

Dorn made his way listlessly back again and re-entered the library by means of the window. At any rate, this had made a pleasant little break in the most dreary monotonous evening ever remembered. He was half-inclined to stay outside there and join in the man hunt. But then he thought of that immaculate suit he was wearing, and decided that on the whole he was better off where he was. He sat there gazing into the darkness till the church clock struck one, waiting and perhaps hoping for something to happen. Just as he was about to close the window the crack of a rifle broke the silence. Then there was a shout, followed by another shot.

Dorn could hear a confused voice in the distance, then a figure flashed from the bushes and came headlong in the direction of the open window. It was no convict this, but a man dressed in a suit of dark grey with a smart cap on the back of his head. He came forward eagerly enough, furtive and desperate, and stood in front of Dorn with his hand on the window-ledge. Dorn could hear him panting with his exertions. Then, without any warning or invitation, the fugitive fell over the window-sill fairly into the room, and as coolly as his condition permitted softly pulled the window down.

CHAPTER VI

OLD FRIENDS

"Put that lamp out," he whispered. "Blow the lamp out and pull the blind down, Dorn."

There was a certain quick ring of command in the stranger's voice that caused Dorn mechanically to obey. Not that he was not nervous and uneasy, because he was. Dorn was by no means the sort of man that heroes are made of, and even if he had been so naturally, the life he had been leading of recent years would have taken all the nerve and courage out of him. But the fact that this man knew him was ominous. The way in which he spoke subtly conveyed the impression that one scoundrel was talking to another. With a hand that trembled, Dorn pulled the blind down and lowered the flame of the lamp. He would have put it out altogether but for certain prudent instincts.

"Who are you?" he asked hoarsely.

"Never mind that for the moment," the fugitive replied. "Yes, perhaps on the whole you are right. You always were a cunning beggar, Dorn. If you had put the light out suddenly, those devils outside would have spotted at once that something was going on. And I expect your reputation is pretty well known in this neighbourhood."

Dorn listened with a certain rising feeling of irritation. He knew that he was safe now from any violence at the hands of this audacious intruder. This man was in desperate straits, and he was certain not to be rash enough to lay hands on one who was shielding him from authority. And, moreover, though Dorn could make nothing of the blurred outline of the stranger's face, he could see that this man was not in convict garb, and that he had hit upon another adventure altogether. And with it all was the feeling of annoyance that we all experience when we recognise a voice without being in a position to connect it with its owner. And that was what Dorn felt. He was wondering where he had heard that voice before.

"But look here," he began.

"Shut up, you fool," the intruder interrupted. "They have got a pretty good idea where I am. One of those chaps outside must have seen me cross the open, or he wouldn't have fired. It was a bit of infernally bad luck running straight into the arms of those fellows. But then it's been one of my unlucky evenings. Ah, here they come. Push me under that sofa, behind that pile of papers. Ask them to come in. Tell them that you heard the shot fired and that somebody ran by just as you were pulling down the windows preparatory to going to bed. Now, go on; don't keep them waiting."

Dorn pulled himself together. On the whole, this was a congenial job. Here was some scoundrel who knew him, some forgotten accomplice in crime to whom he was doing a good turn, and there might be a corresponding advantage in it somewhere. Therefore Dorn proceeded to open the front door and admit a couple of policemen, together with a man in his shirt sleeves, who might, from his appearance, have been an upper servant.

"Sorry to trouble you, sir," one of the policemen said. "But this is Mr. Gregory Smith's butler. There was an attempt to burgle the house about an hour ago, and the burglar was traced as far as your grounds. By good luck some prison warders were hunting for a convict here, and the fellow ran into them. They very nearly had him, and we think he must have got into your house somehow. One of the windows was open—"

"It was," Dorn said. "I was speaking to the warders some time ago, and I have been sitting in the open window of my library ever since. I had just closed it, and was turning the lamp down with the idea of going to bed, when I heard a couple of shots fired. So, you see, there can be nobody here. We'll go round the house if you like, but I don't think you'll find a single door or window unfastened."

The policeman hesitated for a moment, obviously impressed by evidence as direct as this, before he suggested that it would be just as well to look around, which they did under Dorn's guidance, only to retire a few moments later fully convinced that there was nothing further to be done so far as the inside of the house was concerned. They disappeared presently, with many apologies, leaving Dorn to return eagerly to the library, where he had turned up the lamp.

"Now come on," he said. "Come out and let me have a look at you. You seem to know me well enough, but I prefer not to have all the advantage on one side."

With a laugh the stranger crept out from under the couch and stood there before Dorn, a fine, upright, handsome figure of a man with regular features and a pair of flashing black eyes. He was quite well-dressed, exceedingly neat and natty with his small black moustache and tiny pointed beard, obviously a gentleman to outward appearances, and a man certainly accustomed to move in good circles. His long slim hands were assuredly those of an artist.

"Well, don't you know me?" he asked.

"De Barsac," Dorn cried. "Victor de Barsac, as I am a living sinner. Now, tell me, what is the most famous sculptor in Europe doing here like this? And tell me, why is the spoilt child of princes and the darling of society up to this sort of thing? Oh, come de Barsac!"

"Well, you never know," the other man said, as he dropped into a chair. "I am supposed to be a man in the enjoyment of a princely income, and, to a certain extent, I am. But there never was enough money in the world for me, and there never will be. Light come, light go, you know. I tell you, Dorn, I am fairly up against it. I haven't a score of pounds in the world I can call my own, and moreover, if I can't lay my hand upon a few hundreds within the next few days, then I am as good as a convict. You remember, it was always the same with me. Now, how many years was it since we were in that little business together? It must be quite ten."

"Oh, never mind that," Dorn said impatiently. "What are you doing here?"

"Well, at present I am the guest of that distinguished scientist and eccentric millionaire John Bevill. I suppose you know his name well enough."

Dorn started, but controlled himself quickly. It was no policy of his to tell this old acquaintance in crime what he knew about the wealthy John Bevill.

"Of course I know his name," he said. "But what are you doing in his house?"

"Well it's like this. Bevill has a perfect menagerie at Baron's Court, and when I asked him to let me come down and make a study of some of the animals he was good enough to put Baron's Court at my disposal. He is not there himself. He is hidden away in some secret retreat, where he is finishing a book, and has left me and one or two other friends of his in charge of the house. Here I am, a potential millionaire, living on the fat of the land in a famous mansion and hard up for a five pound note!"

"No treasures there?" Dorn asked cynically. "Nothing you can lay your hands on?"

"Heaps of them, my dear boy, heaps of them," de Barsac smiled. "But that's too dangerous a game. The stakes are too big for that. I daren't touch anything there, and all the more so because Bevill is quite an old man and I know that I am down on his will for a thumping big legacy. And that's why I don't want him to know my desperate position. I had to have money, so I planned a little burglary of my own—by no means the first—on a house in this neighbourhood, and I should have got away with the stuff all right but for a bit of sheer bad luck. I was practically caught by that old butler and made a bolt for it in this direction. Then, when I got in a tight place, I thought about you, and that's just where my luck was out again, for I ran bang into the arms of a lot of warders who are looking for a convict. If I hadn't happened to have seen that window of yours open, I should have been nabbed to a dead certainty with the tools in my pocket. My word, what a sensation that would have been for all my dainty society friends! But I think it's all right now. 'Pon my word, you look pretty snug here, in spite of all I hear from certain shady acquaintances to the contrary. Come, give me a drink and a cigar."

"I am very sorry," Dorn said. "I haven't so much as a glass of beer in the house. And I smoked my last cigar yesterday. There isn't a pipe of tobacco on the premises. You seem to be up against it pretty hard, but at any rate you have got comfortable quarters where you have everything to your hand. I have struck a rotten bad patch. Literally I am down to my last few shillings, and I'm hanged if I know where the next are coming from. Haven't you got a cigarette?"

De Barsac laid a silver cigarette case on the table and Dorn grasped it with avidity. The Spaniard watched him with a cynical smile and a certain narrowing of his eyelids.

"Let's sit down and talk," he said abruptly. "So far as I can gather, we both seem to be in the soup together. You are no fool, Dorn, and there was a time when you didn't want for courage. Now, I must have money, and a lot of it. So far as I can see, so must you."

"I'd sell my soul for it," Dorn said hoarsely.

"Very well. Then you can come in if you like. It ought to be worth anything up to two thousand pounds—perhaps more. I have mortgaged all my commissions; in fact I can't raise an honest penny anywhere. So I must try the other track. Only I must have you with me, where I can show you the ground. Now, suppose you come over to Baron's Court to-morrow and stay the night. I can give you all the de Rothschild's cigars' and vintage champagne you can drink. Oh, dash it, you can bring back a case or two if you please, and as to a few boxes of cigars, well, they're yours for the asking. But mind, you must be careful. There are two other men staying in the house, not our type at all. But one of them is about as cute as they make 'em. Not that they will interfere with us. I am only giving you a word of warning. I can send a car over for you and we can go into our plans carefully. It's dangerous, I don't mind telling you that, but the stakes are immense. Now, in one word, Dorn, are you on?"

Dorn held out a hand silently.

CHAPTER VII

BARON'S COURT

Dorn sat in the luxurious library at Baron's Court facing de Barsac, who lounged in a big chair opposite him and discoursed more or less casually on the scheme that he had laid out. It was yet fairly early in the afternoon, and Dorn had arrived in the car which had been sent for him directly after lunch. He had come prepared to enjoy himself and hoping to do a fine stroke of business at the same time. He sat there with a choice cigar between his lips, well content with his surroundings and determined to take the gift that the gods had provided, and enjoy them as long as he possibly could. So with the prospect of comfortable quarters before him, and the anticipation of a dinner the like of which he had not enjoyed for a long time, he was quite prepared to wait upon events.

He had come over there with that complete wardrobe of his much as if he had been an honoured guest who had been invited indefinitely, and, indeed, so far as he was concerned, he proposed to make it as indefinite as possible.

"Upon my word," he said, "you seem to have fallen upon your feet here, de Barsac. You are, to all practical purposes, the master of a fine house without any of its responsibilities. But how long is it going to last?"

"I haven't the remotest idea," de Barsac said coolly. "As long as I can make it, you can depend upon that. You see, this is my position. I have mortgaged my commissions for about a year ahead by drawing money on account, so that I can't put my hand upon a shilling. I told you last night that I wanted some money desperately, so desperately, indeed, that I had to run a big risk, as you know."

Dorn flicked the end off his cigar. He had his own schemes to think of, and the question he proceeded to put carelessly enough to de Barsac meant a good deal to him.

"Um—yes, I understand," he said thoughtfully. "It is always my position. And I suppose the amiable old man wouldn't be disposed to help you?"

"Well, he might. He is very eccentric, but hot-headed and generous where he takes, but, at the same time, he doesn't entirely lack worldly shrewdness. Now, he regards me as a successful man, which, indeed, I am, and a great sculptor, which, without egotism, I am also. But if he knew the truth, he might possibly prefer my room to my company, and then I should be finished."

"But you say he is generous?"

"Oh, amazingly so. Never listens to a story of distress without putting his hand in his pocket."

Dorn smiled to himself. All this sounded very promising for his own little scheme.

"Well, I suppose we shall have to make the best of it," he said. "Now, we are quite alone here, where nobody can hear. Tell me what you have got in the back of your mind."

De Barsac hesitated. Evidently he did not care to utter his thoughts aloud, and, indeed, the scheme that he had in the back of his mind was so black a one that he hardly liked to mention it to a confederate even as unscrupulous as Dorn.

"Not yet," he murmured. "I haven't thought it out quite. It's very dangerous, so dangerous indeed that if anything came to light we should both have a strong chance of finding ourselves—well, don't ask me to be more definite."

"In goal, do you mean?" Dorn whispered.

"Yes, in gaol, and perhaps worse than that. You know what I mean."

Dorn wriggled about uncomfortably. Just for a moment his heart seemed to stand still. For there was no mistaking the dread significance of de Barsac's words. And, unscrupulous as he was, Dorn shrank back from the idea of taking life, for that was unquestionably what de Barsac meant. There was every evidence of it in the droop of his voice, in the averted glance of those sinister eyes of his and that compression of his lips.

"But we need not go into that yet," he said. "All I want to know is whether you are with me or not."

Dorn bent eagerly forward.

"I don't like it," he whispered. "I don't like it in the least. But there's one thing I like less, and that is the miserable poverty-stricken life that I have been leading for the last year or two. I never know from day to day how am going to live to-morrow."

"Well, don't talk about your scruples," de Barsac said.

"Scruples. Bless the man, I haven't one. 'Pon my word, I believe I was born without any. But this is a serious thing. I don't mind crime, I don't mind running the risk of imprisonment if there is a sporting chance on my side. But when it comes to taking life—"

"Who said anything about the taking of life?"

"Oh, nobody. Not in as many words. But you and I are here alone together and we understand one another, and that's what you meant."

"Well, suppose I did. What then?"

"Well, then, we shall have to discuss it some time or another. How much do you expect, I mean how much do you expect this eccentric old gentleman to leave you?"

"Anything between forty and fifty thousand pounds—perhaps more. And I want it now, Dorn."

"And you don't mind how you get it?"

De Barsac nodded gloomily.

"That's about what it comes to," he said. "I must have the money, and if you can help me, why I don't mind giving you a quarter of it. So now you understand. Only it will have to be very carefully thought out."

Dorn helped himself to a fresh cigar.

"I see that," he said thoughtfully. "Now if you and I were alone together here with the old gentleman it might not be so very difficult. But what about the other people in the house? Who are they, and how long are they likely to stay?"

"Ah, that I can't tell you," de Barsac exclaimed. "As a matter of fact, there are two of them, and I believe they both intend to remain here till Bevill returns. One of them is Sir Watney Gibson."

"Indeed!" Dorn said with some show of interest. "I suppose you mean the famous surgeon? The rather hot-headed Irishman who is always indulging in controversies with his confreres in the scientific papers."

"Yes, that's the man," de Barsac said. "He is hot-headed and impetuous, I know; but, at the same time, he is a long way from being a child in worldly matters. He gives you the impression of simplicity, but I should be very sorry to make an enemy of him, and the man who tried to deceive him would assuredly get the worst of it. His companion is a certain Lionel Markham, a young Oxford man who acts as his secretary. I believe they are down here on some scientific errand. They don't trouble about me, and I don't trouble about them. I have got a big barn out here in the grounds fitted up as a studio, and there I spend most of my time. It's a funny sort of household on the whole. Of course, I know it is magnificently furnished and everything here is of the very best. A man like you, who appreciates a good dinner and a bottle of the right sort of wine, will understand that presently. But Bevill thinks more of his animals than all the rest of the world put together. With the possible exception of Tring Park. Baron's Court boasts the finest private menagerie in the kingdom. And that's why I am down here. I never touch anything, but animals, as you know, and I am making a particular study just now of some remarkably fine tigers. You see, I understand them. I have been studying all sorts of animals. With the exception of one particular vicious brute, there isn't a cage here that I haven't entered. And that is where my opportunity might come in."

Dorn's eyes gleamed.

"I think I understand," he said. "You mean some sort of accident? An accident that might happen to anybody who chanced to be with you some day—"

Dorn's voice trailed off as he spoke, and he saw that de Barsac avoided his glance.

"Well, something like that," the latter muttered. "It's all infernally difficult and whichever way I look I can see danger staring me in the face. That's why you may be able to help me. You were always a very cunning chap, Dorn. Think it over. There's time at least for you to do that."

Dorn sat there drawing nervously at his cigar and glancing round the luxurious room as if in search of inspiration, when the door of the room opened and a strange object came in. At the first glance it seemed to Dorn that he was looking at a man, and then, in the light of what he had just learnt, he saw that it was an ape, or rather a chimpanzee, a queer, wizened, misshapen creature in evening dress, a caricature of a man with long hairy arms and a preternaturally solemn face. It was so strange and unexpected that Dorn fairly started.

"What the deuce have you got here?" he stammered.

De Barsac smiled as he saw the startled expression on the face of his companion.

"Perhaps I had better make the introduction with due formality," he said gravely. "Let me introduce you to Vim, the most remarkable simian in the world. To all practical purposes Vim is a man; he can do everything but talk, and, indeed, Bevill swears that he has a language all right if anybody could only understand him. Apart from that, he lives just the same sort of life as you and I. He dresses for dinner, and comes down to meals with us, where he eats and drinks discriminately and takes a cigar afterwards. He has the bad taste to rather dislike me in the house. Here, Vim, come and shake hands with this gentleman."

The chimpanzee crossed the room and placed his hairy paw in Dorn's reluctant fingers.

"Heavens, what a household!" the latter murmured.

CHAPTER VIII

AT DINNER

A thin drift of cigarette smoke sifted over the dining-table at Baron's Court, where four men were seated in deep enjoyment of the coffee and liqueurs that followed a perfectly served meal. At the upper end of the table de Barsac, in his capacity as deputy host, lounged back idly in his chair, for he liked to sit there for half an hour or so after the evening meal talking idly on the events of the day. The big room was half in shadow, with a couple of lamps casting pools of light on flowers and ferns and fruit, on the ruby flush of wines in Venetian decanters and glinting on certain matchless old silver and priceless Sevres. Here and there, on the dark walls, a spot of light gleamed upon the electric bulbs that stood like lighted shrines in front of Bevill's famous pictures. It was one harmonious scene of luxury and refinement and wealth, and suggested nothing of the tragedy that was hanging like a black and sinister cloud over that fine old house.

Seated at the head of the table there, de Barsac looked the role he was playing to the life. He gave the impression of power and strength and success in every line of him. His handsome face was lit up with a pleasant smile, though there were people who declared that his eyes were a little too close together and that those strong lips of his were thin and cruel. But then, no great man is without his enemies.

The elderly man seated opposite to him, the man with the youthful face and quick, restless manner, was Sir Watney Gibson, the famous surgeon, and perhaps, in his fierce moments, the most pugnacious man that ever made a reputation in Harley-street. Always ready to fight for his theories, and somewhat intolerant of the opinions of other people, he was yet one of the kindliest of Irishmen and a veritable boy in heart, despite his seventy odd years. But if any criminal ever deluded himself with the idea that this manner covered a native simplicity, then that criminal would have been mistaken. For more than one of them had found his way from the Central Criminal Court to the dock owing to the brilliant and amazing research of Watney Gibson. The young man on his left was his distant relative and assistant, Lionel Markham, a young Oxford man who was just beginning to make a mark for himself.

The figures round the table were completed by the chimpanzee, who lounged there with a cigarette in his mouth and a tiny liqueur glass at his elbow, a quaint imitation of a man of the world in a mood of relaxation. Those queer little eyes of his seemed to be taking in all that was going on around him, and when the others laughed he threw back that wizened head of his and laughed too. He looked quiet and amiable enough now, though he had his moods and his little displays of temper, during which the whole household gave him a wide berth, for he had the strength of a lion and the tenacity of a bulldog. But these intervals were few and far between, and a reproachful glance from his beloved master was usually sufficient to restore the great ape to his normal serenity of mind.

Sir Watney, out of the corner of his eye, was watching Vim with keen interest.

"I tell you you are wrong," the great surgeon broke out into a sudden explosion. "Bless me, de Barsac, do you think I don't know? Why, I am just as well acquainted with the habits of animals as my old friend John Bevill. I tell you yonder creature, to all practical purpose, is a man. Look at him. Do you mean to tell me he doesn't know what I am saying?"

The ape seated there grinned and chattered.

"There, what did I tell you?" Gibson went on. "Ah, my boy, if we could only translate his language, we should know all about the missing link. I don't care a hang what the authorities say, I tell you, to all practical purposes, Vim is a man. Why, he's got the same teeth we have, and the same feet and hands. If you will give me some of your modelling wax, I will take an impression of his fingers and show you what I mean. You call it a paw, I say it's a hand. Look here, de Barsac, I wish you would do me a favour. You're about the only man I know who can do it. I want you to let me have an exact impression of Vim's arm in bronze. You'll know all about it when I go for that ignoramus Watson in next month's 'Scientific Review.' Will you do it for me? Or if you get the wax I'll take the impression now. What do you say?"

"Oh, I'm agreeable," de Barsac smiled. "It's all in my line, of course. I haven't touched anything but animals for years. That's why I am down here. I only wish I could afford to make a change sometimes."

Sir Watney burst into a roar of laughter.

"Oh come, none of your modesty, my boy," he said. "There isn't a man in Europe in your line who's making half so much money as you are. You must be drawing the income of a prince."

De Barsac smiled as he rose and rang the bell.

"Ah, that's all very well," he said. "But if you happen to spend the income of a king at the same time, that doesn't go very far. Yes, I rang, Jackson. Go into the studio and bring me back a large piece of modelling wax."

The well-trained servant returned presently with the wax, and for the next half-hour or so Sir Watney was busy taking the exact impression of Vim's hand and forearm. At first it had not been an easy job, for the great simian showed certain signs of resentment; but presently, as he glanced into the smiling faces around him, he seemed to enter into the spirit of the game, and smiled and chattered, till at length Sir Watney professed himself to be satisfied.

"There, my boy," he said. "I flatter myself that's a good job. If you reproduce that properly as you can, you will have the finest model of muscular strength in a condensed form that exists anywhere. And I believe Vim's proud of it. Look at him, grinning all over his face, like some pretty girl who is listening to a piece of subtle flattery."

The party rose from the table presently and scattered themselves about the house. Sir Watney made his way in the direction of the billiard-room, accompanied by his young relative, who had sat unusually silent throughout the whole of dinner. They played a game of billiards, then sat down in the solitude of the big room to a final cigar.

"What's the matter, my boy?" Sir Watney asked. "You're not usually so quiet."

"Well, sir, I'm a bit puzzled," Markham said. "And perhaps a bit uneasy too. Do you know anything about Major Dorn? Have you met him before?"

"Never saw him in my life," Sir Watney replied. "This is a funny sort of household, Lionel, and you meet some queer people here occasionally. I make a point of asking no questions when I come to Baron's Court. And if you take my advice you'll accept things as you find them. I always do. John Bevill is by way of being a philanthropist, and philanthropy finds itself in strange company."

"Yes, I know that, sir. But between ourselves, when we are alone here, how does the Major strike you?"

"Well, if you put it like that," Sir Watney said, "he doesn't strike me at all pleasantly. I don't like the look of the man. He is a gentleman by birth, of course, I know. Anybody could see that. But he strikes me as being cunning and shifty, and he drinks a great deal too much. He must have had quite a bottle of champagne at dinner, to say nothing of other wines and liqueurs. But if it comes to that, I don't care much for de Barsac either. It may be prejudice on my part, but I don't much fancy a man whose eyes are as close together as his. But why do you ask?"

"Oh, I don't know," Markham said. "You will remember before I came to you I had a fancy for going into the City. I spent two or three months in the office of a man called Lupas, who described himself as at general broker. As a matter of fact, he was a money-lender of the worst type and mixed up in many shady transactions, though you may be sure I was not allowed to learn much on that side. I left him finally because that sort of work was not in the least congenial, but I do remember seeing some correspondence which was not intended to fall into my hands between Lupas and a certain Major Dorn, who resided somewhere in Devonshire. I don't know for certain, but I should think this Dorn is a bit of a scoundrel. That's why I asked you that question. It's no business of mine, but I'm certain that fellow's here for no good. I wonder—"

Markham broke off and hesitated. He looked just a little confused and there was a dash of colour in his face.

"Go on," Sir Watney said encouragingly.

"Well, it's like this, sir," Markham proceeded. "When I was taking my holiday on the east coast last summer I amused myself for a week or so playing a small part with a travelling company. You know how fond I am of theatricals. And with this company I met a jolly old chap called Maxwell Frick, an elderly comedian of the Mark Tapley type who used to be at Cambridge years ago. And he introduced me to a girl called Dorn—Sylvia Dorn. A beautiful girl, well-bred and refined, and quite out of her class with a company like that. I saw a good deal of her at the time, and she told me that her home was in Devonshire. My dear uncle, she was a remarkably nice girl, and—well, I don't mind telling you I hope to meet her again. She didn't say much, but somehow I was sorry for her, and if this man Dorn is her father I am sorrier for her still."

"Um! quite a romance." Sir Watney yawned as he rose to his feet. "Good-night, my boy; I'm going to bed."

For a long time Markham sat at his open bedroom window looking out thoughtfully over the silent park. He was disturbed and uneasy in his mind and not at all inclined for sleep. Then he heard a door closed softly somewhere, and presently two figures appeared through the darkness—figures that appeared to be making their way cautiously across the park. Markham's eyes were clear and keen, so that he had no great difficulty in making the figures out as those of Dorn and de Barsac.

"Ah, I wonder what those two rascals are after," he murmured to himself. "No good, I'll swear."

CHAPTER IX

THE SILENT HOUSE

Sylvia stood there irresolutely, with the envelope in her hand. It was a desperate situation, and one that she recognised with a heart that beat fast and a certain dizziness that caused the room to revolve round and make her feel weak at the knees. A cruel situation for a girl to find herself in, and one that, for the moment, entirely overpowered her.

Her first impulse was to sit down on the nearest chair and give way to tears. But then tears were not Sylvia's way; she had been brought up in too hard a school for that. She could be soft and yielding enough when the atmosphere was right, but, on the other hand, she had learnt to look out for herself, and she had always known since she had come to years of discretion that those criminal practices of her father must end, one day, in dire disaster.

But she had always hoped and prayed that when the time came she would be far away from the trouble. And yet here it was, and gripping her in its toils like a serpent. And again there was the cruel and amazing coincidence of the whole thing. It was as if fate had conspired to drag her into it.

Well, whatever happened, she would speak the truth when the time came. She would not stand quietly by and see her whole career blasted for the sake of a worthless man, though he did happen to be her own father. And once she had made up her mind to this, the natural courage of the girl came back to her. Gradually she got a grip upon herself, gradually the room ceased to revolve round her, and every article there came back to her in its proper perspective. She opened the flap of the envelope to look inside and see for herself whether or not her worst fears were realised. And then she discovered that what she held in her hand was nothing but the envelope, neatly slit open, and the letter itself was not to be found. Somebody had opened it, no doubt, and had placed the contents on one side for further consideration. Well, she knew the worst of that, at any rate. And she would have been, perhaps, easier in her mind had she known what had become of the photograph. The letter in itself was nothing by comparison; it was the photograph that would cause trouble for her.

Just for an instant Sylvia was almost tempted to turn her back upon the silent bungalow and seek shelter and safety in the darkness of the night. If she could get away without being recognised, she might still save the situation.

The storm which had lulled for a time broke out with redoubled violence, the thunder crashed overhead, and the storm of rain, driven by the force of the wind, pelted on the windows like a volley of musketry. No, there was no escape that way. With all Sylvia's courage and resolution, she could not face the open country on such a night as this. Therefore, she resigned herself to the inevitable, and, pulling up a chair, seated herself in front of the fire. There must be someone about somewhere, she told herself; the people who inhabited the bungalow could not be very far away. It was impossible to believe the place had been actually deserted. So she sat there for half an hour or more until she heard the door open presently and a moment or two later a man entered the room.

Sylvia could see that his handsome face was wet, that his boots were muddy and sodden, and his neat black suit was dry enough, and he had the air of a man who is quite at home. His face was set and firm, almost like that of a mask; his black hair was brushed back from his forehead, and a pair of singularly lustreless eyes regarded Sylvia without surprise and much as if the new-comer had expected to find her there.

"I beg your pardon," she said. "I had to come here. I was walking through the woods when the storm overtook me, and I came here because I saw a light. As no one answered the door to my ring, I ventured to come inside."

It sounded very unconvincing, even to Sylvia's own ears, but apparently the black-haired man standing there in the doorway seemed to see nothing wrong about it, for he merely bowed in the respectful manner of a well-trained servant and proceeded without speech to arrange one or two articles on the table. Then he turned to leave the room.

"One moment," Sylvia said. "I am afraid you don't quite understand."

"I understand perfectly, madam," the man said. "You came here to seek shelter."

"Certainly, I did," Sylvia replied. "But that is not everything. Would you mind telling me to whom I am indebted for this kindness, and to whom this bungalow belongs?"

"It belongs to my master," the man replied.

"So I presume. But would you be good enough to tell me the name of your employer?"

It seemed to Sylvia that the man looked a little uneasy, but no more uneasy than she felt herself.

"Professor John Bevill," he said.

"Oh, indeed, and is he here?"

"Not for the moment, madam. But he will not be long. He won't be more than an hour at the outside."

With that the reticent individual with the black hair turned his back upon Sylvia and walked out of the room. It was all extraordinary, so amazingly unconventional, that despite her difficulties and anxieties Sylvia could hardly restrain a smile. Still, there was consolation in the knowledge that this silent, well-trained servant had accepted her presence there as a matter of course. Evidently he had regarded her as a lady, and equally he had believed all that she had to say—but by no means the kind of thing likely to happen in the ordinary conventional household. There was nothing for it, therefore, but to sit quietly before the fire and to wait the advent of someone more human than the man with the black hair. And all this time the rain was coming down in torrents and the bungalow was shaking with the force of the storm. Then, presently, it seemed to Sylvia that she could hear the sound of wheels outside, followed by the toot of a horn, and a moment or two later someone else walked into the room.

It was a woman of apparently about fifty years of age, tall and with a kindly face framed in hair that was rapidly turning to silver on the temples. The new-comer flung aside a big cloak, with a hood, and disclosed a typical nurse's uniform. Then she turned with a look of surprise in those dark eyes of hers, but with a tiny smile in them that gave Sylvia fresh courage. It seemed to her, just for an instant, that the smile gave place to a half-startled expression that might, indeed, have been one of recognition; but it was only for a moment, and then the kindly look was back in those dark eyes again.

Here was someone, Sylvia thought, who might be a friend. Here was someone that perhaps she could confide in. She rose from her seat by the fire and crossed the room.

"I don't know what you will say or think to find me here," she said. "But I hope that you won't resent this intrusion."

"On a night like this?" the other asked. "Oh, surely not. You are quite welcome."

"I thought you would say that," Sylvia murmured. "I thought you would say that directly I saw you. I was walking—well, I was walking—oh, perhaps I had better tell you the truth. I was walking to London, because I hadn't the money to pay my railway fare, and I got caught in this awful storm."

"You are very wet?" the other asked.

"I am not in the least wet," Sylvia cried. "I managed to get here before the rain came down in earnest. I saw the light of the bungalow through the trees, and I thought that I might beg shelter for an hour or two until the storm was over. I knocked at the door two or three times, but no one came, and then I began to feel that something was wrong here. I was terrified, too, by the storm and the loneliness, so I ventured to try the door and found that it was not fastened. So I plucked up my courage and came in expecting to find all sorts of horrors here. And then, to my surprise, I discovered that the house was empty. After that a servant—or I suppose he is a servant—came in, and I tried to explain. For some reason or another he took my presence here as a matter of course."

The woman smiled.

"Yes, he would," she said. "Garrass is an excellent servant, but the quietest and most taciturn man I have ever met. I don't think an earthquake would disturb him. A most peculiar creature, who hates everybody in the world except his employer, and for Mr. Bevill I believe he would die. But do sit down and make yourself at home. You must stay the night here now. You will excuse me asking, but have you had anything to eat lately?"

Sylvia's cheeks flushed.

"Oh, that does not matter," she said. "I am not particularly hungry."

"Is that true?" the woman asked. "No, I can see it isn't. Now, my dear young lady, I'm a nurse, and I understand these sort of things. Mr. Bevill won't be very long, and he won't be in the least annoyed if we sit down and have supper before he comes back. He is a bit strange and eccentric perhaps, but one of the kindest-hearted men in the world. When he hears your story I know he will ask you to stay here as long as you like. He always does. Now, do come and sit down at the table. And perhaps I had better introduce myself. I am a distant relative of Professor John Bevill's, and, as you see, a nurse—Nurse Coterell to be exact. You see, I have been taking a holiday for some time, and as the Professor wants a good deal of looking after I came down here to stay with him. He is by no means strong, and working all night, as he frequently does, is rather too much for him. Now, come along, and let me give you a little of this cold chicken and a glass of port. If I were to prescribe for you, I should say that this moment a glass of port is the very thing you want. Come along."

There was a trace of tears in Sylvia's eyes.

"You are more than kind," she said. "Let me tell you my name. I am Sylvia Dorn."

Nurse Coterell looked up swiftly.

CHAPTER X

Just for a moment it seemed to Sylvia that there was something like a challenge in her companion's eye, and, if not, that it was quite plain that the name of Dorn conveyed something to the intelligence of Nurse Coterell.

"You have heard of me before?" Sylvia asked.

"I have heard your name," the other said guardedly. "Do you happen, by any chance, to be related to Major Dorn, of Lanton Place, near Tavistock?"

"Yes, he is my father," Sylvia said.

Again that strange look came into Nurse Coterell's eyes.

"Dear me," she said. "That is interesting."

"I met him once," Nurse Coterell said in the same guarded tone. "But it is a great many years ago, and I don't suppose he would remember it. And so you are his daughter. I wonder why it is that I seem to have seen you before. Your face is quite familiar to me, and yet I could not be any more definite than that. You probably bear a resemblance to some chance acquaintance of mine. You know how we often think we have met people before, when there is no foundation for any belief of the kind. And yet your features fairly haunt me."

Sylvia laid down her knife and fork and played for a moment or two nervously with the stem of her wine glass. She had a deep instinctive feeling that she had found a friend here—indeed, after what had happened, how could she possibly doubt it? As she looked in that kindly face on the other side of the table the impulse to confide her troubles in Nurse Coterell grew more stronger, the idea of deceiving her became hateful. And deep down in her heart, too, she knew the reason why her features conveyed so much to her companion. Evidently this kind-hearted creature was in the confidence of Professor John Bevill, and beyond doubt she had read that artfully heart-breaking, begging letter and, no doubt, had become familiar with the photograph that had accompanied it. A moment or two later—and Sylvia had made up her mind.

"I am going to tell you the truth, Nurse," she said. "Have a good look at me again. Thank you. Now, though you have never met me before, I am sure, it is more than probable that you have seen a photograph of mine. Did you happen to see a photograph very like me, but in stage dress, and made up for the footlights, that was contained in an appeal that reached Mr. Bevill within the last day or two?"

"Why, bless my soul, yes," Nurse Coterell, cried. "My dear child, you have solved the mystery. You are the young actress who wants money to go to America. Well, if that's a fact and your story is anything like the truth, you are certain to get what you want from Mr. Bevill. But I don't understand. The letter you speak of came from an address in London, signed by a man who called himself your father, but I am quite sure the name was not Dorn."

Sylvia flushed to the roots of her hair.

"It seems very difficult," she said, "and very painful to me. But I assure you that I am telling you the truth and that I am Sylvia Dorn. And I have been on the stage, though I can hardly call myself an actress as yet. You see, I have a chance of getting something to do in London, and though I live in a castle, and my father is the head of an old family, I had not the necessary money to pay my fare to London, and that is why I decided to walk. And as to the rest, it is too shameful. Oh, I cannot tell you."

"I think I understand," Nurse Coterell said kindly enough. "Mr. Bevill has all sorts of appeals for money, some of which are genuine, whilst others are downright frauds. I expect that someone has been taking your name in vain. Someone has got hold of your photograph and used that pretty face of yours as a lure to draw money from the pockets of a man who is notoriously simple and kind-hearted. Perhaps it is someone you want to shield, someone you are fond of. Ah, my dear child, it is usually the way that we women are fond of those sort of people, when we care little or nothing for the less showy men who are honourable and upright enough. Yes, I see it is something of that kind; I can see it by the look in your eyes and the flush on your cheeks. But if it is a fraud, as I very strongly suspect, I am perfectly certain that you are no party to it."

"I thank you from my heart for saying that," Sylvia cried. "Indeed, indeed, I am no party to it. I knew what was happening, but it was too late to interfere. And now that you know the truth, will you help a little further? Will you try and induce Mr Bevill not to take proceedings—"

Nurse Coterell laughed aloud.

"Oh, he would never take proceedings," she said. "Why, if the individual you speak of, who has been using your photograph to put money in his pockets, were to rob John Bevill of the last shilling he had in the world, he would only smile and suppose that the thief was driven to it."

Sylvia found herself breathing a little easier. So far as she was concerned, she had told the truth, and, at the same time, contrived to shield her father. She would take good care that he did not benefit by that letter, and now, that being assured, she could go on with the supper that she so badly needed with a more tranquil mind. And yet the whole extraordinary coincidence left her a little strange and dizzy.

"Isn't it an amazing thing," she cried, "that out of all the houses in England I should have come here to-night? And yet there are so many people who sneer at coincidences. Now, that photograph of mine. I knew it was here, because when I came into the house and looked round for some clue as to the identity of the inhabitants, I found that envelope lying on the table there in my own handwriting. I was tricked into writing that letter. But it is an amazing thing altogether."

"The most amazing thing I ever heard," Nurse Coterell cried. "But, very fortunately, that picture of yours fell into the right hands. Mr. Bevill was most interested in it. He locked it up in his safe, with the intention of seeking out the original and helping her. My dear child, your photograph made a vast impression on him. I won't go as far as to say he fell in love with it, but it really was something like that. And you will fall in love with him when you meet; for everybody does."

"I am afraid you will think I am rather curious," Sylvia said. "But what is an old gentleman at his time of life doing out on a night like this?"

"Oh, more kindness of heart. A farmer in the neighbourhood had met with an accident just at a time his wife was ill in bed. So nothing would do but that the whole lot of us must go over there at once with all sorts of comforts and things till the doctor could make arrangements to have the poor man properly looked after. We have been there all the evening. But the car may be back at any moment now. There it is."

A few minutes later and Professor John Bevill himself came bustling into the room. He was a tall man with a scholarly stoop of the shoulders and a big, amazingly intellectual face in a perfect forest of white hair. He flung his wraps on one side and advanced cheerfully to the supper table.

"Well, that's all right, Sara," he said. "I left them all happy and comfortable with a doctor and two nurses in the house, and, God bless my soul, who have you got here? Who is this young lady who has been kind enough to bring the sunshine of her presence into my bungalow? And where have I seen her before? The lady of the photograph!"

"Perhaps I had better explain," Nurse Coterell said. "It is a most romantic story, and quite worthy of a place in a novel. Now listen, uncle."

Very rapidly the speaker went over the events of the last hour or so, laying particular stress upon all that Sylvia had said, and with much tact and delicacy skating over the things that Sylvia had not said. But the old man seemed to understand, for he rose gallantly from his seat and held out his hand to his visitor.

"I think I have got sufficient intelligence to grasp the situation," he said. "And I am not going to embarrass you with a lot of awkward questions, my dear young lady. If you want to shield somebody who has not scrupled to do you harm to put money in his pocket, then that is no business of mine. But from what I gather you need a friend badly, and I want to tell you at once that you have found that friend in John Bevill. The idea of a delicate little creature like you walking to London! I never heard anything more ridiculous in my life. No, I don't mean ridiculous, I mean courageous. Now what you are going to do is this. You will stay here and conduct those negotiations of yours by correspondence. You will stay here as Nurse Coterell's guest and mine till everything is settled. No, I don't want to hear another word. Now, sit down and get on with your supper which I interrupted so unkindly. Sara, I declare I am as hungry as a hunter."

"But aren't you very wet?" Sylvia asked.

"Not in the least," Bevill replied. "It stopped raining a quarter of an hour ago; as a matter of fact, it's brilliant starlight. Here, let's get on."

With which Bevill proceeded to make a hearty meal. He rang the bell presently, and the table was cleared by the taciturn servant, who moved about as if he were a piece of oiled machinery. Then the fire was made up again and the door closed, whilst they sat round the blaze talking as if they had been friends for years. It was getting quite late when there came a knock at the door, and Garrass came in creeping softly across the floor and whispered something in Bevill's ear.

The Professor jumped to his feet.

"At once," he cried. "Get both cars round without the slightest delay. We must go back to Baron's Court at once, Sara. I can't tell you exactly what has happened, but we must go. And of course this young lady will come with us. We can't leave her here alone. Please don't ask any questions. Run away and get your wraps on without the slightest delay."

CHAPTER XI

IN THE MOONLIGHT

Sylvia listened almost placidly to this strange statement of Bevill's. After what she had gone through the last hour or two, nothing seemed impossible or out of the question. What was going to happen in the next hour or two she neither knew nor cared. By sheer good luck, and because these people had accepted her statements implicitly, she had averted what a little time ago had appeared to her to be a terrible danger. No longer was there any chance of her being compelled to face a police inquiry in connection with an attempt to obtain money by false pretences. And now she knew that, whatever happened, her father would be safe so far as Professor John Bevill was concerned.

Therefore, beyond a certain sense of bewilderment and a feeling of regret that, tired as she was, there was no rest for her yet, she was quite prepared to be up and doing and take whatever part was assigned to her in connection with this remarkable household. She rose to her feet, but with a kindly glance Bevill motioned her back to her chair again.

"There is no occasion for you to trouble, my dear," he said. "My niece here will make all necessary arrangements and Garrass will look to the rest. I am only too sorry to be compelled to disturb you."

"Oh, please don't consider me," Sylvia said. "You have been too kind to me already. I am not very tired either. And if you like, I should be quite prepared to stay here alone. I assure you, I am not in the least afraid."

Nurse Coterell had already risen to her feet and had bustled out of the room, but she came back presently with the information that it was a brilliant moonlight night and that the two small cars were already outside.

"Then we had better get along," Bevill said. "You start, Sara, with Garrass, and drive straight to the house, and I will bring Miss Dorn along with me."

According to this programme they set off presently along the high road in the direction of Tavistock. It was likely to be a long journey, and indeed it was, for the moon began to slide down in a blue and tranquil sky and the first streaks of the dawn were coming up from the east some time before their destination was reached. From time to time Sylvia stole a glance at her companion, and though it seemed to her that he was looking just a little stern, he still bore his benign expression and kept up a flow of conversation on the way. Without appearing to be in the least curious, he contrived to learn a good deal about his companion, and seemed to be particularly interested in what she had to say about Maxwell Frick and the cinematograph company that mercurial individual represented.

"Now that is exceedingly appealing," he said. "And it gives me an idea. Strange that I never thought of it before. I wonder if you would help me?"

"I shall be only too pleased," Sylvia said, "if you will tell in what way."

"Well, it's like this, Miss Dorn. You see, at Baron's Court I have one of the finest private menageries in England. I have all sorts of animals there, both wild and domestic—indeed, I have spent a small fortune on them. For this is my hobby. I have been studying wild animals all my life. I have spent most of my time abroad, studying them in their native state; and I flatter myself that my researches have not been altogether in vain. I have spent nearly three years practically alone amongst the monkeys. With the exception of Professor Garnier, I know more of those creatures than any living man."

"And you want me—"

"Yes, I think so," Bevill interrupted eagerly. "I want you to arrange if you can for these friends of yours to make photographic studies of my animals. There is a splendid opportunity, and it won't cost them anything either. Now, do you think Mr. Frick would be agreeable?"

"I am quite certain he would," Sylvia said. "Especially if he can see his way to make a story out of it for the camera. I suppose you see what I mean. Didn't you say that you had a wonderful monkey?"

Bevill broke out enthusiastically.

"The most wonderful in the world," he said. "Vim is practically human. I suppose you have heard of those two famous apes called Max and Moritz?"

"Oh yes," Sylvia said. "I saw them some years ago when I was a child. They were wonderful."

"I don't think they are any more wonderful than Vim," Bevill said. "He can do anything but speak, and I believe, if I had the time, I could learn his peculiar language. I used to hope that I could teach him ours, but that was a dream. But he can do anything. He has his own bedroom and his own bath and looks after his own wardrobe. He eats and drinks practically the same as we do, and sits up to the table and appears to join in the conversation. At any rate, anything that amuses us always amuses him. He has his likes and dislikes just like human beings, and also has occasional outbursts of temper. And then, I must confess, he wants looking after."

"Is he dangerous?" Sylvia asked.

"Well," Bevill said thoughtfully, "I have never seen him actually dangerous, and only on the verge of it once or twice. But I am afraid that if any foolish person played a practical joke on him he might get out of control. And he is as powerful as any three men. But I don't think we need worry about that. No sensible person would ever attempt such a thing. Now, it occurred to me that if some of Mr. Frick's literary friends like to write a story or two round my animals, especially Vim, they might be able to do a good deal with it."

Whereupon Bevill lapsed into silence and drove a considerable distance before he spoke again. And Sylvia, sitting there, turning the events of the evening over in her mind, was equally silent. She was trying to picture to herself what sort of a household Baron's Court was, and what sort of a man he was who dragged people across country at this hour in the morning for what was apparently no better than a caprice. And when Sylvia was still debating this point the car pulled up in front of two massive iron gates, flanked on either side by long stone walls surmounted with three strands of barbed wire. In the moonlight behind the gates Sylvia could see a small lodge nestling amongst the trees. The whole thing was so familiar and yet so strange and visionary that she found herself rubbing her eyes and wondering if she were not reconstructing some half remembered dream.

And then it came to her with a flash. Of course, she had been to Baron's Court before. And this was Baron's Court, where she had come in a despairing attempt to see its owner and from whence she had been turned away civilly enough but quite firmly by the apple-cheeked lodge-keeper who had refused politely to let her pass through the gates. It was the same scene right enough, though, in the waning moonlight and in the early dawn, it looked just a little different.

From away in the distance somewhere, apparently at the back of the wide spreading park, came a plaintive cry or two, and then a deeper note that seemed to proceed from some angry animal. Then, too, there was a snarling cry that ended in a chatter of rage, and Bevill seemed to grow rigid.

"It's Vim," he said. "Now, what is the matter with him, and why is he roaming about the park at this time in the morning? He ought to be in his bed."

As Bevill spoke he leapt from the car and proceeded to hammer upon the gates. He rattled the bars again and again, but no response came from the people in the lodge.

"That's a very funny thing," he said. "What on earth's the matter with the woman? She's such a light sleeper as a rule. And besides, she knows that I'm accustomed to coming in at all hours of the day and night. You see, Miss Dorn, I have to make a strict rule that these gates are never left open. There are occasions when some of my wild animals get loose, and if one of them happens to enter the road I should find myself in no end of trouble with the authorities. What's become of the other car? They ought to have been here twenty minutes ago. They must have passed through the gates. I am beginning to think there is something wrong here."

"Is that why you came?" Sylvia asked.

Bevill did not appear to hear the question. He was rattling the bars again now, and displaying an irritation and anxiety that was beginning to get on Sylvia's nerves. Then, with an agility that would have done credit to a younger man, he climbed perilously over the high gate and dropped on the inside. Then he proceeded to hammer on the door of the lodge, until it was opened presently by a woman with her head in a shawl who looked out stupidly with her mouth open.

"What's the meaning of all this?" Bevill demanded.

"Eh, what's that?" the woman asked.

Bevill placed his hands upon the woman's shoulders and fairly dragged her into the open. Her eyes were half-closed, her lips were parted, and her face was pale and drawn. Then gradually she seemed to come to herself, as an intoxicated person might do in the fresh air, and she gazed at her master with dawning intelligence in her eyes.

"I am very sorry, sir," she stammered. "But I don't know what's the matter with me to-night. I was all right when I went to bed, and now I feel fairly dazed. Just as if somebody had been drugging me. My head is ready to split."

Bevill asked no further questions. He procured the key of the gate and brought the car inside. He was looking stern enough now as he shut off the engine and handed Sylvia out of the car.

"I think we'll walk the rest of the way," he said curtly. "Mrs. Leach, you go back to bed. I'll see to all this to-morrow. Come alone, my dear."

In absolute silence Sylvia walked by the side of her companion along the thick avenue, under the shadows of which it was intensely dark, till they came in sight of the house. Then suddenly Bevill pulled up and dragged Sylvia backwards into the shelter of a patch of laurels.

CHAPTER XII

THE SCARECROW

The assault was so unexpected that Sylvia could only wonder if Bevill had been suddenly afflicted with a phase of madness into which she seemed to have been plunged during the last few hours. She could see nothing except a little patch of moonlight on the far side of the avenue, could hear nothing but the hard breathing of her companion, and presently catch his whispered words to the effect that she must be quite silent and all would be well. That there was some great danger close at hand she realised. Perhaps some wild animal had escaped and was even at that moment stalking them through the bushes.

Then suddenly that strange chattering sound broke out, a chatter that was more than half-snarling rage, and a queer figure, like some misshapen human being, darted out from the shadow of one of the big trees and went headlong to the ground. The strange monstrosity rose again, and then Sylvia's amazed eyes made out the outline of a huge ape that seemed, so far as she could see, to be fastened by a long chain to the base of one of the big trees in the avenue.

"What is it?" Sylvia whispered. "What is it!"

"Don't be more frightened than you can help," Bevill murmured. "It's Vim. And, by Heavens, someone has played a trick upon him. I didn't think it possible that anybody could be so foolish. You remember what I told you just now?"

"Oh, I remember," Sylvia shuddered. "How cruel!"

"Worse than that," Bevill said angrily. "I don't know who is responsible for this outrage, but his life would not he worth a moment's purchase if Vim were free at this moment. Unless, perhaps, he is caught in a trap. On the whole, it is rather a good thing I came home this evening. There is something going on here that I cannot fathom. Someone has taken advantage of me. Well, anybody can do that up to a certain point. You stay here, my dear."

Bevill advanced into the open, followed a yard or two behind by Sylvia, who, despite the terror she was feeling, could not remain under the cover of the trees. She saw Bevill go forward quite cautiously and heard him call the monkey by name. The big chimpanzee stood up to his full height and beat his paws on his breast in a frenzy of passion. Then he sprang forward, and but for the chain about his foot, would have undoubtedly attacked the person that in ordinary conditions he loved best in the world. Bevill had only just time to spring back and save himself from the infuriated beast that struggled so hard to get at him.

And in this way the best part of half an hour passed, until gradually and by slow degrees, keeping just at a safe distance, Bevill managed to pacify the maddened ape, until at length it was safe enough to stroke him as he was now lying whining and imploring at his master's feet. He had been fastened there by a long chain, the end of which had been wound twice round the base of the tree, so that another few minutes elapsed before the animal was free. He was placid and quiet enough now, whining and fawning on his beloved master and evidently grateful for his release. Where he had tugged at his chain, one of his feet was cut and bleeding; there was not a vestige of clothing upon him, and for the time being at least, he had lapsed into his primitive state. Sylvia watched it all with a strange mixture of pity and loathing in her heart.

"He's all right now, my dear," Bevill said. "But if I had gone too near him when he was mad with fear and anger, most assuredly he would have torn me in pieces. And he can do it, too. There's not a man in the world who would have a chance in an encounter with Vim. What I can't understand is how he ever allowed anybody to fasten that snap lock round his foot. But somebody is going to account for it. Vim!"

The big animal came fawningly to his master's feet and looked into his face with an expression that was almost human.

"Vim," he repeated. "Come here and shake hands with the lady. She is a great friend of mine, and I want you to know her. Shake hands, my dear; don't be afraid. Don't show any fear of him, and he will respect you all the more. If you display any signs of that sort he will think you despise him."

Greatly daring, or so it seemed to her, Sylvia held out her hand, which Vim took respectfully enough and then proceeded to make her a courtly bow. After that he skipped on ahead as if he had quite forgotten his recent troubles. Bevill turned to follow when a cry from Sylvia stopped him.

"What's that?" she said. "Who is that standing there, just out in the moonlight? Can't you see a man there?"

"It certainly looks like one," Bevill said.

As he spoke he stepped across the open patch of moonlight in the direction of the figure. Sylvia following close behind. For a minute or two they regarded that rigid outline with a certain puzzled astonishment.

"Why, it isn't a man at all," Sylvia said. "It's a dummy, a scarecrow."

"So it is," Bevill cried. "Are we both mad, or dreaming, or what? What does it mean? Yes, a stuffed figure wearing an old suit of clothes of mine. I recognise that old Norfolk jacket. It's the one I always wear when I go into the pumas' cage. You see, animals go a good deal by sense of smell, and when I am wearing that coat I can do anything with my pumas. And I should like to know what all this means. But come along, my dear, I am very sorry. You must be utterly worn out with all this excitement, to say nothing of the fact that you were walking the whole of yesterday. I hope by this time the others have turned up. Let's get back to the house."

It was practically daylight by this time, just on four o'clock in the morning, and the sun was rising behind the avenue. Outside the main portico of the great house the other car was standing, and in the hall Nurse Coterell was anxiously waiting the advent of Bevill and Sylvia.

"Oh, here you are at last," she said. "I was wondering what had become of you. I was afraid you had had a breakdown."

"Oh, we've been here the best part of an hour," Bevill said. "We found an extraordinary thing in the park, which I will tell you all about after we have had a few hours' rest. Vim here has met with an adventure."

Vim chattered as if making an attempt to join in the conversation with the rest.

"Here, don't you interfere, Vim," Bevill said. "You go off to your bedroom. Off you go."

The big animal grinned, but trotted off obediently and then was seen no more.

"But where have you been?" Bevill asked. "When we reached the lodge gates you had certainly not been through. I had the greatest difficulty in waking Mrs. Leach up, and when I did, she had every appearance of a person who has been intoxicated for a month. I should very much like to know what is going on here. Something very strange, I am sure. Do you happen to know who is staying in the house?"

"I haven't the least idea," Nurse Coterell said. "Probably a few of Mr. de Barsac's friends. He generally does as he likes here in your absence. I'm not usually ill-natured, uncle, but if Baron's Court belonged to me Victor de Barsac would never be inside it. I don't like that man; I don't like the way he looks at you; I don't like the expression of his eyes. Oh, I know he's a great man, and perhaps the finest sculptor in the world, but I distrust him."

"Ah, a case of Dr. Fell, I suppose," Bevill said. "Well, there's no accounting for a woman's prejudices. But you haven't answered my question. You ought to have been here first, whereas we were a long time in front of you."

"Well, we took the wrong turning," Nurse Coterell said, "and went out of our way for some miles. Luckily, I have the front door latch-key in my pocket, and that's how we got in. I don't suppose any of the servants will be down for the next couple of hours, and I don't see any reason why we should disturb them. You go to your room, uncle, and get an hour or two's sleep. I will look after Miss Dorn. I have taken all her things into the dressing-room behind my bedroom, and will make her comfortable there. Now, come along."

Sylvia was thankful enough, a few minutes later, to find herself in a spacious dressing-room, where she flung herself on the bed just as she was with every intention of sleeping for hours to come. It was broad daylight now, and through the open windows she could hear the singing of the birds and the call of lambs in distant pastures. And presently, as she tossed about there, she began to realise that it would be a long time before sleep visited her eyelids, though she closed her eyes and turned her face resolutely from the light.

But it was all in vain; the strangeness of her surroundings, the recent adventure, and the amazing happenings of the night before chased one another through her restless brain, till at length she rose from her bed and wandered out in the corridor in search of a bathroom. This she found presently and, refreshed with a plunge into cold water, went back to her room, where she dressed herself as carefully as she could, and then creeping down the stairs opened the front door and passed on to the wide terrace that overlooked the park.

She did not dare to go too far with the memory of last night before her, but stood in a secluded corner of the terrace behind a thicket of flowering shrubs in pots, looking out across the landscape, where presently she saw two figures coming, as she thought, cautiously in the direction of the house. Then, as the figures passed her and disappeared under the big porch, she rubbed her eyes with amazement, not altogether free from fear.

One man she did not recognise; the other, beyond the shadow of a doubt, was her own father. She stood there holding her hand to her head for a few minutes, trying to grasp what all this meant, then she started as the echo of footsteps came in her direction along the terrace. A moment later she was looking into the surprised eyes of a young man.

"Lionel—Mr. Markham," she stammered.

"Why, Sylvia, Sylvia Dorn," Lionel Markham cried. "What amazing good fortune has brought you here?"

CHAPTER XIII

ON THE TERRACE

Sylvia smiled faintly enough, for just at that moment it seemed to her as if nothing mattered, and nothing in the world could be of the least importance. She was too dazed to stop and analyse her own feelings, too utterly indifferent to mind or to wonder at the extraordinary combination of circumstances that had brought her face to face with Lionel Markham.

"How do you do?" she said feebly enough.

Then the stupid banality of the remark appealed to her sense of humour, and she laughed unsteadily.

"I couldn't think of anything else to say," she went on. "Really, Mr. Markham, I am so utterly bewildered that I don't know what to say. And here we are, standing face to face at this hour in the morning as if it were the most natural thing in the world."

"Well, so it is," Markham smiled. "I knew perfectly well that I should meet you again, and I have been looking forward to doing so, though you did treat me badly."

"Badly? What do you mean?"

"Well, didn't you? For some little time up north you and I were the best of friends. Then you suddenly vanished without saying good-bye. Don't you call that treating me badly?"

"Well, I think perhaps I had better confess," Sylvia smiled. "I had to go. We all had to go, for the matter of that. The theatrical tour was an utter failure. We were badly treated as well. So I went back home, I managed that somehow, and I suppose all the rest of us scattered."

"I think I understand," Markham said. "And since then you have been doing nothing, I suppose. Well, it doesn't matter now. We have come together again, and this time I'm not going to lose sight of you, Sylvia."

He looked down into her face with an expression in his eyes that she knew and remembered so well, and a little flush rose to her cheeks.

"Perhaps I had better explain," she said.

And there and then, slowly and hesitatingly, but firmly enough, she told him everything. There was nothing that she disguised from him, not even the shameful story of that begging letter. It was not a pleasant confession, and one that she told with burning cheeks and downcast eyes, but it was finished at length, and in a strange, inconsequent way Sylvia felt all the happier for it. For she knew perfectly well that in Lionel Markham she had something more than a friend. And she had a feeling, too, that the time was coming when she would need a friend sorely enough. By great good fortune she had made one already in the shape of John Bevill, but then he was old and confiding, and lacking in knowledge of the world.

"I cannot tell you how sorry I am," Markham said gravely. "You poor unhappy girl!"

"Please don't speak to me like that," Sylvia said. "Please don't pity me or I shall break down altogether. I feel that I have had more than I can stand. But you'll help me, won't you? You won't think any worse of me for what I have said?"

"I will help you to the end of the world," Markham cried. "Sylvia, I want you to believe that there is nothing I would not do for you. And yet I don't see exactly what I can do. I have little or no money."

"As if that mattered," Sylvia said.

"Oh, but I think you'll find it matters a great deal. Now listen to me. There is something very wrong going on here, something criminal and underhand which spells danger to somebody, though as yet it is difficult to say who. Your father—"

Markham hesitated. It seemed difficult enough to speak his mind to Dorn's daughter.

"Go on," Sylvia said. "Don't let us have any misunderstanding. You hesitate because you are afraid of hurting my feelings. You are afraid of saying too much about a man to his own daughter. There is no occasion for all this delicacy; I know my father. He is capable of any wickedness. It hurts me to say so, but we shall gain nothing by hiding the truth."

"I am sure of that," Markham said. "And you know it. I must have been a poor hand at expressing my feelings if I did not show you when we were together that time I cared for you. Ah, Sylvia, that is a feeble way of expressing it. And though we have been parted all this time my feelings have undergone no change. I love you, Sylvia; I shall love you now and always."

As Markham spoke, Sylvia looked up in his face with an expression in her eyes that he could not misunderstand. He could not comprehend her feelings of admiration and gratitude, the blessed sense of having found a loving friend to protect her in the crisis of her life. Quite simply she put her hand into his, and he bent and kissed her once quietly and tenderly upon the lips.

"There," he said as he released her. "Now we understand one another. Whatever happens, Sylvia, it will be you and I together to the end now. We are going to the bottom of this trouble and save your father if we can. And I should like to do something for that unfortunate mother of yours too. We shall see. And meanwhile, perhaps it will be just as well if this understanding of ours remains a secret between us."

"I was going to suggest the same thing," Sylvia said. "Because I think I shall be able to help you. Oh, I am not afraid; honestly I think I have as much pluck as most girls. And despite everything that has happened, I am proud to think that I am a Dorn."

"I am quite sure about your courage," Markham said. "Who could doubt the pluck of a girl who starts to walk half across England in search of work? And now let me tell you the other side of the story. Let me tell you why I am here, and what is taking place in this amazing household. Now, listen carefully, and don't interrupt, because time is getting on and we may be disturbed at any moment."

Whereupon Markham told his story as briefly as possible; while Sylvia listened with all her ears.

"What are you afraid of?" she asked.

"Well, frankly, I don't know," Markham said. "But I mistrust that man de Barsac, though I believe Mr. Bevill thinks highly of him, and I don't understand why your father is here. I feel sure he is up to no good."

"I am sure he is," Sylvia replied. "It is a shameful thing to say, but wherever my father is, he is up to no good. I am very much afraid that he and this de Barsac have some business on hand which will certainly not be to Mr. Bevill's advantage."

"I shouldn't be surprised if it is rather worse than that," Markham said. "If it were merely a case of conspiracy to rob that confiding old gentleman, I should not so much mind. But there are darker forces at work here. Take the case that you told me just now about that extraordinary animal Vim. Who was it that chained the ape to the tree? and who was it that dressed up a scarecrow in what I call Mr. Bevill's working clothes? I tell you I don't like it, Sylvia, I don't like it a bit. I must think it all out quietly. I wonder if that extraordinary individual Garrass can help me."

"I wonder," Sylvia said. "Is he really devoted to his master? He is so quiet and taciturn that he almost frightens me. Can you trust him?"

"Oh, I have no doubts on that score," Markham said. "I don't know what strong bond there is between those two, but I am quite sure that Garrass would take his life in his hand any day to help John Bevill. Bevill is the one subject in the world on which he speaks eloquently. But we can put that out of our minds for the moment. What are you going to do?"

"What am I going to do?" Sylvia echoed.

"Yes, what are you going to do? You can't very well stay here. Unless I am greatly mistaken, there is going to be stern work at Baron's Court, and I wish to heaven I could see in which direction. Now, I think the best thing to do is to go home, go home and wait till you hear from that eccentric individual Maxwell Frick again. He will probably come down here within a day or two about that cinematograph business of his, and then you will be able to come here in the ordinary way without anybody asking questions. Wouldn't it be just as well if you got away home before your father knew that you were in the house?"

"But isn't it too late?" Sylvia asked. "Remember, Mr. Bevill knows who I am, and so does his niece. My name is bound to be mentioned. I must see my father, and let him know that though I have told about the letter he will be safe; indeed, so far as he is concerned, I have not told the whole truth. Mr. Bevill may guess, but I have not told him that it was my father who dictated that shameful letter. And I want to let him know that I have done my best not to expose him."

"Very well," Markham said. "Perhaps you are right. And now I think I had better leave you."

He turned away a moment or two later and left Sylvia to her distracted thoughts. She sat there for some time, looking out across the park and thinking over the strange events of the night before, until the breakfast bell rang, then turned in the direction of the house. As she crossed the hall in the direction of the dining-room, she came face to face with Major Dorn. He gave her one quick glance of astonishment, and something that seemed to Sylvia very like fear, before he spoke to her.

"What are you doing here?" he demanded. "What is the meaning of this? I suppose you know whose house you are in? If you have come here to betray me—"

"I have done nothing of the kind," Sylvia replied coldly. "I am not going to explain, but so far as Mr. Bevill is concerned you are safe. If he guesses, he will do nothing. But you will not get that money, whatever happens. Mr. Bevill will give you nothing. And I am not going to interfere with you. I am going back to my mother presently, and you can go your own way. You are safe for the present; but if you'll only take my advice, which of course you won't—"

"We'll have this out presently," Dorn threatened.

"We shall do nothing of the kind," Sylvia cried. "And don't forget that I have warned you."

She turned on her heel and left him.

CHAPTER XIV

ROGUES IN COUNCIL

Dorn lay luxuriously back in a big arm-chair in the room where de Barsac had set up his studio, and smoked his cigar with the air of a connoisseur. He had lunched well, a little comforted by the knowledge that Sylvia was no longer under the same roof as himself, but there was just the shade of anxiety on his face and a moody gleam in his eyes. De Barsac sat opposite him, with a cigarette between his lips.

"Well, what do you make of it?" he asked.

"I'll be hanging if I know," Dorn said irritably, "I don't like it a bit. So far the whole scheme has been an absolute failure. It's too dangerous altogether. Now, who would have expected that that confiding old idiot Bevill would have turned up in the middle of the night and just at the moment when we particularly didn't want him? Look at the fuss he made about that confounded ape of his. Just for all the world as if there was any harm in what you did. How on earth can you get your studies of animals in their savage state unless you make experiments? And I don't like the way in which that conceited young ass Markham asks questions. We shall have to be careful, my friend. You are too sanguine. You take too much for granted, your point of view is the only one in the world, and you are too fond of thinking everybody is a fool except yourself. The scheme is good enough if you give it time. But if you rush it as you are doing, it'll all end in disaster. And what sort of a disaster I don't need to put into words."

De Barsac flicked his ash off carelessly.

"Oh, that's all right," he said. "Bevill is as innocent as a child. And, besides, Gibson and that conceited secretary of his will be gone in a day or two. And once they are out of the way we shall be able to work things as we like. It is a devilish odd thing that they should have picked up your daughter in the way they did. I had no idea she knew them."

"Oh, that was a mere accident," Dorn explained. "She is a headstrong, impulsive sort of girl who must not be spoken to, and she—well, she ran away from home. Actually started to walk to London. Got caught in a storm by the way, and by the blindest chance hit upon the old man's bungalow. It night have been a serious matter, but as things have turned out, it doesn't matter except that her stupidity cost me a good many sovereigns that I can ill afford to lose."

"Oh, so you've been trying some little game of your own," de Barsac grinned. "All right, I'm not going to ask any awkward questions. The young lady has gone now, and we needn't trouble about her any longer. What we have to do now is to get Sir Watney Gibson and his secretary out of the way, and once the house is quiet we can manage all right."

"There you go again," Dorn exclaimed. "Didn't you hear all that talk at lunch-time about a cinematograph company coming down here? If the old man persists in this new hobby of his, we shall have those infernal actors swarming all over the place for weeks. I tell you, there is no time to be lost."

"You are about right there," de Barsac said grimly. "There certainly is no time to be lost. I must have a big sum of money by the end of this week. That scoundrel Henderby Lupas is putting the screw upon me. I can't put him off any longer. As you have met him before, you know the class of man I have got to deal with. As a matter of fact he is coming this afternoon, and may be here at any moment. I had a letter from him this morning with the Exeter postmark, so I suppose he's got another victim in the neighbourhood. I have told them to send him here directly he comes, I think I'll get him to stay a day or two if it is only to prove to him what a firm hold I have on the old man, and perhaps when he sees that he will be disposed to give me a little more time. If he doesn't—"

De Barsac shrugged his shoulders and lapsed into silence. For the next hour or so the two men smoked moodily without the interchange of a further remark, until someone rapped on the door of the studio and a thin, tall, wizened man with a face like parchment came twisting into the room and nodded curtly to de Barsac before he took a seat. Then he stretched out his hand coolly and helped himself to a cigar, after which he turned to Dorn and favoured him with a long stare.

"Ah, another old friend," he said in a voice that was low and husky and penetrating as the sound of a saw. "Major Dorn, unless I am greatly mistaken. Ah, Major, it is a long time since you and I did business together."

"Not too long for me, you old rascal," Dorn said. "What ill wind blows you here?"

With the end of his cigar Lupas pointed to de Barsac, who was eyeing him with no friendly gaze.

"Our friend the famous sculptor," he laughed. "The greatest man of his kind in the world. The friend of princes, the darling of all the ladies in England's fashionable drawing-rooms. The man who makes the income of a king, and spends it twice over. The man who ought to be rich, but is really poorer than the meanest city clerk; because not only is he up to his eyes in debt, but he has done that which the law calls wrong. And I can say this because Major Dorn is his friend, and because Major Dorn is not immaculate himself."

"What do you mean?" Dorn asked threateningly.

Lupas looked at the speaker out of a pair of eyes that gleamed malignant as those of a snake.

"Now, don't you try and bully me, my gallant warrior," he said. "I know, and if I liked, I could lay you by the heels too. There are few successful scoundrels in England whose history is not known to me. And when I am in the presence of the head of the begging letter fraternity, why, I take off my hat to him. But no nonsense, please."

"Here, don't let's quarrel," de Barsac said, as Dorn collapsed uncomfortably in his seat. "There's no occasion for any wrangling. Lupas, you want money?"

"I do," Lupas snapped. "And what's more, I am going to have it. Ten thousand this week, my boy."

"Oh that's all nonsense," de Barsac expostulated. "Now how much do I owe you altogether?"

"Say five times the amount."

"Oh, is that all? I thought it was more."

"It's more than you can pay," Lupas retorted.

"This week, yes. Next week, no. I'm not going into details, Lupas, but you shall have your money within a fortnight."

"Ah, you have been telling me that once a week for the last year," Lupas sneered. "Now, I'm not unreasonable. Show me a fair chance of getting my own back, and I am quite prepared to wait. In the circumstances, I can afford to."

"I should think you could," de Barsac cried. "Now, it's like this. You can see the sort of place I'm living in. I'm not going to say it's my own, because it isn't. But it will be, Lupas, it will be."

"Ump!" Lupas said. "I'd like to have proof of that. Of course I know that Mr. John Bevill is an immensely rich man, and that you are a great favourite of his. But there's many a slip betwixt the cup and the lip, my boy, and I don't see why I should wait indefinitely."

"And suppose you don't wait, what then?" de Barsac drawled. "You can only make a bankrupt of me."

"I can send you to gaol," Lupas hissed. "I can disgrace you in the eyes of Society; I can break you like a reed, and I'll do it, too."

"But not if you get the money."

"No, not if I get my money. I'm not vindictive; at least, not till I find out that a man has swindled me, and then if he can't make good, God help him. Revenge is a passion that never appealed to me. But, on the other hand, I don't spare a man who has robbed me. Now, come, I'll make you a fair offer. I am prepared to stay down here a day or two, and if I ascertain that there is anything in what you say—"

"Then you'll wait," de Barsac interrupted eagerly. "You can stay in the house, you can live on the fat of the land—a thing you are fond of at other people's expense—and you can see for yourself on what terms I am with Mr. Bevill. I happen to know that his will is locked up here in his safe, and it won't be my fault if you don't get a look at that interesting document. Perhaps that will satisfy you."

"It would certainly go a long way," Lupas admitted. "You must be on very good terms with Mr. Bevill if you can invite guests under his roof like this."

"He does just as he likes here," Dorn explained. "Mr. Bevill is only here by a sort of accident. He has placed Baron's Court entirely at de Barsac's disposal during the summer, and he spends most of his time writing in a little bungalow of his. You will be quite satisfied in staying here, Lupas."

"Well that's settled, then," Lupas replied. "And now I would like to have a look round and see the place. You may not think it, but I am very fond of those old houses. Some of these days I'll have one of my own."

"Well, go," de Barsac said. "Wander about at your own sweet will. I'll come out presently when I have finished the business I have got on with Major Dorn."

Lupas strolled away a minute or two later and sauntered along the terrace in the direction of the house. He stood there a minute or two admiring the view, till the sound of footsteps attracted his attention, and he turned to find himself face to face with Lionel Markham.

"Mr. Henderby Lupas!" Markham exclaimed. "Will you kindly explain what you are doing here?"

"Is that any business of yours, Mr. Markham?" Lupas retorted. "If you wish to know, I am a friend of de Barsac's, and he has asked me to stay here a day or two."

"I don't think so, I really don't think so," Markham said icily. "There must be limits even to the strange type of animal that comes occasionally to Baron's Court. Now, you and I know one another; I had the honour of being in your employ once. I didn't have your confidence, of course, but I remained long enough to discover the fact that Henderby Lupas is the greatest scoundrel in England. In common justice to Mr. Bevill, I cannot allow you to stay here; and if you force me, I shall have no hesitation in speaking quite freely. Now, you go back to de Barsac and tell him that you are not going to stay here."

With which Markham turned away and left Lupas standing there baffled and in a cold fury.

CHAPTER XV

With a definite course of action marked out in his mind, Markham strode along the terrace in the direction of the studio. There, without any particular ceremony, he broke in upon a whispered conversation between Dorn and de Barsac, who regarded him with anything but favour.

"Is there anything I can do for you?" de Barsac asked. "Just at the moment, however—"

"I quite understand," Markham said. "I am evidently intruding. But, in the circumstances, I could do nothing else. That man Lupas is a friend of yours?"

"Well, that depends what you call a friend," de Barsac drawled insolently. "It is an expression that is very much misused. For instance—"

"I am not here to argue any abstruse philosophy of friendship," Markham broke in impatiently. "I suppose that when you ask a man to stay under your roof, or at any rate under the roof of a house where you yourself are a welcome guest, you would not object to the word I use. Therefore, for the purpose of what I am saying, Lupas is a friend of yours."

"Is that a challenge?" de Barsac asked. "Because, if it is, I am quite ready to accept it. For the sake of the argument, Lupas is a friend of mine."

"Thank you," Markham said. "Now, de Barsac, you are a man of the world. And, being so, do you usually allow yourself to abuse the hospitality of a gentleman?"

De Barsac rose threateningly to his feet. There was a gleam of anger in his eyes as he turned upon Markham. But all this was lost upon the younger man, who returned the glance with a cold contempt.

"You had better sit down again," he said. "You are a fairly powerful man, I know, but in that respect I think I have the advantage of you. You are not in good training. I am. Now, sit down."

With a shrug of his shoulders de Barsac dropped back into his seat again. For he was beginning to ask himself questions. He was wondering how much this young man knew, and therefore he grew a little more conciliatory.

"All right," he said. "After all, what is there to quarrel about? But you must admit, my dear Markham, that your manner is not ingratiating."

"Neither was it meant to be," Markham retorted. "I understand that you have given this man Lupas an invitation to stay here for a day or two."

"Well, why not? For the time being, at any rate, Baron's Court is my own house. It has been placed at my disposal by Mr. Bevill, who, to all practical purposes, is my guest at the present moment, though he is under his own roof. And that being so, I have every right—"

"Yes, so long as Mr. Bevill is not here. And again, we have ladies present."

"Are you speaking about my daughter?" Dorn asked. "Because, if so, she has either left Baron's Court already, or she will be on her way before very long. And really, Mr. Markham, I think that as a father I am the best judge of the sort of people my child should associate with."

"You certainly ought to be," Markham said with emphasis. "But, well—frankly, I rather doubt it. Still, that's not the point. The point is that Henderby Lupas is a slimy scoundrel that no honest man would touch with a pair of tongs. I know what I am talking about, because for some months I had the misfortune to be in his employ. I was long enough with him to learn something of his methods, and as soon as I found them out I left him. In the City of London there is no greater rascal, and I cannot help feeling, de Barsac, that you are aware of it."

"Indeed I am not," de Barsac said. "And that's a very serious statement, Markham—a statement that no man ought to make without definite proof. Of course, if you are in a position—"

"I am not going into that," Markham said. "If you want me to give you documentary evidence, I haven't got any. But I assure you that I know what I am talking about; and if you persist in keeping that man here, then I shall make it my business to tell Mr. Bevill all that I know about him. Our host is a kind-hearted, unsuspicious man, but he can put his foot down upon occasion, and I am quite sure that you don't want to quarrel with him especially for the sake of a worthless rogue like Lupas. The man's presence is an outrage, an insult to all concerned. I might have gone to Mr. Bevill at once, but out of consideration of your feelings I have come here to tell you this. You may have had dealings with Lupas, very likely you have, but that is no reason why he should thrust his hateful personality into a house like this. And with that I have about finished. You can't say I haven't warned you."

With which Markham turned on his heel and left the two other men to their reflections. For a minute or two they stared at one another before de Barsac spoke.

"Well, what do you think of it?" he asked.

"Unpleasant, deuced unpleasant," Dorn replied. "And, besides, he means it."

"Not the slightest doubt about that," de Barsac said. "The question is, how much does he know?"

"You have hit the right nail on the head there," Dorn said. "How much does he know? For my part, I should say a great deal. He spoke like a man who is absolutely sure of his ground. And the first question is, is your friend Bevill as big a fool as he looks?"

"Oh, he's pretty simple. But he has his likes and dislikes, and he can be quite firm on occasion if he wants to. And besides, Lupas is not an engaging personality. We shall have to go slow, Dorn."

"Of course we shall," Dorn replied. "You know all the difficulties of our position—difficulties that may be absolute dangers before long. And that being so, we must not allow anything likely to prejudice to reach the ears of Bevill. You will have to tell Lupas the truth. You will have to get rid of him, however unpleasant the consequences may be. Make it plain to him that his presence under this roof is likely to prejudice your interests. Besides, he can stay in the neighbourhood if he likes. There are plenty of farmhouses about here where they put people up at this time of the year. And I don't suppose that young Markham objects to your friendship with Lupas as long as he doesn't come here. In other words, if we can get rid of him, nothing more will be said. And we do know what a poisonous old rascal he is."

De Barsac debated the point in silence for a few minutes before he rose to his feet.

"It's most infernally awkward," he said. "But, all the same, you are quite right. It would be a fatal thing if I did anything now to shake the confidence that John Bevill has in me. Besides, there are other reasons."

"Yes," Dorn said darkly. "There are."

"Well, come on, let's go and see Lupas and get it over. He won't like it. But when he comes to realise that it will be to his own material advantage in the long run, I don't think he is likely to object."

Outside Lupas was pacing up and down the terrace in an angry frame of mind which he made no attempt to disguise. He turned almost furiously upon the other two.

"Look here," he said. "Are you master in that house, de Barsac, or is that insolent young hound who has just ordered me off the premises?"

"Oh, he has tackled you, has he?" Dorn asked.

"Well, that's a mild way of putting it. He came up to me as if I were some tramp and ordered me off. Told me that if I didn't go, he would tell Mr. Bevill all about me. And now I want to know who is master here."

"Well, I am," de Barsac said with rather an uneasy laugh. "You see, Lupas, I am in rather an awkward position. I am practically the tenant here for the time, but I pay nothing and John Bevill foots all the bills. Usually, he gives me a free hand as to who I can ask here, and he would raise no objection to you if Markham hadn't been here. But then, unfortunately, he is here, and has just informed me rudely enough that if you don't clear off the premises he will disclose your disgraceful past to Mr. Bevill. If he does, there is certain to be a scene, because Bevill can be quite firm on occasion, and he has a niece of his here in the house. Look here, Lupas, don't do anything foolish. You've just got to put up with it. If that young man was in your employ for some months, as he says he was, he is bound to have picked up a good deal of information regarding your methods of business. I hope you won't mind this plain speaking, but we are three men of the world together here and a large sum of money is at stake. Your money as well as mine, remember. Now, what are you going to do? Brazen it out and find yourself escorted off the premises at the finish? Stick it and run the chance of losing all the money I owe you?

You'll never be as foolish as that. For the time being, that young man is top dog, and the sooner you realise it the better. Take it lying down for the moment."

"Very well," Lupas said between his teeth and drawing a deep breath as he spoke. "My time will come. I'll make this insolent young dog suffer for this, or my name is not Henderby Lupas. I am not accustomed to be insulted like this."

"Yes, and I will help you," de Barsac said. "That young man must be got out of the way. I won't rest satisfied till I have got even with him."

Dorn shuffled about uneasily, for there was a menace in de Barsac's voice that suggested violence. And violence, was a thing that was antagonistic to Dorn's nature.

"So that's settled," he said with forced cheerfulness. "You leave it to me, de Barsac. I'll find your friend Lupas some comfortable quarters here where we can see him if necessity calls for it. And, by Jove, I should not like to stand in young Markham's shoes."

Lupas smiled at this somewhat vague flattery.

"You are quite right there," he said. "Oh, I'll get even with him. I'll teach that young upstart to interfere with my arrangements. And now, don't you think we had better set about to find somewhere I can stay."

CHAPTER XVI

A GLIMMER OF REASON

Sylvia had been back for two days at Lanton Place, waiting to hear something from Maxwell Frick. That she would hear from him sooner or later she knew perfectly well, especially when he discovered that she had not made her way to London. But that mercurial individual had his periods of forgetfulness, and it might be some days yet before any sign came from him. Therefore she set herself down to wait in patience till the time came when she could go out into the world and get her own living once more. Meanwhile there was consolation in the knowledge that her father was not at home. She knew perfectly well that so long as he had free and luxurious quarters at Baron's Court he was not likely to return to the gloom and desolation of Lanton Place.

That he was up to some mischief, or perhaps worse, Sylvia did not doubt for a moment. At any rate, her courage and the force of circumstance had prevented him from robbing John Bevill, and therefore that was something to the good. So Sylvia set herself down to wait and watch and look after her mother as best she could. Deep down in her heart was a warm affection for that unhappy woman, for Sylvia alone knew how she had suffered at the hands of a bad man and how her strange mental condition had been caused by all that trouble.

At the same time it was a heart-breaking and melancholy business. There were hours, and even days together, when Mrs. Dorn said nothing even to her own daughter. She was grateful for any little kindness; there was a look in those dark eyes of hers from time to time like that in the eyes of a dog when he receives recognition from his master. And there were times when the restless fit came upon her and she wandered out of the house in all sorts of weather, eternally prowling amongst the blackened ruins and ever searching the ashes. And sometimes it seemed to Sylvia there was worse than this—times when her mother wandered about the dim corridors of the old house at all hours of the night; and once Sylvia had gone out into the dawn, where she had discovered her mother, like another Cassandra, brooding amongst the ruins. And once, again, Sylvia had found a pair of her mother's boots, caked in clay and mud as if she had wandered far under the cover of the darkness. She must have gone far afield then, for she slept all the next day like some worn-out animal. It was always the same, never any change in that dark and forbidding household.

It was the third day that Sylvia had been at home, waiting for some sign from Maxwell Frick, and wondering vaguely when she was going to see Lionel Markham again. She had written and posted one or two letters, which she had posted down in the village, and was making her way back through the tangled growth of shrubbery towards the house, when she saw the form of her mother over there in the ruins with the eternal rake in her hand. She crossed over and spoke gently to Mrs. Dorn.

"Come into the house, mother," she said. "Do you know that you have been there for hours? Come and let me make you a cup of tea. Would you like me to play something to you?"

The unhappy woman raised her eyes to Sylvia's for a moment, and then she went on with her work again as if she had not heard, which was probably the case. With a sigh, Sylvia repeated her question. And then, as she turned to go back to the house, she recognised Markham coming in her direction.

"I said I should come over and see you," he said. "Are you glad, Sylvia, or perhaps—"

He broke off abruptly, as he turned and saw Mrs. Dorn standing there, a drab and patient figure in the midst of all that blackness and desolation. He had been prepared by Sylvia for something in the way of a tragedy. But he had not pictured anything as heart-breaking and pathetic as this.

"I beg your pardon," he murmured, "I did not know that—I thought you were alone."

"To all practical purposes I am," Sylvia said with an unsettled little smile. "Isn't it sad, Lionel?"

Markham could only shake his head and glance uneasily at the dusky figure grubbing in the ruins.

"Oh, she won't hear you," Sylvia said. "When she is doing this she can never hear anything."

"But why—why—"

"Oh I don't know," Sylvia said. "This sort of thing has been going on for years, ever since the fatal night of the fire when the house was burnt down, and my unhappy mother lost her reason. She is looking for something, though nobody knows what—indeed, I doubt if she knows herself. But occasionally she talks to herself, and then one hears little bits about jewels and valuable things that are missing. I fancy that she is doing all this for my sake. She has delusions that she has lost something which she was saving up for me—something that she concealed from my father, who would certainly have taken it had it been discovered."

"Can't you rouse her?" Markham asked.

"Very seldom. But I can try. Mother, here is a visitor who has come to see you. Mr. Lionel Markham."

Very slowly and as if the words had come to her from afar off, Mrs. Dorn stood upright and gazed with a peculiar intentness of expression into the young man's face.

"I knew your father," she said.

Sylvia started back in surprise. For the words were sane and commonplace enough, the first coherent words that she had heard her mother utter for many years. Then, as if she were engaged in some ordinary occupation, Mrs. Dorn went back to her work again, leaving the other two embarrassed and amazed. She rose again presently and spoke once more.

"Your father was a friend of ours," she said. "He was a banker; wasn't he?"

"Yes," Markham stammered. "He was."

"And one of the best and kindest of men," Mrs. Dorn went on. "Ah, if he had been alive now there would never have been all this trouble. But he died suddenly. Let me try and remember. He was found dead in his own park, shot through the head, and they called it suicide."

"I always doubted it," Markham said.

"He was murdered—murdered, I tell you," Mrs. Dorn said in a voice that was little more than a whisper. "I can't tell you how, and I don't suppose anybody will ever know, but he was murdered. Strange, very strange after all these years that his son should come here making love to my daughter."

Markham fairly staggered back, and Sylvia cried out in surprise. The whole thing was true, but then, how did this unhappy woman with her clouded intellect go straight into the centre of the truth? And she spoke, too, as if it were the most natural thing in the world, spoke without looking at the others and going on restlessly with that never-ending search of hers at the same time.

And then she spoke again.

"Ah, they think I know nothing," she said, as if speaking to herself. "They think I am blind and deaf. But I know, I know. You come from Baron's Court, don't you?"

The astonished Markham gasped a reply.

"Yes, I thought so. My husband is over there. And another man called de Barsac. Beware of him, Lionel Markham, beware of him. He is a bad man, an utterly bad man. I knew him years ago. How many years ago was it? It seems to me to be hundreds. I was young and handsome then, and I had all the world at my feet. And because my head was turned, and they flattered me, I married Major Dorn. Ah, a bad day's work, a bad and bitter day's work."

She broke off abruptly and went back to her work again. And from that moment she did not speak again. It was as if she had grown deaf and blind again to the world.

"I am afraid it is hopeless," Sylvia whispered. "She will go on like this till she is tired out. And really, it is a kindness not to worry her. Come in the house and let me give you a cup of tea."

In a bewildered and puzzled silence, and with a heart aching in sympathy for these two unfortunates, Markham followed Sylvia along the weed-grown track that led to the house.

"It is extraordinary desolate here," he said presently. "And yet this place might be made a perfect paradise. Sylvia, I cannot tell you how sorry I am."

"Don't," Sylvia said. "Please don't. I really can't stand it. I must go my way, Lionel, and I must do the best I can till the sun begins to shine. And surely it must shine for me some of these days."

"It shall," Markham declared. "It shall be the business of my life to see to that. But how strange it all is! Here is a woman like your mother, apparently hopelessly insane, but who sees into the heart of things as none of us can do. Now, fancy her guessing that I was making love to you. And fancy her remembering about the tragic death of my father and all about that man de Barsac, whom, by the way, I have always believed to be a scoundrel from the first. Well, it's a warning. And, if you will give me a cup of tea, I will get back again. Have you heard anything from those theatrical people? Have you heard anything from your father?"

"That's not at all likely," Sylvia said. "There is very little chance of us seeing him so long as he is living in the lap of luxury at Baron's Court. And as for Maxwell Frick, well, he will communicate with me when he recollects. You can quite understand, Lionel, how anxious I am to be doing something; indeed, I must do something before long. My mother doesn't realise how desperate things are in the house. We have only a few shillings between us, and there isn't a single tradesman within twenty miles who would trust Major Dorn with as much as a loaf of bread."

Half an hour later Markham was striding down the road in the direction of Baron's Court, and presently at a sudden turn, he came face to face with the smiling features and striking wardrobe of Maxwell Frick himself.

"Aha, my gallant youth," the actor cried. "And what are you doing here? Have you found her out, my boy? Following her to the ends of the earth, I suppose? That's good. Well, I'm on my way to see Miss Dorn myself. Oh yes, it's all right. I have got her contract in my pocket. And between you and me, my boy, she's worth every penny of it."

CHAPTER XVII

Markham was pleased enough to meet Maxwell Frick again, for the little he had seen of that genial Bohemian he had liked well enough, and besides, was he not bringing him good news for Sylvia, whom he had gone out of his way on more than one occasion to benefit? So that he hooked his arm in that of Frick and began to retrace his footsteps.

"I am very glad to hear what you say," he said, "because the news you bring is more than welcome. I know that in your kind-hearted way you have taken the greatest interest in Miss Dorn, a common interest as great as mine."

"Ah, my boy," Frick smiled. "And that's a good deal, isn't it? I don't wish to pry into other people's affairs, and you can tell me as much or as little as you like, but I think you know what I mean, and I am very pleased to find that you are down here. She is a real nice girl, and—well, I don't think I need say any more. But from what I can hear it is rather a funny household, isn't it?"

"Dreadful," Markham said. "But perhaps you may be able to judge that for yourself in a few minutes. Now, between ourselves, Frick, I take more than a usual interest in Miss Dorn's affairs, and that's as far as it is necessary to go for the moment. Now, you are a man of courage and resolution, I believe, and perhaps a little later on I shall have to ask your assistance in a matter that involves personal danger."

"Is that really so?" Frick asked. "Well, you can count me in. I love adventures. And though I am getting on a bit in life I don't think there is much that I am afraid of. Are you coming back with me?"

"I don't think so," Markham said. "Now you go and get your business over and I will wait for you here. Where do you happen to be staying to-night?"

It was quite characteristic of the comedian that he had not the slightest idea where he was spending the night. Possibly he might walk back to Tavistock and find a lodging there, but he had quite an open mind on the subject.

"In that case, you had better come back with me," Markham said. "Where are your belongings? At Tavistock Station? Then we will pick them up and taxi out to Baron's Court. I want to introduce you to Mr. John Bevill, who takes the keenest interest in this cinematograph venture of yours. He is the man I told you about, the man who has the finest private menagerie in England. He is very keen on having a series of pictures taken of his wild animals, and I thought perhaps you might be able to do a good deal of business on behalf of your firm. Now could you work up some sensational story and bring in those animals? Has not your firm a sort of stock author, who turns his hand to that sort of thing? Do you see what I mean?"

In his impulsive way Frick fell in love with the scheme and began to enlarge upon it.

"That's a rattling good idea, my boy," he said. "Yes, we have got the very thing you speak of. A sensational writer who will throw together a good plot in no time. Of course I came down here as a sort of advance agent to get everything ready for the big Dartmoor drama we are filming, and from what I have heard, Lanton Place will make a magnificent background. We shall want to take it over practically, but of course we shall bring all our portable studios and all that kind of thing. But that animal story of yours is a great idea, and if Mr. Bevill will only put me up for a night or two we can discuss the preliminaries at once."

"He will be delighted," Markham said. "Now, you get on and finish your business with Miss Dorn, whilst I sit on the stile here and smoke a cigarette."

It was quite an hour later before Frick came back full of enthusiasm for what he had seen, and absolutely certain that the venture was going to prove a tremendous success.

"It's great, my boy, great," he cried. "That melancholy house with the blackened ruins will make a glorious background. I have never felt more depressed in my life. But we will alter all that presently. When we put up our temporary buildings and get our company down here, we'll make things hum at Lanton Place and put money in the pocket of the proprietor at the same time. From what I have seen, I should say he badly needs it. By the way, he's over at Baron's Court, isn't he? What sort of a man is he?"

"A blackguard," Markham said curtly. "A cold and calculating scoundrel, who lives entirely for himself. He was, at one time, a comparatively rich man. Once upon a time Lanton Place was one of the show houses in the neighbourhood. But it is a melancholy story, and I don't intend to dwell upon it. But you will see the man for yourself presently, and you can make your own arrangements."

"In that case, he ought to be pleased to get twenty pounds a week," Frick said. "As we shall probably be here for six months he ought to jump at it."

As Markham prophesied, Frick received quite a warm welcome at Baron's Court. He found Bevill eager enough to go into the matter and quite ready to place the whole of his menagerie at the disposal of the Syndicate. But just for the moment Dorn and de Barsac were by no means pleased at the advent of the florid little man, who seemed to take everything for granted and who talked freely enough about his plans. But when presently he approached Dorn with his offer, the latter was amiable enough, and long before dinner a rough contract was drawn up and signed on both sides.

"That's all very well for you," de Barsac muttered. "It ensures you a comfortable living for the next months, and that is all you seem to think about. But, after all, it's nothing in comparison with the big scheme we have on hand."

"No, but it's a good deal to me," Dorn retorted. "And besides, what does it matter? This man Frick and all his company will be at Lanton Place, so that they are not likely to interfere with us."

"Oh, indeed," de Barsac sneered. "That's all you seem to know about it. But, as far as I can understand, it will be the best part of a month before Frick has made all his arrangements at Lanton Place, and meanwhile it looks as if he had made up his mind to make himself quite at home here. You heard what passed at tea-time? You heard Bevill ask Frick to regard this place as his own, and furthermore, he was invited to bring some out-at-elbows novelist who will loaf about here for weeks writing some silly story round the menagerie. And we shall have cinematograph operators and goodness knows what besides running about all over the place as if it belonged to them, and making themselves a general nuisance. It's very unfortunate."

"You're not blaming me?" Dorn asked. "It's no doing of mine, and even if I had not been here at all Frick would have turned up just the same. If I had been fool enough to refuse these people the run of Lanton Place, they would have found some other suitable spot. Anyway, it can't be helped, and we shall have to make the best of it."

De Barsac listened moodily.

"It's very unfortunate," he said. "And you know perfectly well that for our purpose we want the house entirely to ourselves. The fewer people here the better. If we could afford to wait a few months or so, it wouldn't much matter, but you know how impatient Lupas is."

"Lupas is a fool," Dorn exclaimed. "If he doesn't mind what he's doing, he will spoil everything. Now, were you talking through your hat, or did you really mean it when you told Lupas that you could get him a sight of old Bevill's will? If you could only do that—"

"That's possible," de Barsac said. "I happen to know where it's kept, and I might possibly get hold of the key of the safe. That's not a bad idea of yours, Dorn, and I will see what I can do. It ought to be to-night."

"Why not?" Dorn asked.

Meanwhile the delighted Professor, together with Markham and Frick and Sir Watney Gibson, was conducting his guest over the menagerie. They went from cage to cage, past the lions and the tigers and the other feline animals, until at length the whole collection had been exhausted. They were a fine lot altogether, and Frick was loud in his admiration. He looked round the wide-spreading park with its little hills and valleys and thick belts of trees here and there, and expressed himself as quite satisfied with what he called the atmosphere.

"Yes," he said, "we ought to be able to make a big thing of this. If you don't mind, Mr. Bevill, I'll get Stafford Hatton down here to-morrow. That's the man who writes up all our scenarios. He's a wonderfully clever chap if you can only keep him off the drink, and he'll write a story round those animals that will be simply great. Is your park safe? I mean, could you manage to get some of those beasts out into the open? Have you got any keeper who could handle them if they were once out of their cages? You see what I mean? If we could photograph them in the open the pictures would be far more effective."

"There's nobody who could do that but myself," Bevill said. "There isn't a single cage here I am afraid to go into. But how my beasts would behave if they were once out in the open, I can't say. I don't think it would be particularly dangerous for me, but it might be a serious matter for your operators."

"Oh, I don't know," Frick said thoughtfully. "You see, we've got a new dodge now whereby we can get up cameras and direct them from a distance by an electric process. For instance, if you drove one of your animals through that thicket yonder they could be photographed automatically whilst the operator was a long way off—I don't know, but I rather fancy we could work that sort of thing in any light, even in moonlight. But that we can go into later. Just fancy that magnificent beast yonder prowling through the wood as if in search of prey whilst all the time he has been driven. It would make a splendid picture. You see, we could fix up half a dozen cameras and work them simultaneously by the process I speak of. Indeed, I don't see any other way of doing it. Still, of course, if there is any danger of the animals escaping—"

"They couldn't," Bevill said. "They couldn't possibly get outside the park. You see, there's a high wall all round specially built for the purpose."

"That's good," Frick cried enthusiastically. "This is going to be one of the biggest things on earth."

CHAPTER XVIII

John Bevill and his strange assortment of guests sat round the dinner table later on in the evening discussing the subject of the wild animals in the menagerie and all connected with them, the talk being led enthusiastically by Frick, who declared that the Baron's Court menagerie was about to take history or something like it. He was immensely taken, too, with Vim, who sat by his side smoking his cigarette with the air of a connoisseur and sipping his liqueur like a man of the world. Vim seemed to have settled down again now; he had lost all the snarling vindictiveness that he had displayed the last day or two, and appeared to be taking the keenest interest in what was going on around him.

"It's great," Frick said. "Absolutely great. And if Stafford Hatton doesn't say so, I shall be greatly mistaken. He can work Vim here into the plot—indeed. I don't see how we are going to do without him. By the way, Mr. Bevill, how does this amazing ape of yours get on with the other animals?"

"Oh, excellently," Bevill said. "He is on the best of terms with all of them. He goes in and out of their cages with me. I don't know whether he talks to them or not, but most of them seem to understand him."

"Vim isn't an animal at all," Sir Watney Gibson remarked. "I told you that before. He is a human being. His outward appearance is not all one would exactly expect from a human, but he's got a soul somewhere, and I am firmly convinced that he knows all we are talking about. And if he could speak, he would tell us so. Look at his hands. I know you people call them paws. But they used to be paws with us a few hundred centuries ago. By the way de Barsac, how are you getting on with that model that you were going to do for me?"

"What model?" de Barsac asked.

"Well, the model of Vim's hand and forearm that I measured for you a night or two ago. You took the impression in wax. You can't have forgotten."

"Really, I beg your pardon," de Barsac said. "But all the same, I had forgotten it for the moment. You see, I have been so very busy the last day or two. But I can promise to let you have it to-morrow."

"That will be quite all right," Gibson said. "I should like to take it with me at the end of the week."

De Barsac's eyes lighted up for a moment, a fact that was not lost on Markham, who sat quietly smoking his cigarette and watching everything carefully.

"You are leaving us then?" de Barsac asked.

"Yes, I am sorry, but I must," Gibson said. "I have got to give evidence next week in that Annondale murder case. A most mysterious affair, but I think I shall be able to help the authorities to hang the man they have laid their hands on."

"Very interesting," de Barsac drawled. "Why is it that all the world is so fascinated with a man hunt? Do you happen to be on in this scene, Markham?"

"No, I'm not," Markham replied. "Mr. Bevill has asked me to stay on for a few days, and seeing that Sir Watney has no need for me, I am remaining."

As he spoke Markham could see that this piece of information was by no means pleasing to de Barsac. He sat there moodily smoking and sipping his port, until at length the little party round the dining table broke up, and de Barsac, with Dorn, strolled off in the direction of the studio. The rest of the party made their way to the billiard-room.

There they sat, talking and chatting for the best part of an hour or so, until Sir Watney announced his intention of going to bed, and shortly afterwards Mr. Bevill followed his example. For a little time Markham and Frick smoked their cigars in ruminative silence.

"Now what do you think of it all, Frick?" Markham asked. "Amazing household, isn't it?"

"Oh, I don't know," Frick replied. "I have been knocking about all over the world for the last thirty years, and if I only had the ability to put my experiences on paper I could tell of a great many more extraordinary experiences than this. But, all the same, you are quite right, it is an amazing household. I felt, to-night, when we were at dinner, as if I were dreaming. Every time I looked at that amazing ape I wanted to rub my eyes and ask myself whether I was awake or not. I saw those two monkeys they used to call Max and Moritz, but neither of them were anything like as human as Vim. But is he always quiet like that? Doesn't he break out sometimes? By Jove, if he did, he would be able to wipe the floor with the whole household before anybody could interfere."

"I believe he has his moods," Markham said. "And in connection with your question a strange thing happened early yesterday morning. Mr. Bevill had occasion to come back here from his bungalow in the New Forest and he found Vim tied to a tree. Heaven knows who was responsible for that idiotic mischief—probably de Barsac, as far as I can understand. You see, de Barsac confines himself almost entirely to the study of animals, and from what I can gather he wanted to see Vim in a royal rage. Well, he managed that all right, but Miss Dorn told me it nearly cost Bevill his life. It's not a very pretty story, and it shows up de Barsac in a very cruel and cold-blooded light. Perhaps I had better tell you the story. It's worth listening to."

"I don't like that a bit," Frick said when at length Markham had finished. "And I don't see the point of dressing up a dummy for the purpose of infuriating the animal. But then, I am a creature of moods and impulses, as you know, and perhaps I have taken an unreasonable dislike to de Barsac. I dislike him quite as much as I do Major Dorn. Oh, I know he's handsome enough and a great favourite with the women, but I mistrust that sleek appearance of his, and I can see the tiger behind those brown eyes. Hang me if he doesn't walk like a tiger. I calculate I'm as good-natured and hospitable as most people, or I should be if I had anything to be hospitable with, but if I were Mr. Bevill, I should have given de Barsac what the Americans call his walking ticket long ago. But look here, Markham, isn't there more in this than meets the eye? You hinted some little time ago that there was something very wrong going on here. Is de Barsac at the bottom of it?"

"Well, if I were in the witness-box, I should say no," Markham replied. "But between one man and another I have my doubts. I believe that there is some very sinister underhand business going on between those two scoundrels, and Mr. Bevill is going to pay for it. What is going on I haven't the remotest idea, but I'm going to find out. That's why I'm staying on here. I have talked it over with my uncle, and he thinks it would be just as well. You heard de Barsac ask me if I was leaving on Saturday with Sir Watney, and you may have noticed his expression of disappointment when I told him that I was staying on. Did you notice anything?"

"Yes, I did," Frick said. "I'm a pretty easy-going chap, but there is little that escapes my attention."

"Ah, then you are something like my uncle in that respect," Markham said. "He is hot-headed and impetuous enough, and most people regard him as a scientific enthusiast who can see nothing beyond the end of his nose. But I pity any criminal who banks on that. Once Sir Watney's suspicions were aroused, he has the tenacity of a bull dog, and there is not a detective in London who has a clearer vision than he. He pretends to take no great interest in what de Barsac is doing here, but I believe he does, all the same. He listens and asks absent-minded questions, and then months afterwards he brings up the subject again, and then you realise that he has been following a closely-reasoned train of thought for months. If de Barsac imagines that he has a child to deal with, he is making the mistake of his life."

Markham led the way up the stairs a few moments later, putting out the lights as he went, and said good-night to Frick outside the latter's bedroom door. Once alone, Frick turned on the lights and proceeded to light a cigar. It was characteristic of the man that he had put off his correspondence till the last moment; but then, as it was an invariable habit of his to turn night into day, he dragged his portmanteau from under the bed and proceeded to unearth the necessary writing materials. Then for the next two hours or more he set himself down industriously until everything was finished and a big pile of letters lay on the table by his side. He rose presently with a yawn as a clock somewhere downstairs was striking the hour of three, and commenced to prepare himself for bed.

He would have one more cigarette before turning in, he decided; but though he searched everywhere, there was no sign of a match to be seen. For once in his life he decided that the electric light was not entirely an unmixed blessing. He remembered that on a little table in the hall he had noticed a box of matches when he came upstairs. He fumbled along till he found the switch in the corridor and turned on the light. Then he crept very quietly down the stairs and, running his hand along the edge of the table secured the matches. As he did so, however, his hand came in contact with a big brass tray that fell on the polished floor with a resounding crash. Almost immediately a light somewhere at the back of the hall went out, and Frick could hear a smothered curse from somewhere near by, followed by the sound of retreating footsteps.

Evidently there were thieves in the house. Without the slightest hesitation Frick reached for the big brass tray and beat upon it with his fists until the whole house resounded with the hideous din. Bedroom doors began to open, and presently figures appeared on the stairs.

"What has happened?" Bevill demanded.

"Burglars," Frick said. "In the library."

Surely enough the library door was wide open, and when they came to look round it was seen that the door of the old-fashioned fireproof safe had been forced. But nothing had gone apparently until Bevill gave vent to an exclamation, and he shook his head as he went through the papers in the safe for the second time. He was looking grave enough now.

"Have you lost anything?" Markham asked.

"Yes," Bevill said. "My will has gone."

He turned away without further comment, apparently not noticing what struck Markham as strange—that, despite all the clamour, there was no sign of de Barsac or Dorn.

CHAPTER XIX

AN ERROR OF JUDGMENT

"Are you quite certain?" Markham asked.

"Well, I can look again," Bevill replied. "It's a most extraordinary thing altogether. There are a good many valuables here, but not one of them appears to be missing."

"Perhaps I was a bit too soon," Frick explained. "I had better explain. I came down to look for a box of matches. I hadn't been to bed, as you see, and I thought that I would have another cigarette before turning in. Naturally I had a good deal of correspondence to attend to, and I always do that sort of thing late at night. I had just finished and was creeping quietly downstairs in search of a box of matches which I remembered seeing on a little table in the hall, and in getting them I accidentally knocked down that brass tray. It made a good deal of noise, of course, and I expect that it frightened the thieves. Probably they had only just begun. That might account for nothing being missing."

"But something is missing," Bevill protested. "I have just told you that I cannot find my will. I placed it there a couple of months ago alone on this little top shelf, and you can all see for yourselves that it is no longer there. Moreover, I have not opened the safe since the day I placed the document inside. It's a most extraordinary thing altogether. I don't see how anybody could benefit by taking the document. It is certainly of no use to anybody as long as I am alive."

"It is strange," Sir Watney Gibson said. "But how did the thieves get in the house?"

"Oh, that's quite simple," Markham said. "You will see that the window is open. They must have come and gone that way. But it might have been worse."

"So it might," Bevill agreed. "And, in the circumstances, nobody is any the poorer. They are quite welcome to what they have taken; besides, it will be no difficult matter for me to execute a new testament. Really, gentlemen, I am very sorry to give you all this trouble. There is nothing for it now but to go back to bed and leave further discussion till the morning. It certainly is a matter that I must investigate."

Markham listened in silence, though it seemed to him that he might have said a good deal had he liked. In the first place it appeared to him as strange that, despite the noise Frick had made in rousing the household, there had been no sign, so far, of either Dorn or de Barsac. Everybody else had crowded into the library, and it seemed impossible to believe that the two men in question had slept through that hideous din. Then, just as everybody was disappearing in the direction of their bedrooms. Dorn appeared at the head of the staircase, followed a moment or two later by de Barsac.

"What is going on?" Dorn asked with what seemed to Markham to be an exaggerated yawn. "I was fast asleep just now when it seemed to me that I heard a hideous crash, followed by another one, and I woke up. Thinking it was all a dream, I turned over again, and then I noticed a light under my door and I heard the sound of voices."

"Much the same thing happened to me," de Barsac observed. "What's the matter, Bevill? Have burglars been making a raid on the house?"

"Something like that," Bevill said. "They got in through the library window and raided my safe."

"And is anything missing?"

"Only one thing," Bevill explained. "Those thieves have gone off with my will. Why they wanted a useless document like that passes my comprehension. There are a lot of valuable things in the safe, too, but not one of them has been touched. Mr. Frick suggests that they were alarmed before they had time to touch the valuables."

"What an extraordinary thing!" de Barsac said. "Fancy wasting all that time and taking all that risk for the sake of a paper not worth sixpence. At any rate, you can make a new will to-morrow if you like."

De Barsac spoke quite easily and naturally as he stood there clad only in his pyjamas, as indeed was Dorn. In the doorway, half in the shadow, Markham stood, watching everything keenly. He noticed something presently that brought a flash into his eyes and the suggestion of a smile to his lips, but he said nothing as he turned presently and followed Sir Watney Gibson up the stairs in the direction of the latter's bedroom.

"Can I come inside for a moment?" he asked.

"By all means," Gibson said. "Now, my boy, what is it? You have found something out, and want to tell me."

"I think I have," Markham said. "It's only a little thing, but it might lead us a long way. Now, you heard everything that went on. Do you really believe that those thieves ran all that risk merely for the sake of getting away with Mr. Bevill's will? What is the use of it to them, now they've got it? It is perfectly valueless as long as the old gentleman is alive, and if he were to die to-morrow they would be bound to produce it."

"Not necessarily," Sir Watney suggested. "Suppose that whoever took it knew the contents of that document. Let us suppose for a moment that Mr. Bevill intends to leave a large sum of money to someone outside his own family. And let us suppose, further, that these audacious thieves have some pressing reason why the money in question should not reach the hand for which it is intended. They probably count upon the fact that Bevill is a careless man who would put his will away and think no more about it, which is just the sort of thing he would do. Then, if anything happens to him, the will is missing, and all the old gentleman's property naturally goes to his next-of-kin. Now, this next-of-kin, as I happen to know, is a ne'er-do-well nephew to whom Bevill does not intend to leave a penny."

"Then you think the case is clear?" Markham asked.

"Well, at any rate, my theory is plausible," Gibson said. "It looks to me as if the scapegrace nephew knew exactly what had happened, and had come down here with the intention of getting hold of that document. Once he did that, he would feel himself perfectly safe. He would destroy the will and wait for his uncle's death. Depend upon it, my boy, that is exactly what has happened. If the thief had had five minutes more, he would have got away safely and no one any the wiser. Really, I don't think we need worry any more about it. I rather gathered from Mr. Bevill's manner to-night that he has some notion of the truth, and that's why he did not make any fuss about it. At any rate I can ask him in the morning. And, as things have turned out, the thief has only had his trouble for his pains."

Markham shook his head quietly.

"That's not my idea at all," he said. "If you will give me two or three minutes, I will tell you my theory. Now, didn't it strike you as rather strange that neither de Barsac nor Dorn put in an appearance this evening till most of us were on our way upstairs again?"

"Oho," Sir Watney said. "Go on."

"Well, they came down last of all. Now, I defy anybody to remain asleep in the house whilst Frick was making that hideous din on the tray. It was loud enough to waken the dead. It brought everybody in the house downstairs with the exception of those two men, whom we both mistrust and suspect. And when they did come they were a little too natural. Did you notice how Dorn yawned and de Barsac rubbed his eyes? It was acting in a fashion; of that I am certain. Innocent men would have showed some sign of alarm, but they were not even curious. And there is another thing I noticed. The two top buttons of Dorn's pyjama coat were unfastened, and distinctly saw a white shirt and a waistcoat beneath. In other words, he was wearing his pyjamas over a portion of his clothing. Now, why should a man be doing that at three o'clock in the morning?"

"Is that a fact?" Sir Watney asked.

"Yes, I am prepared to swear to it. I suggest those men went out through the library window at the first alarm, and stood outside waiting till everything was quiet again. If the worst came to the worst they could have stepped in the studio and slipped in the house to-morrow morning when the servants came down. No doubt they stood outside the window there in the darkness, perhaps listening to what was going on, or what is more likely still, found a ladder somewhere in the garden and contrived to reach a bedroom window that way. At any rate, I feel quite convinced in my own mind that those two rascals know all about it."

"Well," Sir Watney admitted, "with what you say, it certainly presents the case in a fresh light. There is one thing against your theory. I happen to know that Bevill thinks a good deal of de Barsac, and it is his intention to leave him a large sum of money. Moreover, de Barsac knows it, and this being so, what on earth does the man want to run a risk like that for? Why should he steal a document that is worth a small fortune to him?"

"That we have to find out," Markham said. "That is why I am going to stay on here after you go. There is some deep conspiracy here that I mean to get to the bottom of. What it is I haven't the remotest idea, but I feel it in my bones that it means danger to Mr. Bevill. However, it is no use to discuss the matter further, so I'll get along to bed."

There was no sign on the face of de Barsac when he came down in the morning to show that he had been in the least disturbed by the events of the previous evening. He and Dorn appeared to be in unusually good spirits, discussing the burglary from the point of view that Bevill had made a mistake, and that in his absent-minded way he had placed the missing will somewhere else, and had forgotten all about it.

"Just the sort of thing you would do, Bevill," de Barsac said. "I can remember one or two occasions in point."

"Well, perhaps I might," Bevill agreed. "I am prepared to swear I didn't, but possibly I am wrong."

"Of course you are," de Barsac laughed. "You will find eventually that your will is in the hands of your lawyer. Solicitors never part with those kind of things if they can help it. And, by the way, Sir Watney, I shall finish that cast for you this morning. I'll bring it in at lunch time, and you can pick it away in your portmanteau."

"Oh, really?" Gibson said. "That's interesting. I shall value it highly, and, unless I am greatly mistaken, it will help me to startle society before long."

Gibson spoke lightly enough, but the time was at hand when his prophecy was more than fulfilled.

CHAPTER XX

AN ANXIOUS CONSULTATION

Once de Barsac and Dorn were alone together in the studio the mask dropped from their faces and they sat regarding one another with deep anxiety.

"Well?" de Barsac demanded. "What's to be done? It was your suggestion. You got me into the mess, and I shall expect you to get me out of it again."

"What's the good of talking like that?" Dorn demanded. "You were just as keen on it as anybody else. It was a bit of cruel bad luck, and if that blundering fool had not have come down the stairs we should have been safely back in our bedrooms within five minutes and no one any the wiser. And besides, you've got the old man's will."

"A precious lot of good that is," de Barsac grumbled.

"Oh, isn't it? Upon my word, you talk like a child. We have got it, and no one else knows anything about it—that is, no one outside the house. Of course, Bevill will make another will, and naturally enough, you will figure in it for the same amount as you figured in the last."

"Yes, that's all very well," de Barsac retorted. "But his suspicions are roused. He knows perfectly well that no ordinary burglar would have any use for a paper like that. And, mind you, when he is roused, Bevill is by no means the innocent child you take him for. If he gets the slightest inkling of what is going on, I can say good-bye to that legacy. And here is Lupas, not more than a mile away, fretting and fuming and ready for mischief at any moment. If that meddling interfering young Markham drops a hint as to Lupas' real character to Bevill, I am done. The old man will see at once that I am in Lupas' hands, and if he once learns that he won't leave me a single penny. He's got to make a new will now, even if it is only to protect himself against that nephew of his, who will come into everything if Bevill dies to-day."

Dorn smiled pityingly.

"Really," he said, "you are not half so clever as I took you to be. Can't you see that we must play up to Bevill's dislike for that nephew of his? There's our salvation. You told me about that nephew a day or two ago, and when I was dressing this morning the whole pretty scheme dawned on me. When I was in the park before breakfast I took the opportunity speaking to the old man, and adroitly mentioned his nephew. He rose to it like a shot. He swallowed the whole thing like a glass of milk. Before I had finished with him he was perfectly satisfied that his nephew, or some scoundrel employed on his behalf, had come down here to steal the will. I want to so arrange it that the old man should voice his suspicions before witnesses. If we can do that—and it's quite an easy matter—we shall have done a fine morning's work."

"In what way?" de Barsac asked.

"Really, my dear friend, you are very stupid this morning. Supposing we get Bevill to do that, and supposing that anything happens to him afterwards—I mean such as an accident or a sudden death? Do you follow me?"

"Go on," de Barsac said hoarsely. "Go on."

"Well, Bevill is found dead in the park, say," Dorn went on in a whisper. "He has met with foul play. If this happens to him, who would be the first person to be suspected? Why a dissolute nephew who lives in London and comes down here occasionally demanding money and generally causing a scandal. It is known that the old man has disinherited this nephew by will. It is known that the will has mysteriously disappeared from the safe, following an audacious burglary. And, moreover, it is known that, in the presence of witnesses, the old man has suggested that the nephew is a thief. Can't you see how suspicion will be directed in one channel, almost to the exclusion of everything else? My dear fellow, here is fate actually going out of its way to help us."

For some time de Barsac appeared to debate the point in his mind, then gradually his face cleared and an ugly smile spread itself from his lips.

"You are a cunning devil, Dorn," he said. "I think the most cunning that I ever met. I flatter myself that I am pretty shrewd in these matters, but, upon my word, I am a perfect child compared with you. But all the same, we made an awful hash of things last night, and, on the whole, it would have been far better if we had let matters alone. And, so far as Lupas is concerned, we are no better off than we were before."

"Ah, that is where you are wrong. Lupas knows nothing about what went on last night, and as he cannot possibly come here. He is not in the least likely to know. Therefore we can take that precious document and show him, and he will see for himself that you have told him nothing more than the truth when you said that you would benefit largely by Bevill's death. He will see it in black and white, and with any luck he will never learn how you got hold of the document. So, you see now, that when young Markham put his foot down, and practically ordered Lupas out of the house, he was doing us a good turn."

"Yes, as things have turned out, you are right," de Barsac conceded. "But he suspects us."

"Oh, let him," Dorn said impatiently. "Leave it to me. I think I have shown you how all these misfortunes of ours have turned out blessings in disguise, and, after all, Markham has no reason to suspect us, except that he knows that I have business dealings with Lupas. Oh, there's nothing to worry about, everything is going our way, and It will all come right in the long run. Really, I am glad that thing happened last night, though it was touch and go."

"It was that," de Barsac grinned. "I shan't forget in a hurry how you looked last night when I stood on your shoulders trying to get in my bedroom window. Or how shaken you appeared to be when I dragged you up after me. Still, it's all over now, and there's not a living soul in the world who could trace that burglary to us. What do you say to walking over to Lupas' quarters and showing him the paper?"

"Just what I was going to suggest," Dorn said. "He must be impressed by it, and if you play your cards properly he might be disposed to let you have a further advance. At any rate, you might try it on."

"Oh, I'll certainly do that," de Barsac grinned. "As a matter of fact, I am down to my last sovereign. I have drawn every penny of advance commission, and I don't know where to turn for a little ready money. Of course, I might borrow a bit from Bevill, but knowing what is at stake I dare not do that. You see, the old boy regards me as a rich man, as indeed I ought to be if I wasn't such a fool. But seeing that I have always posed before him as a capitalist, any suggestion to the contrary might do me serious harm."

"Of course it would," Dorn agreed. "But at any rate, you can try Lupas, and if it turns out trumps you might let me have a hundred or two to go on with."

"Oh, I'll certainly do that," de Barsac said. "Whatever my failings are, I am always generous enough to my friends. And, upon my word, you will have earned it. That is a really fine idea of yours about the nephew. Now, come on, go and get your hat, and we'll stroll across the fields and interview the lion in his den."

They made their way across the fields a few moments later in search of Lupas, whom they found presently seated in the sun in a pleasant orchard reading his paper and smoking under the shadow of a tree. He glowered with no expression of friendliness on his face, and his greeting was not in the least auspicious. He looked up sulkily.

"Well," he asked, "what do you want?"

"Oh, I like that," de Barsac said with a forced laugh. "Here are we, come all this way to see you, to cheer you in the sylvan solitude, and you receive us in this fashion."

"Well, what do you expect?" Lupas asked. "Here am I, actually wasting my time in the company of a lot of country clodhoppers, when I might be making money in London. It's all very well for you people, living on the fat of the land yonder, but I have got to be considered, and don't you forget it. Now, have you done anything?"

"Yes, I flatter myself we have done a good deal," de Barsac said. "You wanted to have a look at a certain document. Wasn't that the idea?"

"I wanted to know if it was in existence," Lupas snarled. "I have heard those fairy tales before. Half the young men in London who come borrowing money from me have expectations—on paper. And when I ask to see those papers they are rarely forthcoming. Oh, Henderby Lupas is a scoundrel, of course, a rascally old money-lender whom any sprig of nobility can insult. They come into my office and call me Shylock, and all sorts of pleasantries which they think I am bound to put up with and yet half of the young devils would rob me without the slightest hesitation if I only gave them the shadow of a chance. I know them, and I know you too, de Barsac. If you could get out of your obligations to-morrow, you would do so like a shot."

"Nice amiable temper you are in this morning," de Barsac laughed. "I rather judge, from what you say, that the document you mention exists only in my imagination."

"Well, I'd like to see it," Lupas sneered.

By way of reply de Barsac produced the document and placed it in the hands of the money-lender. Lupas put on his spectacles, and read it carefully line by line until he had fairly mastered its contents. Then, for the first moment, his grim air relaxed and he grew almost civil.

"Well, it appears to be all right," he said.

"Appears to be all right," de Barsac cried. "It is all right. And a nice job to get hold of it. I ran the risk of losing everything, including your money. But it's all right now, and I can keep that document as long as I please. Now, look here, Lupas, I want money."

"As usual," Lupas sneered.

"As usual, as you say. Now, on the strength of that document, I want you to lend me another two thousand pounds. You can charge me the usual rates, but I must have the money."

"You can have it on one condition," Lupas said. "And I'll send you a cheque from town to-morrow."

"What's that?" de Barsac asked.

"You must leave this document in my hands."

"All right," de Barsac said recklessly. "All right."

CHAPTER XXI

ON THE ROAD

De Barsac swung along by the side of Dorn, whistling to himself and having every appearance of a man who has succeeded in some great endeavour. The mere fact that his financial difficulties were at an end for the moment was all sufficient for him, but Dorn apparently did not share this opinion. He was going to benefit himself, and, indeed, he needed the money badly enough, but he appeared to be anxious and ill at ease—a fact upon which de Barsac rallied him.

"What the matter?" the latter asked. "Upon my word, there's no satisfying some people. Here you are, the richer by two hundred pounds which you have, obtained merely by the asking for, and yet you look like a man who has been robbed instead of one who has had a fine slice of luck."

"I quite understand all that," Dorn said. "And I am much obliged to you for your kind intentions. But you are so rash, so infernally impetuous."

"The artistic temperament," de Barsac said airily.

"Oh, curse the artistic temperament. That recklessness of yours will get you into serious trouble one of these days. I don't think you care two-pence about to-morrow so long as you have got a few pounds to go on with to-day."

"Why should I?" de Barsac asked.

"Oh well, I suppose it's no use talking. You'll go on like this till you land yourself in gaol. I don't doubt your courage. When it comes to personal danger, I would rather have you with me than anybody I know. But you take some frightful risks. I like to see my way clear, I like to see the way out, and I prefer, if possible, to know what the other fellow is doing. Never trust anybody as far as you can see, is my motto. Take Lupas, for instance. Wouldn't he throw you over to-morrow if it suited his purpose? Would he hesitate a moment to betray you? Not he. Now, you see what you have done. He only wanted to see that will, which was quite sufficient for all practical purposes, and goodness knows, we took a hideous risk enough to get it. And directly it comes into our hands, you part with it. You needn't have done so if you had refused to surrender it. Lupas would have let you have the money just the same. As it is, you have gone out of your way to strengthen his power over you. Ah, my friend, some of these days you will be sorry for that."

"Sounds prophetic," de Barsac said.

He was to find out how prophetic it was before long. Meanwhile he would have dismissed the whole thing as hardly worth another thought, but Dorn was not so easily shaken off.

"Very well," the latter said. "I won't labour the point. Now, look here, there's no time to be lost. We shall have a house full of people at Baron's Court before long, and before they come we must do something. I propose we walk into Tavistock and lunch quietly at some hotel there and settle our plan of campaign. It's no use putting things off from day to day, every hour makes our task more difficult; and if we are going through with the thing, the sooner it is faced the better. Now, listen to me."

For half an hour or so they walked quietly along the road, whilst Dorn talked in a husky voice that was little more than a whisper. He spoke with his head hung down, glancing from side to side as if half fearful that the woods had ears, whilst he unfolded his scheme that reduced even de Barsac to silence and rendered him grave almost to the verge of timidity. Then they walked the rest of the distance in absolute silence, after which they lunched generously. But it was a quiet and moody meal, with each man avoiding the other's glance and each of them furtive and sinister. Then they proceeded in the direction of the chemist's shop, where Dorn purchased something which necessitated his signing the chemist's book, which he did in an assumed name, after which they turned their faces once more in the direction of Baron's Court. They reached the lodge gates at length, to find the big iron barriers opened and a couple of cars standing just inside. Besides these was a big trolley, heavily laden with all kinds of strange appliances. By the gate stood Garrass with a gun in his hand.

"What's the meaning of all this?" de Barsac asked.

"The people from London," Garrass explained in his curt way. "The people who take the photographs. They are going farther on in a day or two, but just at present some of them are in the park with their cameras."

"Very lucid," de Barsac said. "And, by the way, Garrass, I have not heard you say as much before. You are becoming quite an orator. But what are you doing here with a gun in your hand?"

"They have turned out one or two of the animals, sir," Garrass said. "Trying to get a photograph or two, I believe. My master was quite anxious for them to begin at once."

"Yes, he would be," de Barsac said. "Like a child with a new toy, of course. I suppose you are keeping guard in case one of the beasts breaks away?"

Garrass nodded and said no more. De Barsac and his companion turned away and walked up the avenue in the direction of the house. Before they reached the big portico they saw something move in a thicket a quarter of a mile or so away, and immediately afterwards a big puma slunk across the open and was lost to sight in a mass of undergrowth. Dorn glanced apprehensively over his shoulder and quickened his pace.

"Is Bevill quite mad?" he asked.

"I believe he is at times," de Barsac said. "There is something of the comic opera about all this."

"It is most infernally dangerous," Dorn said. "With all those servants about the house, and the men and boys in the gardens, it's criminal. Suppose anything happened, as it easily might?"

"It doesn't matter two-pence as long as nothing happens to us," de Barsac said lightly. "It's a confounded nuisance, all the same. Look, there goes the old man yonder, right across the opening with that ape of his by his side. He'll get killed himself some of these days. I believe he regards that savage beast of his as absolutely harmless."

"I don't like it," Dorn muttered. "I don't like it a bit. Let's get inside; we shall be safe there."

De Barsac smiled at the troubled expression on the face of his companion, but followed him all the same without further hesitation. They shut themselves in the studio, where they sat smoking and casually discussing their plans until through the window they could see Bevill, together with Frick and the rest of them, coming along the avenue in the direction of the house. Evidently the exciting adventures of the day were over, and obviously Bevill was in a state of pleasurable excitement, for he strode along at the head of the little procession with Vim equally delighted by his side.

"Well, I suppose we shall have to humour him," de Barsac said. "But all this is exceedingly unpleasant for us. Upon my word, I've a great mind to throw the whole thing up altogether."

"What's the use of talking like that?" Dorn asked. "You couldn't do it if you would. We shall have to see this thing through now, whatever happens. Just think what it means to go back. You could no more pay Lupas than you could turn one of those bronze statues of yours into life. And if you don't pay him he will prosecute you. And once that's done, you are of no more account than the meanest tramp on the road. I don't like even to hear you talk like that."

De Barsac shrugged his shoulders as he rose to his feet and moved towards the door. At the same time he picked up a heavy object in bronze and placed it under his arm.

"What have you got there?" Dorn asked.

"Oh, that's the cast for Gibson," de Barsac explained. "A fine piece of work, though I say it myself. It's complete in every detail, and you could put it on to the scale without finding it vary a hundredth part of an inch. Upon my word, Sir Watney ought to pay me for this."

They drifted into the house presently for dinner, where they found the strange house party had been augmented by another guest, a tall thin man with an eager, enthusiastic face and a wonderful flow of words, who was introduced as Mr. Stafford Hatton, the popular novelist. The individual in question seemed to be thoroughly at home, which indeed he was, for he was eminently a Bohemian of the old-fashioned type and accepted all the gifts of the gods with a cheerful alacrity. He helped himself from time to time to the wines that went round the table and dilated at great length upon his work.

"We are only at the beginning of it," he said. "The cinematograph, gentleman, is going to be one of the greatest educators. Of course, I know at present it is mainly used to extract coppers from the pockets of small children interested in the adventures of Deadwood Dick, and Hawkshaw the Detective, but that is so much pioneer work. It is only a toy at present, but then there are early stages, so were the wireless telegraph and the telephone. I have just been telling Mr. Bevill that we are going to make history here. It's a great pleasure to have so enlightened a gentleman and so liberal a patron to work with. But he will get his reward later on. Yes, thanks, I will have another glass of port."

For a good hour or more Hatton talked on until at last the fountain of his eloquence seemed to dry up, and he settled himself down seriously to the decanter of port which he kept absent-mindedly by his elbow. With a smile and a shrug of his shoulders, Sir Watney Gibson glanced across the table in de Barsac's direction.

"What have you got there?" he asked.

"Ah, that's your model," de Barsac said. "And I am vain enough to be exceedingly proud of it. I should say that, on the whole, it is the best piece of work I ever did. Every hair and muscle and every nail is true to scale. Take it and put it by the side of Vim's paw, and you will be able to judge for yourself. Then tell me what you think of it."

Sir Watney reached out for the heavy bronze object, and he proceeded to compare it with what he called the hand and forearm of the chimpanzee that was seated by his side. It was not altogether an easy job, for Vim appeared to be unusually restless and fractious for him, and not altogether too good-tempered. But Sir Watney finished at length, and broke out into loud praise at the excellence of the work. Markham, watching everything carefully as usual, noticed the sudden light that lit up Dorn's eyes and wondered what it meant. But he was to know all about that in good time.

CHAPTER XXII

A STRANGE OUTBREAK

"What's the matter with Vim to-night?" de Barsac asked. "He has already broken two glasses and a dessert plate. What's the matter with him?"

"I don't know," Bevill said anxiously. "Ever since I came back he has been quite a different animal. He has been moody and restless, as if he were in some sort of pain. I have been wondering if his teeth want attending to. He was just like this two years ago when I had to have a special animal doctor down from London to see him, and he was of opinion that Vim was suffering from an abscess at the root of his teeth. And that really was the matter. It cost me no end of a lot of money to get a dentist to operate, but we managed it eventually, at the Zoological Gardens in London. And that was the cause of all the trouble. But for days afterwards the anaesthetic upset the poor beast, and he was positively dangerous for a time. Just like he was last year when he managed to get hold of a bottle of Benedictine and drank more than half of it before Garrass discovered what was going on. Garrass, you remember that, don't you? You recollect what a time we had?"

Garrass, waiting solemnly and watchfully behind his master's chair inclined his head respectfully, but said nothing.

"And Vim is like that again to-day," Bevill went on. "Perhaps he has picked up something that doesn't agree with him. He was fairly quiet all the afternoon, though a bit excited when we were getting those cameras into position, but nothing noticeable. Did you see anything, Dorn, when Vim followed you into your bedroom just before dinner?"

"Not I," Dorn said carelessly.

Just for the fraction of a second the speaker looked up in de Barsac's direction and caught his eyes. It was all done in a flash, but there was one person at the table who did not fail to notice it, and that was Markham. He had been sitting there, all through dinner hardly speaking a word, and watching everything that was going on. He would have been puzzled, perhaps, to say what was uppermost in his mind and what he was looking for, but it seemed to him that there was some mysterious influence in the air, some sinister undercurrent that centred in Dorn and de Barsac and radiated from them like an unseen wave. And all this rendered Markham anxious and uneasy and, at the same time, worried him all the more so, because he could not put his finger upon anything practical to go on. All he knew was that there were mysterious influences at work, and that they boded ill for the kindly, generous old man who sat there at the head of the table smilingly dispensing his own hospitality. And though Markham had confided his suspicions to Sir Watney Gibson, that usually astute individual appeared to have forgotten all about it, for he was laughing and talking with Dorn and de Barsac as if they had been friends for years. But then, Markham reflected, Sir Watney was a seasoned old man of the world, who never allowed his feelings to show themselves, which was a fact that had rendered him the terror of many a barrister who was defending a prisoner in a case where the great scientist was giving evidence on behalf of the Crown. In such cases Sir Watney had never been known to lose his temper, and therefore, perhaps on the present occasion he might be going out of his way to throw dust in the eyes of the two polished and gentlemanly scamps who sat facing him at the top of the table.

The dinner came to an end at length, and the little party scattered, Dorn and de Barsac going off in the direction of the studio as usual, whilst Sir Watney and his host made their way to the library, leaving the rest to amuse themselves in the billiard-room. There Hatton flung himself down on a comfortable lounge and helped himself liberally from the whisky and soda that Garrass had deposited there. Frick shook his head benevolently at his literary friend, and suggested that in view of work on the morrow the casual Bohemian had better be careful.

"Oh, that's all right," Hatton said. "I always know when to leave off, especially when I have a story to write. I have got it all clear in my mind, and I shall probably work on it for the best part of the night."

"How far have you gone?" Markham asked.

"Oh well, we have done practically nothing up to now," Frick said. "We were only trying a few experiments this afternoon, more to please Mr. Bevill than anything else. The man in charge of the cameras set up a couple of them to try the electric machinery, and I understand from what he says that he got one or two successful snaps of those pumas this afternoon, but that's all in the nature of elementary work. To-morrow we shall set up a travelling photographic studio with dark rooms and all the rest of it on that piece of waste ground just outside the gates, and then I hope we shall show you something good."

"I don't quite understand," Markham said. "What's the idea? Are you going to drive those animal through the covers and take photographs of them as they go by, working cameras hidden in trees with some electric arrangement?"

"Oh, that's not a bad rough way of putting it," Frick said. "Mind you, we didn't come down here originally with that intention at all. What we really have to do is to work out a big drama with a scene laid on Dartmoor, the centre of which is a dark and mysterious household—in other words, Lanton Place, which is an ideal household. We are going to have escaped convicts and prison warders and all that kind of thing, and a real big scene in the ruins of Lanton Place. But that's Hatton's job. When he has been over the ground and studied it he will be able to write up a story that few men could surpass. Meanwhile, during the fortnight or so when he is busy getting his local colour, we can fake up a series of splendid animal pictures for Hatton to write a story round later on. I don't quite know how it's going to be done yet, but of course there will be a hero and heroine. And, by the way, what a lovely heroine Miss Dorn will make."

It was all exceedingly interesting, so interesting, indeed, that Markham, forgetting all his dark thoughts and suspicions, sat there, talking and asking questions for the best part of two hours, until the rest of the house had sunk into silence, and everybody appeared to have gone to bed. Frick was full of the most entertaining reminiscences, and Hatton, after resolutely putting the whisky and soda on one side, suddenly, became both an interesting and intellectual companion. The big clock in the hall was striking the hour of one before Markham rose reluctantly to his feet and suggested that it was time to go to bed. They were just putting the lights out and making a move in the direction of the hall, when suddenly from somewhere on the ground floor came an urgent cry for help.

It was repeated three times in quick succession, each call more urgent than the last, and with it mingled strange snarls and cries that seem to have come from some infuriated animal. Markham put on the lights again, and, followed the other, dashed down the corridor in the direction of the library, from whence the cry proceeded. It was intensely dark there, and nothing could be seen, though assuredly enough there was some struggle going on in the dim recesses of the room. Markham put his head in through the door.

"What's going on here?" he demanded.

"The lights! For heaven's sake, put up the lights!" a panting voice broke out. "The switch is just inside the door. Don't hesitate, or I am done."

With a strange feeling of horror upon him, Markham fumbled along the edge of the doorway until his hand came in contact with the switch and the whole of the big room was flooded with light. He saw Bevill, clad in nothing but his pyjamas, standing in a corner of the room, with the table in front of him. He had caught up one of the heavy chairs and was holding it above his head. A yard or two away, crouched on the floor as if ready for a spring, was Vim—Vim, changed out of all recognition. His eyes were gleaming with madness; he showed his teeth in a hideous grin. As Markham yelled, Vim dragged himself slowly to his feet and rubbed his paws across his eyes in a strange resemblance to a man who is waking from a nightmare. Then, all the murderous rage seemed to fall from him like a garment, and he flung himself forward on his face, whining piteously like a dog asking mercy from some angry master.

Bevill came from behind the table, white and panting with his exertions, and laid his hand on the shoulder of the chimpanzee. Vim seemed to tremble at his touch.

"Get up, boy," he said. "Get up, it's all right now. There, I'm not angry with you."

Vim crawled to his master's feet and lay there, whimpering and crying in the fashion that was strangely human. There was something almost pathetic in his grief.

"You came only just in time," Bevill said. "It was entirely my own fault. I ought to have known better. You could see for yourself at dinner-time that there was something wrong with the animal, probably the reason I assigned. When I went to bed an hour ago, I shut Vim in here as usual—he always sleeps on the couch in the corner there, you know. Then I said good-night to de Barsac and Dorn and we all went to bed. I had occasion to come down here a few moments ago to get a book I had forgotten, and, instead of slipping into some clothes, I ran down here in my pyjamas. Vim has never seen me in them before, and directly I came into the room he went for me. If he had killed me, it would have been no one's fault but my own. He rushed at me before I was able to turn the lights on, and I had just time to get behind that table. I am very sorry to cause you all this alarm, but it's all right now. You see how sorry the poor beast is. He can't do enough to express his penitence. It might have occurred to me that he would not know me; he has never seen me in a sleeping suit before. Oh, yes, it's all right."

Bevill's last words were addressed to Dorn and de Barsac, who, disturbed by his cries, had come downstairs and were standing in the doorway listening to the explanation of the extraordinary scene that had taken place.

"A lucky escape," de Barsac said. "Still, there's no reason why we should stay here."

As he turned away Dorn laid a heavy hand on his arm.

"Come to my room," he whispered. "I have got something to say to you. Everything seems to be going our way just now. We've got it in the hollow of our hands. A little bit of audacity on our part and we are rich men."

"Lead the way," de Barsac said hoarsely.

CHAPTER XXIII

MRS. DORN'S DISCOVERY

John Bevill's enthusiastic expectations were not destined to be realised quite as soon as he had expected. There had been a great deal more to be done than Frick was aware, so, instead of a series of properly developed films showing the vagaries of the various animals in the park, nothing had materialised beyond an odd picture here and there, which, so Frick said, was largely due to the defects in the electrical arrangements. The cinematograph operators, on the other hand, declared that Frick had been in too much of a hurry, and that he was quite wrong in making all those extravagant promises. They could do nothing on a large scale, they said, with regard to animal pictures until they were in a position to use more power, and this, of course, they could get by accommodating their machinery to the dynamo that supplied Baron's Court with electric light. Once that was done, they had no doubt as to the result, but it would take a few days, and in the meantime, Mr. Bevill would have to possess himself in patience. The cameras were all there and the mechanical appliances in proper working order, but they must have more power. Then, with the aid of Bevill and his keepers, they hoped to do great things both by day and night in the park.

Meanwhile, the majority of the company had begun to settle down in the neighbourhood of Lanton Place. There was fair enough accommodation for them in the adjacent farmhouses, where they were welcomed freely enough and subjected, of course, to hundreds of curious questions. Hatton had gone off on to the moors to study the locality day by day, with a view to the elaboration of what he called his scene plot. And on most of these occasions he was accompanied by Major Dorn, who had deemed it prudent to go back home again, and keep his eye upon the business side of the arrangement. Dorn had been largely influenced in this decision by the fact that de Barsac had been summoned in London for a week or to in connection with an important commission that was being freely discussed in the columns of the daily press. Once more de Barsac was in the limelight, and Dorn smiled cynically to himself as he read those florid paragraphs.

For he knew only too well that there was something behind all this that the public little dreamt of. He knew how important it was that de Barsac's movements should be chronicled day by day, and how imperative it was, at the same time, that he himself should not be at Baron's Court just now. So he stayed quietly at Lanton Place, interested, or so he pretended, in Hatton's movements and keeping closely by the side of the latter day by day.

And Sylvia was busy enough. There was always something to do in the outdoor studio which had been erected in the grounds of Lanton Place. There were odd photographs of interiors, little scenes of odds and ends which, sooner or later, would form a part of the big story, All this, of course, was done under the eyes of Frick, who was going back to Baron's Court at the end of the week with the intention of making good his promise to John Bevill. And so a busy fortnight passed.

There were a good many hours in the day, of course, that Sylvia had entirely to herself, and Lionel Markham made the most of these. Most afternoons he cycled over to Lanton Place, taking care not to be there when Dorn was present, which was not a difficult matter, seeing that the weather was fine, and that Major Dorn spent the best part of the day on the moors in company with Stafford Hatton. It was lovely summer weather, too, so that there was no occasion to waste any time inside that gloomy old house.

"Are you enjoying it?" Markham asked one afternoon as he and Sylvia sat on the edge of the moor amongst the heather. "Do you like the work?"

"Ah, my dear boy, if you were in my particular position you would like any work," Sylvia smiled. "It makes one forget. Of course it is trying, and the glare of those big electric lights goes to my head sometimes, but I am getting used to that. And, besides, I am earning quite a large income. Fancy me with fifteen pounds a week to spend! A little time ago I should have been pleased to have earned as many shillings. But, at any rate, it keeps us quite comfortably now."

"And your father?" Markham suggested.

"Oh, he never dreams of troubling about us. He is getting more than I am, but not not penny of his money goes into the house. He said, as I was doing well and could not possibly spend anything down here, I might, if only as a duty, pay the household accounts out of my salary."

"And you are doing so?"

"My dear Lionel, I do so, if only for the sake of peace and quietness. I am grateful to have all these people round me—grateful to feel that I am living the life of an ordinary human being, and glad of the chance of getting away from the misery and desolation of it all. It's a bit monotonous at times, but then it is a good opening, and I think I shall stick to it. I ought not to grumble."

"Stick to it always?" Markham asked.

"Why not? A beggar like myself can't pick and choose."

"Well, I hope it won't be for long," Markham said. "It won't be my fault if it is. For the time being, at any rate, I am entirely dependent upon the salary that my uncle pays me, but I on not going to be content with that. I have been promised something that will bring me in a good many hundreds a year, and when once that is settled I am going to take you away from Lanton Place altogether."

"But my mother?" Sylvia said. "Oh, I couldn't possibly go away and leave her all alone."

"Of course you couldn't. I wasn't going to suggest anything of the kind. She can come with us. We can have a nice little place on the outskirts of London, where you could look after her, and perhaps with a change of scene, away front this dreary spot, she may recover entirely. I think she would. I don't think you need trouble about your father. He will always contrive to get a living."

And so they talked on there, in the golden sunshine, laying their plans for the future and thinking nothing about the morrow or what it was likely to bring forth. They parted presently, and Markham turned back in the direction of Baron's Court with his head in the air, dreaming dreams of the future.

Some way down the road he came face to face with Henderby Lupas, who was plodding along the highway in the direction of Lanton Place. He favoured Markham with a scowl and a curt nod of recognition as he passed by.

"Oh, so that old rascal's still in the neighbourhood," Markham said to himself. "I wonder what mischief he is up to down here. I wonder if he is in any way connected with the mysterious things that are going on at Baron's Court. I'd like to know. By Jove, I will know."

Acting on the impulse of the moment, Markham turned his cycle round and followed Lupas at a discreet distance. He saw the latter making inquiries at Lanton Place and then go off in the direction of the moor. A minute or two later and Sylvia came out of the house.

"You are back again?" she asked.

"Yes," Markham explained. "I followed that man who has just been to your front door. Do you know him?"

"Only that his name is Lupas," Sylvia said. "He has been here twice before. I think he is one of my father's mysterious friends. A hateful-looking man. He wanted my father this afternoon in a great hurry, and has gone to look for him. I thought he was very much upset about something."

"Oh, well, never mind him," Markham said. "I only wanted to know. I happen to have met Lupas before, and I can tell you nothing to his credit."

"Do come inside for a minute or two," Sylvia said. "My mother wants to speak to you. She has just come in out of the garden in a state of great excitement for her. Directly she did so she asked for you. It's a very strange thing since she has never mentioned your name since the very first day you came here. When I told her you had been and gone, she was greatly distressed. She wanted me to run after you and bring you back. It took me quite a time to explain that you came on a bicycle."

"Do you know what she wants?" Markham asked.

"I don't know, but I think she has found something. She had something that looked like an envelope in her hand. But do come and see her for a minute."

Mrs. Dorn sat in the dingy, melancholy dining-room with her face in her hands, gazing into space as if she were seeing some vision there, and ever and again glancing down at a stained and discoloured envelope that lay on her lap. Her sombre eyes lighted with something like intelligence as she caught sight of Markham. She held out her hands.

"So you have come back again," she said vaguely. "You have come back just at the right time. Look at this. It's a letter written by your father to me twenty years ago. I should very much like you to read it."

Markham took the dingy, half-blackened envelope in his hand and proceeded to read it. He saw a few curt business lines obviously written by a clerk acknowledging the receipt of a small locked black box and signed on behalf of a firm of private bankers with the signature "Richard Markham."

"Where is that box?" Mrs. Dorn demanded. "In that box was Sylvia's fortune. Where is it?"

"I am afraid I can't tell you," Markham stammered. "But I can make inquiries. When my father died, his affairs were in the most extraordinary state of confusion. He never ought to have been a business man, he was never intended for a banker. I know that in a cottage belonging to me there are all sort of odds and ends of boxes and packages that were removed from the old home and possibly yours might be amongst them. But I should say not. This is an official letter from the bank, and the box would have been there, of course. And everything connected with the bank was wound up long ago. Do you mean to say that you sent my father a little black box?"

Mrs. Dorn clasped her head wearily.

"I don't know," she said. "I don't know. It was clear enough a minute or two ago, and now it's all gone again."

She dropped her head on her hands again, and Markham could not get her to speak another word.

CHAPTER XXIV

MISSING

Meanwhile, Lupas tramped on in that dogged, obstinate way of his for a mile or two across the lonely moor in the direction which Dorn had gone, plodded on with his head hung down and his jaws moving, as if he were some bulldog with his teeth fixed to the throat of his enemy. He made a very sinister and forbidding object on the peaceful landscape as he trudged forward, until at length he came upon two figures seated by the roadside. One was Dorn, smoking a choice cigar, the other was Stafford Hatton inhaling his everlasting cigarettes and rattling on in that inconsequent way of his. He glanced up humorously at Lupas.

"Oh," he said. "'By the pricking of my thumbs, something wicked this way comes.' Say, Major, is this cut-throat brigand looking for you or for me?"

Dorn shrugged his shoulders resignedly.

"For me, I am afraid," he said. "My dear fellow, that is a London money-lender called Lupas. Now, between two men of the world I don't mind telling you that I have had sundry dealings with him. And evidently he has come here looking for me—a most thoughtless thing to do on a lovely afternoon like this when all nature is smiling peacefully. So, if you don't mind, perhaps you will stroll on in the direction of Lanton Place and I'll overtake you presently."

Dorn spoke lightly and frivolously enough, but inwardly he was feeling terribly uneasy as he noticed the thunder cloud on the features of Henderby Lupas. He knew that something must be wrong, indeed, to induce the town-bred money-lender to walk all this way on a blazing hot afternoon. Still, the matter had to be faced, and his smile was easy enough as he asked Lupas if anything was wrong.

"Wrong?" Lupas snorted. "Everything is wrong. Now, you must listen to me. I have been over to Baron's Court to see if I could find de Barsac, and they tell me he has been in London for some days. Back late this evening, I believe. I suppose he has been keeping out of my way."

"Nothing of the kind," Dorn retorted, with more heat than appeared to be necessary. "Nothing of the kind. De Barsac has a big commission which you can see for yourself if you read the paper. He had to go. But what's the use of all this? Tell me, what are you driving at?"

Lupas sat down and produced a cigar.

"Well, it's like this," he said. "On the strength of that will you and de Barsac managed to get hold of in some way I agreed to wait, and, what's more, I lent your friend a further sum of money."

"Knowing the conditions, of course."

"Oh, well, I thought I did. But, for once in my life, I was wrong. Now, I don't take any risks. I never knowingly took a risk in my life. It occurred to me after I had parted with that last lot of money that there might be trouble over that will. Mr. Bevill might have found out that it had been stolen or 'borrowed' or something of that kind, and in that case I wanted to know what he intended doing. If he found out anything, his suspicions would naturally be aroused. And after all, it's quite easy for a man to make a fresh will. It was up to me, therefore, to discover if the old gentleman intended to do anything of the sort, and I took steps accordingly. I found out the name of his solicitors, and in their employ is a clerk who owes me money. I have never pestered him for that money, because a clerk in the employ of a big firm of solicitors is often in a position to supply valuable information. Therefore, I put the screw on, and the man came to see me."

"Go on," Dorn said anxiously. "Go on."

"Oh, I'm going on fast enough," Lupas said. "As I feared, John Bevill discovered his loss. From what I gather he is under the impression that a scapegrace nephew of his stole that paper. And therefore Mr. Bevill sent full instructions to his lawyers to draw up a new will. I have seen that will, all ready engrossed for signature. It isn't signed yet, but it may be at any moment, and this time it will not be kept in a flimsy safe. It will be retained in London."

"And what's all this to do with me?" Dorn asked uneasily. "I suppose the will is practically a copy of the old one, in which case you have got nothing to worry about."

"Quite wrong," Lupas said. "It isn't a bit like the old one. Every penny of the money is left in trust for a certain purpose, after which it goes to someone else. A girl, I think it is. Her name is not mentioned, but she is the only daughter of somebody or another who used to be on the stage. I didn't trouble much upon that point, because it makes no difference to me whatever. But what I did notice was that de Barsac's name was never mentioned. Whether the old man's suspicions are aroused or not I don't know, but it is quite clear to me that Bevill has changed his mind so far as de Barsac's legacy is concerned. If he dies to-night, de Barsac would not benefit by a penny. And I should be the poorer by over forty thousand pounds. And I am not the man to sit quietly down and be robbed of a sum of money like that.

If this latter will is signed to-day or any time, we are all done. I am done. And I am not the man to be fooled in this fashion. Now, tell me straight out how you got hold of that document."

Dorn hesitated and stammered, he prevaricated and lied, but gradually Lupas dragged the whole truth out of him. It was not a pleasant story, and sounded so serious that Lupas lost all trace of his anger.

"Well, you have made a nice mess of it between you," he said. "Of course the old man's suspicions are aroused. He probably knows a great deal more about you and de Barsac than you think for. If you had told me this at first, de Barsac would never have got another penny out of me. I have a good mind to prosecute him for getting that money by false pretences. I had a great mind to go to Bevill and tell him everything. If I did, he might think he was under a moral obligation to repay me all I had lost. I should not have allowed de Barsac to have a penny if I had not been told about that legacy."

"You wouldn't do that?" Dorn asked.

"Oh, wouldn't I," Lupas snarled. "I wouldn't hesitate a moment. I am going to do something."

"And suppose that new will is never signed?" Dorn almost whispered "Suppose something happened to Bevill?"

Lupas looked up swiftly with a queer sinister light in those forbidding eyes of his.

"Suppose nothing," he said. "I am not concerned with the sort of things that happen in sensational novels. Still, it's a practical proposition, and if the old man died before the new will was signed there is nothing more to be said. I should get my money in due course, and our interesting friend de Barsac will be able to congratulate himself upon a narrow escape from something like ten years' penal servitude."

Dorn shuddered slightly. There was something almost grimly humorous in the suggestion.

"Well, give us a day or two," he implored. "Don't do anything till the end of the week. You know how careless Bevill is. I happen to be aware of the fact that he is not likely to go to London for the next week or two, and I can't see how that will can be signed until he does so. The fact is, the old man's full of excitement over this new toy of his—the photographing of his animals in the wild state. You leave it to de Barsac and myself. I believe he is coming back to-night by a late train, and we can talk it over before we go to bed. I'll tell him exactly what you say."

"You had better," Lupas said grimly. "And tell him that I am not going to stand any of his infernal nonsense. Here, this is what I am prepared to do. You had better 'find' that will. Trump up some story to the effect that you have found it in the grounds. De Barsac had better say he had the curiosity to read it. Then he can shed a few maudlin tears of gratitude over his own legacy, and tell the old man that he has been engaged in disastrous speculations and try and induce him to fork out the cash now. You know the sort of game I mean. Play on the old gentleman's feelings, snivel about ruin and disgrace, which, by George, will be true enough if nothing is done. There now, I have shown you a way out of the trouble, and I hope that de Barsac will be correspondingly grateful."

An hour later and Dorn made his way slowly and thoughtfully up the avenue in the direction of Baron's Court. He had thought of an excuse for seeing John Bevill, who, however, was somewhere out in the grounds with Frick engaged in some new series of experiments, for the electric power had been installed and before dark it was hoped that some highly successful photographs would be taken. They would be all in presently to a late dinner, and if Major Dorn liked to stay, no doubt Mr. Bevill would be glad to see him.

All this information Dorn learnt from the taciturn Garrass.

"Very well, Garrass," he said. "I think I'll stay. I can amuse myself in the library with a book for an hour or two. And perhaps you will let Mr. Bevill know when he returns."

Dorn sat there till the light began to fade, and one by one the people began to trickle in from the park. It was now past nine o'clock, and Bevill's hungry guests were wandering about the house, wondering whether or not it would be polite to sit down to the cold dinner set out in the dining-room before their host returned. They did sit down presently at the suggestion of Garrass, who said that his master had probably been detained and that he would be quite upset if his friends waited for him. He very often remained in his absent-minded way at the cottage with one of the keepers till quite late at night, and, indeed, on one occasion he had not come back at all.

"Well, perhaps we had better go on," Frick said. "I hope the old gentleman isn't wandering about the park with all those animals loose. Our cameras will do their work without any attention now. And I don't mind confessing that I am faint for want of my dinner."

The time drifted on till nearly eleven, when de Barsac put in an appearance, having come down by the last train, and motored over from Tavistock. Then the clock struck eleven and twelve without any sign of Bevill, and a moment or two later Garrass burst into the room.

"My master is nowhere to be found," he said. "None of the keepers have seen him, neither has he been at the lodge. I am afraid that something serious has happened to him."

CHAPTER XXV

TRAGEDY!

Markham jumped to his feet, the first of them there to understand that there was something serious. He knew, in the ordinary course of things, that Bevill's absence would have meant little or nothing. For instance, it would have been nothing strange for that eccentric old gentleman to go off in his absent-minded way to the bungalow and there remain for a day or two without advising his friends of his whereabouts.

But this Markham felt by instinct was a different matter altogether. There was a chill foreboding at his heart and a strange coldness down his spine that seemed to tell of disaster. He glanced at the other men in the room, from Hatton and Frick, who were exchanging mystified looks, to Dorn and de Barsac, with a queer feeling, utterly illogical, perhaps, that these latter men could tell him a good deal if they pleased. He knew perfectly well that they were standing there, on the verge of catastrophe, and that something very sinister had happened to John Bevill.

It was all absolutely illogical, of course, but there it was. He knew perfectly well that for the last few hours, at any rate, Dorn had been under his own eye, and that quite recently de Barsac had come off a railway journey.

"What the matter?" Hatton asked. "Is there anything very wrong? I thought it was quite usual for the old gentleman to wander all about the place by himself."

"That's quite correct," Markham said. "But—"

There he stopped, breaking off abruptly, conscious, perhaps, that he was taking too much upon himself, and that it would be much wiser to leave matter to de Barsac, who, to all practical purposes, was his host. He turned to the latter.

"Aren't you going to do something?" he asked. "Surely it is in your hands."

De Barsac shrugged his shoulders. He was perhaps, on the whole, the coolest of the company. Markham could see that his hand was perfectly steady as he pulled at his cigar. His eyes were indifferent, and his features serene enough. Just at that moment Markham's chief regret lay in the fact that Sir Watney Gibson was no longer in the house. He felt just then in sore need of counsel.

"Really," de Barsac said, "I don't see any occasion for all this fuss. Garrass, how many times has your master gone away like this without saying a word to anyone?"

"A good many, sir," Garrass admitted. "But never before have we opened the cages of those animals for the experiments of those gentlemen here."

"But they are not wandering about now?" de Barsac asked.

"I think not, sir. There may be one or two, but the keepers hope to have them all in by nine o'clock. They will be sure to come back for their food."

"Then in that case, I don't see the least cause to worry," de Barsac said. "I daresay Bevill is wandering about in the moonlight, too deeply interested in some scientific problem to come home. Oh, he'll turn up in the morning all right. If we go out hunting him he won't like it. Besides, I suppose he has got the faithful ape with him, hasn't he Garrass?"

"That is so, sir," Garrass said gravely.

"Ah, well, in that case, I think I shall go to bed," de Barsac said. "I have no anxiety."

"I don't take the same view of it at all," Markham said coldly. "Suppose something has happened? There is certain to be an inquiry afterwards, and if so, what will people say when they know that we all went coolly to bed whilst the master of Baron's Court was missing? Come along, Garrass, we'll go at any rate and have a look round."

"You can count me in, too," Frick said.

As Frick spoke he rose and, followed by Hatton, made his way in the direction of the door. De Barsac shrugged his shoulders cynically and glanced in Dorn's direction. It was as if the latter, too, had good humouredly made up their minds to humour a piece of folly on the part of their companions.

It was a perfect moonlight night, warm and dry, so that there was no occasion for any change of clothing before the little party set out on their errand. For the best part of two hours they searched the woods and thickets in the park until it began to dawn upon them that they were looking in the wrong direction. They came, presently, to a little clump of trees sheltering a spring right in the heart of the park, and in the gloom something seemed to stand out like a patch of huddled black and white on the edge of the water. With a little cry, Garrass darted forward and bent down.

"My master," he said hoarsely.

It was even as he said. John Bevill lay there as if he had fallen placidly asleep. His white still face was turned up to the sky, his dress was not in the least disarranged, and those benevolent features of his were singularly peaceful.

He was quite dead; evidently he had been dead for hours. From his appearance he might have sat down there to rest, and had died tranquilly in his sleep. They lifted him from where he lay, and carried him out in the open.

"This is a ghastly business," de Barsac said. "A terrible business. Garrass, run as far as the keeper's cottage and tell him to come along with a hurdle. We must get our poor friend to the house as soon as possible. I am very sorry, Markham. We were wrong, and you were entirely right. We ought to have come here at once. Not that it made any difference. As far as I can see, Bevill must have died as he was crossing the park. A peaceful death, and one that he would have asked for himself. I can't see any signs of violence."

Markham said nothing. For the moment, at any rate, he was too overcome with the weight of the discovery. From the start he had expected something of this kind, but in quite another form. He had feared violence or foul play, but so far as he could judge there was no suggestion of either. The full light of the moon shone down on the dead man's face, a face that was singularly calm and placid. There was no suggestion anywhere of a struggle, the clothing was not disarranged, and there was not so much as a scratch on those pallid features. It was tragedy, dreaded and feared, but it had come in such a strange and unexpected form, that, for the moment, at any rate, Markham could make nothing of it. He drew back partly in the shadow and waited without another word till Garrass returned with one of the keepers, and then the little procession moved silently across the park in the direction of the house. They carried Bevill up to his bedroom and left him there.

"There is nothing to be done till the morning, as far as I can see," de Barsac said. "I don't even see the sense of waking Nurse Coterell up. It will be time enough to tell her in the morning. Garrass, you had better telephone to the police at Tavistock and tell them what has happened. You had better say that so far as we can judge there is nothing wrong, and that your master was found dead in the park a few minutes ago, obviously from natural causes. If the police like to send over here now, they can, but there is no reason why they should not wait till morning. If they decide to come at once I will sit up and wait for them."

Garrass came back a moment or two later with the information that a superintendent of police was already on his way to Baron's Court, and would be there within half an hour. De Barsac appeared to listen rather wearily.

"Well, after all, it is for them to decide," he said. "Garrass, there is no reason why we should keep you up any longer. The same remark applies to you other gentleman."

Markham, however, had disappeared, and a few moments later was followed upstairs by Hatton and Frick, leaving the other two facing each other in the dining-room. Dorn walked over to the sideboard and helped himself liberally to a whisky and soda. His face was very pale and his hands were trembling. He half irresolutely took a cigar from a box, then, changing his mind, lighted a cigarette instead.

"I think I will follow your example," de Barsac said. "Pour me out a drink, will you? A little more, please. This is a shocking business, Dorn."

"It is," Dorn agreed. "A ghastly business. Of course, being a soldier, I know something about these things; but when I saw the poor old man lying dead there—"

Dorn broke off abruptly, swallowed his drink at one gulp and filled up his glass again.

"Well, it can't be helped," he went on more firmly. "After all, Bevill was an old man, and never very strong, I should say. Heart disease probably. Really, when you come to think of it, the most merciful of all deaths. And, to be quite cynical, a piece of luck for you."

"Well, I can't contradict you," de Barsac said. "And besides—but we need not discuss that. The old man was a good friend to me, and in many ways I am sorry. But on the other hand, considering my position—"

"Ah," Dorn said. "You don't know yet what a narrow shave you had. Another day or two and it would have been too late. Perhaps I had better tell you."

"Well, it would be as well, perhaps."

Dorn carefully closed the door, having first ascertained that the house was quiet, and then, in low tones, proceeded to tell de Barsac the story of his interview with Henderby Lupas. It was a story that de Barsac appeared to find interesting, for he never spoke until Dorn had finished.

"By Jove, that was a close call," he said. "It will be a lesson to me in future."

"Not it," Darn said contemptuously. "You always will be reckless and headstrong. Now, what would have happened if John Bevill had lived?"

"Well, I'll tell you," de Barsac, whispered. "I should have lost everything. I didn't like to tell you, but the night before I went to town Bevill told me that he had changed his mind in regard to my legacy, and that he intended leaving me nothing. His idea was that I didn't need it, and as he had lost money himself lately, he was going to make another will. Good Lord, if he had only known the truth!"

CHAPTER XXVI

Dorn wiped the beads from his forehead.

"Why did you not tell me that?" he asked.

"My dear fellow, what's the good? It would only have upset you. You are very clever and very cunning, and in connection with some infernally subtle plot you have no superior. But you certainly lack personal courage. Yours is not the hand to put the finishing touch, and if I had told you, you would probably have been frightened. Well, I didn't tell you, and for the last few nights you have slept all the better for it. As far as I can gather Bevill has been speculating himself, and losing his money. I don't say he has lost all, or anything like it, but his idea was to leave Baron's Court to the nation as a sort of college for natural research, and endow it with the best part of his fortune. He had an idea of leaving a good many thousands to some friend of his, though he didn't say who, and that money was the legacy that ought to have come to me. He went on to say that as I was a rich man I could not possibly want it, and—well, you can imagine the absolute rubbish he talked. If he had lived, I should have been at Lupas' mercy. Now I shall be able to pay that old rascal and get out of his power. It will leave me absolutely penniless, but that's a minor consideration."

"It certainly ought to be with a man who can make money as easily as you do," Dorn said. "However, the danger is past and you are free—till the next time. Now, I suppose you see what you've got to do?"

"Oh, yes. First of all, put that will back where you found it. Lupas must let us have it back for the purpose. He can't well refuse. He knows that it is to our interest not to destroy it or play the fool in any way; he knows that directly the will is proved he gets his money."

"That's clear enough," Dorn said. "I'll run over and see Lupas directly after breakfast. It's not altogether as easy as you think. There are difficulties in the way."

"What do you mean by that?" de Barsac asked.

"Well, you've got to get that paper back in the safe again. And after what's happened, it won't be so easy. Now, for Heaven's sake don't go into this thing as if it were of no importance. I thought it all out before I came here this afternoon. Now, my idea is this. There will be an inquest this morning, probably a purely formal affair, and a good many questions will be asked. All sorts of questions about Bevill's private affairs. Somebody ought to make a preliminary examination of the papers. I suggest that you telephone to Bevill's local solicitor in Tavistock. Let's have him over here early and get him to go through the safe. You can help him, or we both can, for that matter. Then we can shove that will into a draft envelope and put it in under the lawyer's nose so that he can't overlook it. And when he has found it, you can make some remark upon Bevill's absent-mindedness and tell the solicitor that the will was in the safe all the time and that all the fuss Bevill made the other night was totally unnecessary. Now, I dare say you may think that all this is unnecessary fussing. But I don't think so. You never know."

"Oh, all right," de Barsac said. "All right. Have it your own way. At any rate, we can shake hands upon a fine get out from a tight place. And now, don't you think we had better turn in?"

"Yes, but what about the police?" Dorn asked.

"Confound it, I had forgotten all about that," de Barsac said. "You go to bed and leave them to me."

It was shortly after nine o'clock the following morning before the superintendent of police came for the second time with information to the effect that the inquest would be held at twelve o'clock, when the coroner would attend Baron's Court for that purpose. After a hasty breakfast de Barsac got the local solicitor on the telephone and invited him to come over without delay. He arrived in due course, a fussy little self-important man who appeared to be duly impressed with the solemnity of the occasion.

"My name is Grant, Mr. de Barsac," he said. "I think we have met before. You were quite right in sending for me. I have never been entrusted with the administration of the late Mr. Bevill's London property from whence he derives a great part of his income, but apart from that I have enjoyed his confidence for years. Amongst other things, I made his will."

"So he told me," de Barsac lied boldly. Here was the very opening he needed. "So he told me. Now, Mr. Grant, you will be betraying no secret if you tell me that under that will I benefit to a considerable amount. Not that I particularly need money—a man in my position wouldn't—but, of course, I value the gift as an expression of good will from a dear old friend. Now, is that will in your possession?"

"It isn't," Grant said. "It ought to be, of course. It is the bounden duty of all testators to leave their wills in the hands of their solicitors. Such a course saves a great deal of trouble. You see, wills get mislaid. But I need not go into that. For some reason Mr. Bevill preferred to keep his will himself, and the last time I discussed the matter with him he told me that the document was in his safe."

"It certainly was," de Barsac said. "I know that because I saw it there myself. But a few nights ago there was an attempt at burglary, and after the rascals were driven off Mr. Bevill declared that his will had been stolen. I don't think so myself; I don't think that anybody would be such a fool as to run the risk for the sake of a document that can be replaced at any moment. I don't want to stir up any scandal, but Mr. Bevill had a certain scamp of a nephew."

"Yes, Yes," Grant said. "I know all about that. Now, what is your theory, Mr. de Barsac?"

"Well, my theory is that the will is in the safe all the time," de Barsac replied. "In his absent-minded way John Bevill probably put the document in a different pigeon hole from the one he intended. I found the key of the safe a few minutes ago and here it is. Now, I want you to make a professional examination of those papers."

De Barsac talked easily for some little time. As a matter of fact, he was putting the lawyer off till Dorn returned from his visit to Lupas. Nothing could be done until Dorn came back with that precious document. And presently, with a little sigh of relief, de Barsac saw his confederate stroll along the terrace in front of the library window. As he passed he paused to light a cigarette and significantly tapped his breast pocket. It was the signal agreed upon, and a few minutes later the safe was opened and the missing will found in a draft envelope, where it had been placed by Dorn ready to be pushed on to the lawyer, much as a conjurer forces a card upon one of his audience. Grant held it up triumphantly.

"There you are, Mr. de Barsac," he said. "You were evidently quite right. It only proves what I said just now that no client ought to have charge of his own will. I think that I had better take care of this."

"Of course," de Barsac agreed. "You'll have to prove it and all that sort of thing, won't you? Though of course, I suppose in the circumstances it will be quite a long time before the estate is administered. Now, what do you say to a sandwich and a glass of sherry before the coroner comes?"

Dorn and de Barsac left the little lawyer to his refreshments, whilst they paced up and down the terrace discussing matters in confidential whispers.

"Well?" de Barsac asked. "And how did you find Lupas? Was he reasonable?"

"Oh, about as amiable as usual," Dorn said. "I don't think he would have believed that Bevill was dead if he had had to take my word for it. But, fortunately for us, he had heard the news before. When I told him what I wanted, he was quite reasonable enough. Indeed, he seemed to be rather sorry that he had ever handled the thing at all. He's going back to town this afternoon."

"Oh, really? Rather sudden, isn't it? That old fox doesn't want to be identified with us any more than he can help. Well, I don't blame him."

They talked on there in undertones, till at length the coroner made his appearance, followed by the jury and one or two curious neighbours, and an odd representative of the press who had already learnt something of the tragedy. The inquest took place in the library, and after a few words to the jury from the coroner the proceedings commenced.

From the first it was quite evident that this was only a preliminary inquiry. The police had only had the matter in hand a few hours, and though, so far, there were no suspicious circumstances it was possible that the case might not be quite as simple as it looked.

Garrass was the first witness. He told how he had found the body of his late master lying in the park; he spoke of Mr. Bevill's peculiar habits, and how it was no new thing for him to be out at all hours of the day and night either by himself or accompanied by his faithful chimpanzee.

"Isn't it rather strange," Markham whispered to Frick, who sat by his side, "that nothing should have been seen of Vim the last few hours? I knew he went out with his master last night—in fact, he was with him all day. And I don't think anyone has seen him since."

"It is a funny thing," Frick said. "It makes one wonder. Look here, Hatton, you heard what Mr. Markham said. There is a plot for you. The dead man and the missing ape."

Hatton nodded and made a note on a sheet of paper. Then they lapsed into silence again and the dreary proceedings went on. Garrass finished at length and after him other witnesses were called. Then the superintendent of police took a hand. He hadn't got much to say, except that he proposed only to call the police surgeon that morning, and afterwards apply for an adjournment for a day or two. The police doctor came forward. He had made a careful examination of the body, he said, and, as a result, he had come to certain conclusions. When asked by the coroner what his conclusions were, the superintendent of police jumped to his feet.

"I think, sir," he said, "that any technical questions had better be postponed."

"In that case," the coroner replied, "the court stands adjourned till this day week at the same time."

CHAPTER XXVII

A BLOW FOR DE BARSAC

Naturally enough, the tragedy at Baron's Court attracted a good deal of attention, not only locally, but throughout the West of England. Then, gradually the conviction began to spread that there was something behind the mystery that had to be explained. On the face of it there was no ground for this theory that did not prevent people talking, especially in the neighbourhood of Tavistock. And, strangely enough, one of the reasons given for a suggestion that something was radically wrong was that John Bevill's pet chimpanzee was not to be found. And, as a matter of facts, Vim had disappeared, leaving no trace behind him. He was known to have accompanied his master the whole of the afternoon and evening on the day of his death, and, indeed, he had been seen in close attendance on John Bevill as late as nine o'clock on the evening of the tragedy.

And, in some extraordinary way, the story of Vim's attack upon his master a fortnight or so ago had become public property. People whispered that on a certain occasion there had been something like a conflict between the man and the monkey, and that, at another time, the chimpanzee had made a violent attack upon Bevill in the dead of the night. Who started these reports and whence they came, no one seemed to know, but they were freely discussed, and there were hundreds of people firmly under the impression that the eccentric old scientist had met his death at the hands of his strange pet. It was pointed out that Vim was a big animal, possessed of extraordinary strength, and quite capable of killing a man with the greatest ease. So that therefore, in the course of a day or two, most people in that part of the country were ready to declare that this was what had happened, and that in the course of subsequent investigations the truth would be made clear. Meanwhile, there was nothing to do but to await till the adjourned inquest.

Life at Baron's Court was going on much about the same. It was not time yet for Bevill's next-of-kin to take possession, and seeing that nearly every member of the household would be asked to give his evidence, things were going on in the ordinary routine with de Barsac as nominal host. He was amiable enough to everybody. He showed no disposition to get rid of certain people there who had nothing in sympathy with him. He played the host easily and naturally, and seemed to go out of his way to make everybody at home. And, when de Barsac liked, his manners were absolutely perfect.

There was one member of the household who listened coldly enough to these blandishments, and that was Lionel Markham. He lost no time in writing a detailed account of what had happened to Sir Watney Gibson, and invited the latter to come over to Baron's Court as soon as possible. And this being done, and a favourable reply received, Markham set himself down to watch the course of events.

Dorn still lingered on, apparently more for the sake of the companionship for de Barsac than anything else, and Markham noticed that these two were seldom together unless it was late at night or early in the morning. Then, on the third day, they went off on some errand, and Markham decided to follow them. He would have been at some pains to say why—an instinct, perhaps; but he kept carefully out of sight and traced them across the moor, until he saw them meet someone whom he recognised as Henderby Lupas. It was an open spot, where it was impossible to overhear or even see much that was going on without being detected, so therefore Markham retraced his footsteps, wondering what the meaning of this secret conclave meant, and carefully making a note of what he had seen.

He had noted that during breakfast both Dorn and de Barsac appeared to be preoccupied and uneasy in their minds, but, for the moment, he had to content himself with that knowledge, and make his way thoughtfully back to Baron's Court.

The cause of all the trouble, however, was in a short curt note that had arrived by post that morning from Henderby Lupas demanding de Barsac's presence at a given rendezvous as soon after ten o'clock as possible. There was something so menacing in this request that de Barsac decided to obey it without delay, and, as a matter of precaution, took Dorn with him. They found Lupas awaiting them, and if Markham had gone a little farther he would have noticed a little two-seater car without a driver standing amongst the heather. It was in this that Lupas had come down from London, quite alone, and the fact, by itself, did not tend to reassure de Barsac and his companion. It seemed to him that there must be something wrong indeed.

"Well, here we are," he said cheerfully. "And now, what's the matter? Upon my word, Lupas, anyone would think that I had nothing else to do except run after you."

"You will run after me just when and where I please," Lupas growled. "You don't suppose I have come down from London all the way by myself for the mere pleasure of seeing you two. Here I am, neglecting important business and pottering about the country as if I had nothing else to do. I started in the car yesterday morning, and it has taken me nearly all my time to get here. And I came alone, too."

"But why?" Dorn asked.

"Yes why?" de Barsac echoed. "You can afford to come down in style if you like. I know you have got a big luxurious car and a competent chauffeur."

"Oh, I've got all that, of course," Lupas said, "but I didn't want anybody to know where I was going, and I didn't want anybody to know I was going to meet you men."

"Still more mysteries," de Barsac smiled.

"I never take any risks. I suppose it's no use asking you what happened to Bevill?"

"Really, I must resent that tone of yours," de Barsac said. "Anybody who heard you talk might think that there was something underhanded about my poor friend's death."

"As a matter of fact, thousands do," Lupas snorted. "And I don't mind telling you I am one of them. But let that pass. I have no doubt the truth will come out in time."

"The truth is out now," Dorn said soothingly. "There's no mystery. Mr. Bevill died suddenly, probably of heart disease. He was picked up dead in the park—in fact, we were both present at the time. He lay there like one asleep. There were no signs of violence anywhere."

"Well, it was a very good thing for de Barsac," Lupas interrupted. "Some people have all the luck. But in this particular instance the luck is out. And that's what brings me down here. What happened over that will?"

"Oh, we managed to get it back in the safe all right," Dorn laughed. "It was easily done. We had a fool of a local lawyer to deal with, and we so contrived it that the fellow found the will himself. And it is in his hands at the present moment, so I suppose before long de Barsac will get his money, and, of course, you will be paid."

Lupas laughed, a queer silent sort of laugh that seemed to come from the bottom of his chest. He turned those malignant eyes of his upon the other two men and smiled in a way that aroused all de Barsac's fears.

"Oh, stop that, confound you!" he said irritably. "If you have got anything to say, say it."

"You won't he pleased," Lupas sneered. "Like other men of your type, you have been too clever. If you had only left that will alone, everything would have been all right."

"But you would see it," Dorn said.

"I know that," Lupas admitted. "And I am sorry now that I didn't wait a bit. Because it's like this. When Bevill found he had been robbed, he made up his mind that his nephew was the culprit. And that being so, he acted in a business-like manner for once in his life and instructed his lawyers in London to draw up a new will. And this was done."

"Oh, we know that," Dorn said impatiently. "You told me so yourself. You had even seen it. But now that document must be so much waste-paper."

"And consequently the old will stands," Lupas sneered. "All very nice and pleasant for de Barsac, but it's not the fact. The new will was signed."

De Barsac dropped his cigar in the heather and swore aloud. His swarthy features had grown strangely pale and he was trembling from head to foot, like some nerveless coward in the presence of some great danger. It seemed extraordinary that a man of his sanguine temperament and easy-going disposition should have been so deeply affected by an incident that hurt Lupas more than it injured him.

"It's a lie," he said hoarsely.

"It's no lie," Lupas responded. "It's true enough. You blundered terribly. You ought never to have removed that paper from the safe; or, at any rate, you ought to have restored it in such a way as to blind John Bevill to what was going on. But it's no use crying about spilt milk. I tell you that the new will was signed at Tavistock three days before Bevill's death. He would have delayed the matter, only those London lawyers were persistent. Perhaps they saw the danger. At any rate, they sent one of their confidential clerks down to Tavistock with the will, and Mr. Bevill went over there and signed it. That document is now locked up in London, and in due course will be proved. I know what I am talking about, because the clerk I mentioned to you gave me all the information. He even supplied me with a draft copy of the will. And now perhaps you understand why I came down here. I have my own good reasons for not wishing to be seen with either of you, and if you can't draw your own conclusions from that remark you are both bigger fools than I take you to be. But that is not the point. What I want to know is what you are going to do about it. It's merely a question of money with me. Where am I going to get it from?"

"I don't know," de Barsac muttered. "Do you mean to say that my name isn't mentioned in that new will?"

"I do," Lupas said curtly. "And what's more, the money originally meant for you has gone to somebody else. It was evidently one of the old man's impulsive ideas, for he left that forty thousand pounds to a girl friend of his for whom he appears to have been sorry. It is a bequest to her in recognition of her courage and honesty in circumstances that were exceedingly trying. Quite romantic, eh?"

"Anybody that we know?" Dorn asked.

"Oh, certainly," Lupas said drily. "The lucky beneficiary is Miss Sylvia Dorn, of Lanton Place."

CHAPTER XXVIII

MORE LIGHT

Lupas threw out this bombshell with characteristic malice and mocking laughter in his eye.

"Yes, quite a romance, isn't it?" he said. "Fancy that dear old gentleman leaving all that money to the daughter of one of the biggest scoundrels in Devon! I wonder if he knew you, Dorn. Some of these quiet, placid men are very shrewd under their mild exteriors."

Dorn said nothing. He was too amazed by this extraordinary revelation, and besides, that nimble mind of his was already engaged in speculating as to how he could turn this information to his personal advantage. Lupas, watching him narrowly, seemed to follow what was passing in his mind.

"I thought I should astonish you," he said. "And I hope you will be correspondingly grateful for the information. It's an ill wind that blows nobody any luck. Fancy a pretty little scheme to put money in the hands of two scoundrels—"

"Three," de Barsac said. "Three."

Lupas smiled, quite untouched.

"Very well, three if you like," he said. "And after all said and done, it was my money you were scheming for. Still, there you are. You go to all this trouble over a certain sum of money, and the sole result is to throw the proceeds into the lap of a young girl who never expected a penny of it. I am quite convinced in my own mind that, if you hadn't bungled over the old man's safe, it would never have occurred to him to have altered his will at all. And now a word in your ear, Dorn. You know this, but you can't use your information yet. You can't tell your daughter a fact that probably will not be communicated to her for weeks. If you do, all sorts of awkward question will be asked. You will probably be required to say where you got your information from. And now, de Barsac, what are you going to do? I have come down here at a great inconvenience to myself and some risk, if you only knew it, because I could not well write you all this. What are you going to do?"

"For the life of me, I don't know," de Barsac said. "I must have time to turn round."

"I'll give you a week," Lupas said. "And if something substantial is not paid on account by that time I shall move. If I lose my money, I'll get even some way. And don't say I haven't warned you."

With which Lupas rose and went off in the direction of his car without another word. He drove across the moor in the direction of Tavistock, leaving the two conspirators facing one another with blank looks and uneasy glances. They stood thus for a time in absolute silence. Then something in a clump of heather stirred and a queer caricature of a human face in a fringe of red-brown hair looked out.

"By heavens, it's Vim!" Dorn cried.

It was even as he said—Vim, ragged and unkempt, covered with dry mud and dust, and without any vestige of his usual neat apparel. As he caught sight of the two men his eyes concentrated vengefully, and he showed his teeth in a chattering grin. Just for a moment it looked as if he was about to attack the two unarmed men, and it would have gone hard for them if he had. But then something changed in that queer, half-human mind of his, and with a strange melancholy cry Vim turned his back upon them and set off with incredible speed across the moor until he was lost to sight.

"Oh, let's get back," de Barsac said. "This is a real morning of horrors. And yet a few hours ago everything seemed to be just plain sailing. Dorn, what on earth possessed that old fool to leave your daughter that money?"

"Heaven only knows," Dorn said moodily. "Pure luck, I suppose. You know how Sylvia met Bevill, don't you?"

"Oh, you told me that, of course."

"Well, that's all I know about it. I dare say the old man found out something of the truth, and no doubt he was impressed by the girl's resolution and courage. Besides, Sylvia is an unusually attractive girl, and old men are proverbially not blind to such things. However, there it is, and we have got to make the best of it."

"I was wondering," de Barsac said. "Being a mere girl, perhaps your daughter might not object—"

"Oh, wouldn't she," Dorn said. "There's not a more obstinate girl in England. If you think it would be any use for me to come the fond parent with Sylvia, you are mistaken. To be brutally cynical, she knows me."

"She knows a good deal, then," de Barsac sneered.

"Well, at any rate, she knows quite enough not to trust me with a penny. You don't know what she's like when she's roused. I shall get nothing out of her. I know exactly what she'll do. She'll take her mother away and defy me. She might, if the worse came to the worst, offer me a pound or two a week to go and live somewhere else. Ah, if I'd have only known this was coming! But I didn't, and there's an end of it."

With this sort of talk the two discomfited scoundrels made their way back to Baron's Court just in time to see Sir Watney Gibson drive up to the house. They avoided him for the moment, for they were in no mood for the ordinary conventions of life, but the circumstance was disturbing. They proceeded to lunch by themselves, and then, as usual, shut themselves up in the studio, whilst Sir Watney and his nephew paced up and down the terrace discussing recent events in confidential tones.

"Now, tell me, my boy," Sir Watney said, "exactly what you asked me to come down here for. I am amazingly busy just now, though I should have come down for the funeral next Monday, of course. You were very guarded in your letter, so guarded, indeed, that I seemed to read between the lines. I suppose that's why you asked me to come."

"That's right," Markham said. "I thought you ought to be here. And yet, if you ask me why, I couldn't tell you. I am uneasy in my mind; I cannot rid myself of the impression that John Bevill is the victim of foul play."

"But there were no signs of violence."

"Oh, I grant you that," Markham went on. "There are no signs of violence anywhere. The poor old gentleman lay there as calm and placid as if he had died in his sleep. So far, the police surgeon has only made a casual inspection of the body, but I rather fancy he knows something, because the inquest was adjourned so hurriedly just as he had begun his evidence. Now, that was one strange thing. Another thing equally sinister is that Vim has disappeared. Now, why should the chimpanzee go off and hide himself in this way? He was with his master all that evening in the park; he was seen with Mr. Bevill just before dark, when they were apparently on the best of terms."

"Just one moment," Sir Watney said. "Don't forget that Vim tried to attack his master on two occasions. And don't forget that he has had outbursts before, particularly when he had the opportunity of indulging in his favourite liqueurs. I always told Bevill that he would have trouble with Vim some of these days. Now, is it possible—"

"Oh, I don't think so," Markham went on. "I know that the chimpanzee occasionally kicked over the traces, but he loved Bevill as two brothers might love one another. And he was brought up here from quite a small ape till the time he grew up. He might have attacked his master in a moment of ungovernable rage, but if he had done so with his enormous strength he would have torn Bevill to pieces. He could not have helped it. The body would have been fearfully mangled, of course. Now, my theory is that Vim saw something happen to his master, and either came to the spot too late, or was frightened to interfere. He might reason in that curious, half-human mind of his that he would be blamed for the tragedy, and I take it that that is why he has disappeared. As you know, he is a most luxuriant beast, and he would not be out in the open, getting soaked with rain and drenched with dew when comfortable quarters awaited him at home. You may depend upon it that Vim is hiding because he is afraid of punishment."

"But if he hasn't done anything—"

"Ah, but he might be accused of doing something, knowing perfectly well that others knew of his displays of temper. Perhaps I am giving a mere animal too much credit for intelligence. Perhaps you may not agree—"

"Oh, I'm not so sure of that," Sir Watney said. "Upon my word, Lionel, that isn't half a bad theory of yours. You know my opinion of Vim. And what you say has given me a little idea of my own. Now, you and I are alone here together, and we have the greatest confidence in one another. Tell me frankly what you suspect. You think that Vim saw some crime committed, and has been hiding ever since because he is afraid of being punished for the sins of another. That other, of course, would be a human being. Now, who would benefit by Bevill's death? It is a cynical question to ask, but it must he answered."

Markham looked cautiously around him.

"Well, you don't and I don't, as far as we know," he said. "But de Barsac does. You remember that Mr. Bevill was leaving him money. He made no secret of the fact. And you know I strongly suspect de Barsac and Dorn of a conspiracy to get hold of the gentleman's will. You might ask why. And if you do I think I can tell you. In some way or another de Barsac is under the thumb of that scoundrel Henderby Lupas. Owes him money probably. At any rate, they met this morning on the moors secretly, as I know to my personal knowledge. When those two came back they were profoundly dejected. There may be nothing in what I say, but on the other hand, there may be a great deal."

"There may," Sir Watney admitted. "Now, I have ideas of my own on the subject. I think I'll go upstairs and have a look at poor Bevill's body. You stay here."

Markham paced up and down the terrace for three-quarters of an hour until Sir Watney returned. His face was very set and stern, and there was a queer compression about his lips that Markham had only seen there once or twice before.

"Well, sir?" he asked.

"It is anything but well," Sir Watney whispered. "I am not going to say anything yet, but I have made a startling discovery. Now, is there any sort of conveyance here in which we can get to Tavistock? I want to see that police surgeon at once. He'll talk freely to me when he knows my name."

"You have found light?" Markham asked.

"Yes, my boy, a flood of it."

CHAPTER XXIX

THE MARK OF THE BEAST

Markham was naturally impressed by his uncle's manner. It had been a good many years since he had seen the great scientist look so stern and grave. And knowing Sir Watney well, he refrained from asking an explanation.

"I don't think that will be a difficult matter," he said. "But I take it you want this little journey kept as quiet as possible. Isn't that so?"

"Absolutely," Sir Watney said curtly. "Of course, we don't want to make a mystery of it, and if anybody inquires where we are going I shall tell them. But I would much rather that no one knew. Now, what do you suggest?"

"Well, we can have a dog-cart if you like. Or, better still, nearly every morning about this time one of the keepers in the park goes into Tavistock to fetch certain articles for the animals. Why not go with him?"

"That's a very good idea of yours," Sir Watney said. "We will just stroll out across the park as if we were taking a little exercise, and you can explain to the keeper what we need. And there is no occasion to make a mystery of it."

"You have found something out?" Markham asked.

Sir Watney paused before he replied.

"Well, I think so," he said. "I merely remark that I think so. It is just a theory of mine, and at present almost as intangible as the one you were advancing the other day. But in my case I have something definite to go upon, and you had nothing. But it flashed across me just now when I was looking at the body of my poor friend, and I happened to see something that has apparently escaped attention. It may not have been there a day or two ago. I suppose you know that bodies change after death. For instance, if you found the corpse of a man just after he died, you wouldn't be able to see certain things that are plainly apparent a day or two later. That's what I mean in a nutshell. A scar may not show within an hour or of rigor mortis setting in, but it might stand out like a signal a day later. And with that I don't mean to say any more, except to remark that if my suspicions are correct, then we are on the track of the most amazing and audacious crime in the history of criminology. My idea is so wild and amazing that I hardly dare to believe that it is true. However, you will be with me in this matter, and you will know before long whether I am correct or not? Now, come along."

They crossed the park a minute or two later, and during the course of an hour or so reached their destination. Arriving at the police station, they asked for Mr. Grant, the surgeon, and eventually ran him to ground in his surgery. He proved to be an alert little man with a quick eye and intelligent manner. He was obviously impressed when he learnt the name of his visitor and welcomed him effusively.

"This is a decided honour, Sir Watney," he said. "Of course, I know you quite well, and indeed, I am an eager student of your books. Now, tell me what I can do for you, and I need hardly say that it will be a pleasure."

"That's very good of you," Sir Watney said. "I am perfectly certain that you will be of great assistance to me in some investigations I am making. Now you are probably aware that I was a great friend of the late Mr. Bevill's, and, naturally, I was much concerned over his lamentable death. I understand that you were called in."

"I was," Grant said. "I was called in by the police in the course of my professional duties, and I made an examination of the body."

"So I understand. Now, I am not asking questions out of curiosity when I tell you I am anxious to hear if you noticed anything suspicious."

"Well, I hardly know how to answer that question."

"Thank you very much," Sir Watney said shrewdly. "By your hesitating manner you have answered it. Besides, I can't forget that your examination before the coroner was abruptly interrupted by the police. They wouldn't have done that unless you had given them some sort of a hint."

"Perhaps I had better be candid," Grant said. "In the interests of justice it was decided that I should not say all I knew before the adjourned inquest. I didn't make a post mortem because it seemed to me that I was not justified in so doing. Outwardly, at any rate, it looked to me as if Mr. Bevill had died a natural death."

"But you don't think he did?" Sir Watney asked.

"Well, candidly, I don't. I am puzzled. As a matter of fact I was going over to Baron's Court this afternoon to make a further investigation, and, if necessary, hold a post mortem. You see, it's like this. I noticed certain marks on the throat of the dead man, a certain suggestion of pressure, not exactly scratches, but deep indentations that are only apparent to the trained professional eye. They may have entirely vanished by this time; on the other hand, they may have become discoloured, just as if for instance they had been sketched in ink. And, if so—"

"You are quite right," Sir Watney said curtly. "The marks are there exactly as you expected. I saw them there myself this morning. Mr. Grant, despite the fact that my old friend appeared to have died so peacefully, I am firmly convinced that he was strangled. And yet, if that had been the case, there would have been the protruding tongue and the bulging eye which were so conspicuously missing. I tell you that frankly for the moment I am puzzled. But I do believe that my old friend was the victim of foul play, and, what is more, I shrewdly suspect that you share my suspicions."

"I do indeed," Grant confessed. "If those marks are on the throat of the dead man, as you say they are, then, undoubtedly, he was strangled by some exceedingly powerful individual who must have held him by the throat and choked the life out of him as if he had been no more than a rabbit. Directly I saw the body I came to the conclusion, and all the more so because those marks you speak of are now as plain as if my poor friend's throat had been so much putty, holding an impression so clean that, by making a cast of it, we ought to be able to identify the criminal."

"That's exactly what I am working up for," Grant said. "And that's why I have deferred coming up to Baron's Court for a day or two. I had hoped that in the course of time those impressions would grow clearer, and, from what you tell me, they have. But that is not the strangest point. I studied those marks as well as I could through a glass, and the more I studied them the more they puzzled me. They were finger-prints all right, but what amazing finger-prints. What extraordinarily long fingers, and what an abnormal length of thumb. Almost prehensile. I believe such things are found in certain savage tribes, but certainly not amongst Europeans. That's what puzzled me. And if you can throw any light on it—"

"I think I can," Sir Watney said quietly. "Did you ever hear of Mr. Bevill's famous chimpanzee Vim?"

Grant almost bounced out of his chair.

"That's it," he exclaimed. "By Heaven, that's it. What a fool I was not to think of it before! Of course I have heard all about that famous ape. The country folks here tell all sorts of stories about him. They say that there are times when he is positively dangerous."

"Ah, that is mere gossip," Sir Watney said. "Vim is only dangerous when he manages to get hold of a bottle of liqueur of which he is inordinately fond. At such times he was unmanageable, and then Mr. Bevill used to have his hands full. But usually Vim is one of the most attractive animals in the world. If he is teased—but no man in his senses would ever tease an ape."

"But he attacked his master once or twice, didn't he?" the doctor asked.

"Once, I believe," Sir Watney said. "Once quite recently when Mr. Bevill came downstairs in his pyjamas in the dead of night, and the chimpanzee failed to recognise him. That might have happened to anybody. I have known cases in similar circumstances when a man has been attacked by one of his own dogs. And there is an instance on record where a huntsman was killed in his own kennels by foxhounds under like conditions, killed by dogs that were devoted to him."

"Well, after all said and done, Vim is only a wild animal," Grant said. "And it seems to me, Sir Watney, that we have practically solved the mystery."

"On the contrary," Sir Watney said drily, "we are just at the beginning of it. I am telling you this because I shall want your assistance later on. This is going to be the most sensational crime that I was ever connected with. I have my own idea as to exactly how the thing was done, but for the moment, I prefer to keep that knowledge to myself. Now, if you will come over to Baron's Court this afternoon I will meet you and we will go into this matter together. I want it to appear as if you and I had never seen one another before, and I want you to call me in as if casually. What do you say to three o'clock this afternoon?"

This arrangement being made, the conference broke up to reassemble at Baron's Court in the afternoon, in the absence of everybody else, after which Sir Watney and Grant adjourned to the bedroom of the dead man, where they remained for an hour or so. At the end of that time Sir Watney produced something that looked like a human hand modelled in some plastic composition, and handed it over to his companion.

"Now, look at that," he said. "That is the model of a hand something like the one you describe—a hand with wonderfully long slim fingers and a strangely elongated thumb. It is taken from a bronze cast which I have in my possession, a bronze cast taken from life, and the most careful measurements by one of the greatest sculptors of our time. I am speaking of Mr. de Barsac, who is at present a visitor under this roof. You may have heard of him."

"World famous," Grant murmured.

"Quite so. Now, take that cast, which is fairly plastic and oblige me by fitting those fingers to the dark marks about the dead man's throat."

"They fit exactly," Grant whispered. "That is surely the hand that did all the mischief. Is it—"

"You have guessed it," said Sir Watney. "That is an impression of Vim's right hand, or paw, as you like."

CHAPTER XXX

A STRANGE DISCOVERY

Naturally enough, the tragic happenings at Baron's Court had put an end to the work that Frick and his companions had so gaily taken up. Almost immediately they packed up all their belongings and migrated in the direction of Lanton Place. There was no longer any thought of going on with the animal pictures, so that Frick and those under him were free now to devote their attention to the big drama with its scene on Dartmoor, and the sombre background of the old house.

It was on the same afternoon that Sir Watney and Grant were holding their important interview upstairs that Markham went off in the direction of Lanton Place with the idea of seeing something of Sylvia, if possible, and getting away from a spot where, for the moment, his services were not in request. So far as he knew, de Barsac was busy in his studio, closeted with Dorn, as usual, so that the coast was clear, and Markham free to make the best he could of his opportunity.

He found that Frick had not been wasting time. He and his company had already taken possession of the ruins, and all the portable structures had been erected in the grounds. Hatton was away somewhere on the moors and Frick was seated in the door of his tent with the inevitable cigarette between his lips. He greeted Markham with his usual cheerfulness.

"Very glad to see you," he said. "You have come along just at the right time. We had a very busy morning, and I am taking it easy."

"Where are all the rest?" Markham asked.

"Hatton is out on the moors, and I believe Miss Dorn is with him. They are looking for some picturesque lonely spot likely to form a proper background for one of Hatton's grandest ideas. All my operators are in Tavistock. Well, how are they over at Baron's Court? Upon my word, Mr. Markham, I was glad to get away from there, though it seems rather a selfish thing to say, I suppose there's nothing fresh."

"Well, I don't quite understand what you mean by fresh," Markham said. "You don't suspect—"

"Oh, I don't suspect anything," said Frick. "I was merely asking a question. Ah well, he was a dear old man, and I feel as if I had lost a friend. We might have had a fine time there, and have done some grand business into the bargain. We were on the verge of it all right."

"I was going to ask you," Markham said. "Did you get any pictures at all?"

"One or two," Frick said. "We developed a section that was indifferently good. You see, Mr. Markham, we were only more or less experimenting. It was new work for our operators, and they had to get into it."

"Tell me all about it," Markham said.

"Well, I'll try. You see, what we did was to place three or four cameras in trees so that they could command a good view of the open ground underneath. These cameras we could work from a distance with a new electrical plant that I was telling you about. We could shut them off or set them going as we pleased. You remember that our original current was not strong enough and that we had to connect up with the dynamos at Baron's Court before we could get sufficient current. That delayed us for over a week, and a fatal week it was from our point of view. Well, on the night of Mr. Bevill's death everything was in apple pie order and we commenced to take our photographs. At first we were only working on leopards and pumas and smaller animals of that type, with the idea of going on to the lions and the tigers when Mr. Bevill's keepers were more familiar with the handling of savage beasts in the open. The scheme was to lay down small quantities of food at intervals and lure the beasts into the open that way. Then there was some more food farther on leading them gradually round to their cages again. It's a pretty sound programme and looked like working out all right. On the night of Mr. Bevill's death we were photographing from about seven o'clock till just on ten; no one would be anywhere near the cameras, you understand, and all of them being worked from some distance off by electric power. Of course, the keepers were told to keep under cover as close as possible, so that they shouldn't appear in the open and get mixed up with our films, and, therefore, in ordinary conditions, we ought to have done very well. We did get some pictures, I may tell you, one quite a real corker. Two pumas quarrelling over a piece of meat. The real thing, Mr. Markham. Then we shut off about ten o'clock, just as it was getting really dark, and you know what happened afterwards. We found the body of the poor old gentleman, and Hatton and I decided that it would be more decent if we turned our backs upon Baron's Court and came on here. Besides, from a business point of view, Baron's Court was off."

"Yes, I think you were wise," Markham said. "But, from what you tell me, I suppose that you probably have a good many effective pictures on those films of yours."

"I should say that was more than likely," Frick replied. "But I haven't the heart to get them developed, and they would be only fragments after all. I have put them aside altogether for the present. Perhaps, after we have done our big Dartmoor film and things begin to settle down at Baron's Court, the new owner of the property, whoever he is, may be disposed to give us facilities for working the menagerie there into another story that Hatton has got in his mind. Meanwhile, I am representing a business co-operation whose one idea is dividends as soon as possible, and they won't thank me to hang about Baron's Court on sentimental grounds."

"You are quite right," Markham said. "Perhaps later on, when you have time, you may be disposed to develop those photographs, and, if so, I should like to have copies as a souvenir of this terrible tragedy."

Frick gave the assurance readily enough, and presently Markham walked on in the direction of the moor. It was a little time later that he came across Hatton in his most businesslike mood, with a notebook and pencil in his hand. He was seated on a rock by the roadside, scribbling away furiously, and for once in his life indisposed to talk. He was very busy, he said, and intimated quite plainly that Markham's presence just then was entirely superfluous.

"You will find Miss Dorn a little farther on," he said.

With that, he went on with his writing and Markham pursued his way until he found Sylvia. She was resting a little off the roadway, gazing across the moor thoughtfully, so that she fairly started when Markham spoke to her.

"I came to look for you," he said. "I haven't seen you for two or three days. How is the great work progressing?"

"It has hardly begun as far as I am concerned," Sylvia said. "We are waiting till Mr. Hatton has quite finished his story. He wanted a particularly lonely glen for a meeting between the heroine and her lover, the escaped convict, and I brought Mr. Hatton here this afternoon and showed him the very spot. He was so delighted with it that he went off at once and began to work up the scene. I believe we are to have the cameras out here to-morrow and get it done. I have got my dresses, and when the dialogue is finished I shall have to learn it before I go to bed to-night."

"Rather strenuous, isn't it?" Markham asked.

"Oh, I don't know," Sylvia said. "The joy of having something to do is very pleasing. You have no idea how dull life is here. I am beginning to wonder if I shall ever get out of it. Do you think I shall?"

Just for the moment it was on the tip of Markham's tongue to tell Sylvia how near she was to escaping from that gloomy prison house. For he knew all about Bevill's new will, and the legacy it contained, but it seemed to him that just then it was no business of his to betray a confidence, and, besides, it did not much matter, and, in any case, Sylvia was under a contract that she could not break until the great drama was completed. And there was another reason, too, that served as a bridle on Markham's tongue. He was infinitely glad, of course, to know that Sylvia was placed beyond the reach of poverty and anxiety for the rest of her life, but the mere fact of her being an heiress brought out his own poverty in strong relief. He was not the sort of man to live on a woman's money, though Sylvia had been aware of his affection long before there was any prospect of her ever possessing a penny. No, he would not tell her now, he would leave her to find out in due course.

And so they sat there for an hour or so, discussing their prospects for the future in the golden silence of the afternoon, until the sun began to sink down and the dew shimmered over the moorland in the distance.

"It must he getting very late," Sylvia said. "Lionel, it's past seven o'clock! We must be going."

"Just a few minutes longer," Markham pleaded. "It doesn't matter a bit about me; I can get back any time I please, and you can walk back to Lanton Place easily in half an hour."

"Well, another ten minutes," Sylvia smiled. "Lionel, what's that moving over there?"

Something was creeping along in the tangled heather a hundred yards or so away, then a queer wizened face appeared, followed by a brown hairy body, and Vim stood disclosed. He looked cautiously round, as weirdly mysterious as he might have looked in his own native forest, and then, as he caught sight of Markham and Sylvia, he commenced to beat those long hands of his upon his great hairy chest, and from his lips came a long, dismal, almost heartbreaking cry.

"Oh, poor thing," Sylvia said. "Call him, Lionel."

With some misgivings Markham complied. Then Sylvia added her voice to his, and very slowly and cautiously Vim came along in their direction. He walked upright till he was within a few yards of them, then he dropped on all-fours and came grovelling like a beaten dog to their feet. As he looked up imploringly into their eyes, his own actually brimmed with tears and he filled the still air with his cries. He seemed to have a strange fancy for Sylvia, for he crept up to her side and held out his paw to her with a suggestion of surrender.

"Take it," Markham whispered. "I suppose you have heard the story. People are saying that Vim killed his master. People may be true, but it is hard to believe it."

As Sylvia held out her hand, a sudden shot rang over the moor, fired, no doubt, by some sportsman there. The effect on Vim was magical. He jumped to his feet snarling and vicious, then, with a yell of defiance, dashed into the heather and was seen no more.

CHAPTER XXXI

THE DOCTOR'S EVIDENCE

It was natural enough in the circumstances that the wildest stories should have gone round in connection with the tragical events at Baron's Court. In a country neighbourhood there are always simple people ready to believe anything, especially in the case where the dead man had had a great reputation for eccentricity, and, indeed, most of the country people thereabouts would not cross the park at Baron's Court for a King's ransom. But, of course, these had heard all about Vim, and most of them knew the great chimpanzee by sight, therefore it was natural enough that, once the tongue of rumour was set going, there was no end to the many tales that it told. And when it became known that Vim had escaped from the park and was wandering about on the moors, something like a state of terror prevailed. One or two farmers had gone out with guns in their hand with the avowed intention of shooting Vim on sight, for these simple folk firmly believed that John Bevill owed his death to a mistaken kindness for a ferocious animal, and held that until the beast was destroyed there would be no peace in the countryside. It was in vain that those who knew protested; indeed, the more they argued the point, the more convinced the agriculturists were that the culprit was out there on the moors. And so the time went on until the adjourned inquest was reached.

Despite the whispered horrors and unseen danger, a goodly number of people flocked through the gates at Baron's Court, filled with eager curiosity to hear the rest of the story. And with them came not only a local correspondent or two, but representatives of the great newspapers. Directly the coroner had taken his place, Dr. Grant was called.

"I think," said the coroner, "that at the preliminary inquiry the witness declined for official reasons to give us any further information. Am I to take it for granted, doctor, that on the present occasion you are prepared to continue?"

"Up to a certain point, sir," the doctor said. "I can tell you all I know, but in my judgment there is still a good deal to find out."

"Pray, proceed," said the coroner.

"Well, last time I stood here," Grant went on, "I told you that I had made a preliminary examination of the body. And that was the fact. It seemed to me then that Mr. Bevill had died from natural causes, and in the ordinary course of things I should have been prepared to give a certificate to that effect. But now—"

"One moment," the coroner interrupted. "You say you would have been prepared to give a certificate to that effect. What caused you to change your mind?"

"I don't think I did change my mind," Grant replied. "It was merely a suggestion on the part of the police. There had been rumours to the effect that Mr. Bevill had been roughly treated by a pet chimpanzee of his."

"I think everybody has heard that," the coroner said. "So far as I can understand, all sorts of extraordinary stories are going about. I don't think there is a single person in the room who does not know all about that amazingly clever animal. By the way, what has become of it? I understand that, since Mr. Bevill's death, this Vim, as he is called, is wandering at large upon the moor."

"I believe that is a fact," Grant went on. "And I believe also, from what I have discovered, that there is a good deal to be said for the many rumours one hears."

A thrill ran through the eager audience as there words fell quietly from the doctor's lips.

"Perhaps I had better continue," he said. "I made the examination of the body within a few hours of death. From all outward appearances except to the trained eye there was no sign of anything abnormal. Mr. Bevill appeared to have died peacefully enough. Anybody would have been justified in believing that he expired suddenly, as he was crossing the park, of some heart trouble. That the deceased had a weak heart I know for a fact. Once or twice I attended him professionally. Apart from that trouble he was in quite good health, and as he was a man who lived an exceedingly moderate and regular life, I could do nothing for him except to advise him to avoid all excitement and physical fatigue. And this is why, in ordinary circumstances, I should have given certificate."

"Why didn't you?" the coroner asked.

"I am just coming to that, sir," Grant said. "I have told you and the jury how I came to the conclusion in my preliminary examination that Mr. Bevill had died in the ordinary way from a heart attack. But when I came to look closer there were certain marks about the throat of the dead man that puzzled me. They were queer indentations, little lines and depressions in the flesh that had no business to be there. I examined them through a strong glass, and I could make nothing of them. They were suspicious marks, but, so far as I could make out for the moment, in no way responsible for the unfortunate gentleman's death, and therefore I decided to wait to see how they developed."

"Let us have that quite clear," the coroner said. "What exactly do you mean by 'developed'?"

"Well, sir, it's like this. After a time I knew that those marks would deepen in colour. And they did. When I made my second examination they were as plain as if they had been painted there. They appeared on second examination to be rather deep, so deep, indeed, that they might have caused suffocation. And perhaps they did."

Once more a thrill ran round the room, and once more Grant went calmly on with his story.

"Undoubtedly those marks had been made by a firm grip on the dead man's throat. They must have been applied with great force by some one in the possession of enormous power. And yet, at the same time, if that grip had been the cause of death there would have been certain signs on the face of the deceased which were altogether absent."

"What signs do you mean?" the coroner asked.

"Well, for instance, a certain blackness about the face, a protruding tongue, and a staring of the eyeballs. And, besides, a man of merely normal health would certainly have put up something of a struggle if some assailant had tried to choke him. He could not help it. And therefore, in that case, there would have been signs of a struggle, marks on the grass, disarranged clothing, and all that sort of thing. But, as a matter of fact, there were no traces of this. Mr. Bevill was found peacefully lying on his back without so much as his tie out of place. There could have been no struggle, and yet logically, there ought to be."

The coroner was obviously puzzled.

"I don't quite follow you," he said. "Are we to assume, after all you have said, that those marks on the throat had nothing to do with Mr. Bevill's death?"

"Frankly I can't tell you," Grant said. "I am as puzzled as you are. That Mr. Bevill was killed in some way or another I feel certain. I should have no doubt in saying so if those missing signs had not been present. The marks on the dead man's throat are so deep, now that time has developed them, that they in themselves would be enough to cause the tragedy."

"The marks of a human hand?" the coroner asked.

"I don't think I said that," Grant went on. "I said they resembled a human hand, rather a strange human hand with exceedingly long fingers and an abnormal thumb."

The coroner looked up eagerly.

"I think I begin to follow you," he said. "The hand of an ape, in fact."

"Precisely," Grant said. And, as he spoke, murmurs arose from all round the room. "The hand of the chimpanzee, Vim, beyond the shadow of a doubt. I am all the more sure of this because I have had on opportunity of testing my opinion. A little time ago a copy in bronze of Vim's hand and arm, if I may call it so, was made by a famous sculptor, Mr. de Barsac. He is in the room here now, and I have no doubt he can confirm all I say if necessary."

"Quite right," de Barsac murmured. "I did make that cast on the request of my friend, Sir Watney Gibson, who wanted it to reproduce in a book he is writing, and I may say that the cast is true to a hair's breath."

"Very interesting," the coroner murmured. "But, at the same time, rather irregular. We will hear you, presently, Mr. de Barsac, if there is any necessity. Go on, Dr. Grant."

"Well, sir, from that cast I took a mould in some plastic composition, and when it was sufficiently dry I applied it to the marks on the dead man's throat. I may say it fitted exactly. And now you know why I delayed my evidence on the last occasion."

"And you are quite sure," the coroner said. "If what you say is correct, and I see no reason to doubt it, Mr. Bevill met his death at the hands of the chimpanzee. I fail to see how we can come to any other conclusion."

"I haven't quite finished yet," Grant said quietly. "An hour or two ago I should have said so, but before finally making up my mind I have decided to make a further examination of the body. That was only an hour or two ago. When I did so I discovered a tiny fracture at the base of the brain, no larger, perhaps, than half a crown, but quite sufficient to cause death in an old man. As far as I can judge, the blow must have been administered with a loaded cane, or more probably with a sandbag, such as is generally used in America. That is a bag filled with sand, which makes a formidable weapon. The theory I have formed now is that Mr. Bevill was struck a traitorous blow from behind, which probably felled him and fractured his skull at the same time, as I told you. He may have been just conscious enough to struggle to his feet, and grapple with his assailant before he collapsed again. Then, probably, the hand clutched his throat and held him there after he was dead. But I should say he was dead almost before he reached the ground the second time, and if I am correct in that assumption, then there would have been no blackening of the face or protruding of the tongue that I naturally looked for. In other words, the grip on Mr. Bevill's throat was quite superfluous, though his murderer would not know it."

Apparently there was nothing more to be said or done. It would have been merely waste of time to carry the investigation farther. The coroner summed up briefly and the jury brought in a verdict to the effect that John Bevill had been murderously assaulted by the chimpanzee, Vim, and had received injuries which resulted in his death. Then the excited audience poured out to discuss the tragedy at its leisure.

CHAPTER XXXII

ON THE SCENT

The big house was silent again, the excitement of the morning had died away, and Sir Watney Gibson with Markham was walking up and down the terrace, talking over the recent inquiry. Dorn had vanished, saying that important business had called him home, and de Barsac was apparently busy in his studio. So that the two men on the terrace could talk freely.

"Are you satisfied?" Markham asked.

"My dear boy, I am far from satisfied," Sir Watney replied. "It all sounded logical enough, and after what Grant had said the jury could come to no other conclusion. And the coroner, from his point of view, was equally sound. He told the jury that Vim had attacked his master in a moment of savage fury, probably with a heavy piece of wood. Oh, I know it sounds all right. Vim hit Bevill on the back of the head, and probably thinking his work was only half done, clutched him by the throat and held him down till the job was finished, to put it in a cold-blooded way. What else could the coroner say in the face of Grant's evidence? We know that Vim accompanied his master, we know that he attempted violence on him twice in a fortnight, and we know, beyond the shadow of a doubt, that those marks on Bevill's throat were made by the chimpanzee. And if I had not been here John Bevill would have been quietly buried, and, in the course of time, the hideous tragedy would have been forgotten. A few farmers would have got together with their guns and Vim would have been shot, and buried, and there the story would have ended."

"Then you don't think—"

"I don't think anything about it," Sir Watney exclaimed. "The whole thing is wrong."

"But, my dear uncle," Markham protested, "you were indirectly the means of fixing the guilt on Vim. If that cast had never been taken, you would not have been in a position to lend it to the doctor, and therefore—"

"Oh, I know all about that," Sir Watney said impatiently. "Yet, at the same time, they are all wrong. I know they are all wrong, and I am not going to rest till I have proved it. And don't forget this, my boy, the cause of death was not the finger-marks about Bevill's throat, but that neat little fracture at the base of his skull. Keep that clearly before your eyes, and you will begin to understand what I am driving at. I shall be greatly mistaken and deeply disappointed if within the next week or so I have not put a different construction on the case. Now listen. You stay on here for a day or two and keep your eye open. If you see anything in the least suspicious on anybody's part, no matter who it is, let me know at once. I am going to London this afternoon, and you can write or telegraph to me to my place in town. If you see anything very queer, be sure and telegraph. Not from the village post-office, but from Tavistock. I am going to fade quietly away presently, and when dinner-time comes you had best profess not to know that I have gone."

True to his word, Sir Watney went back to town by the afternoon train, and though it was late when he reached his destination he telephoned immediately to Scotland Yard and asked to be put in communication with a certain detective sergeant there. Being a man who was persona grata with the authorities, Sir Watney was attended to at once, and half an hour later was closeted with Sergeant Gideon in his study. And there, over a cigar and a whisky and soda, he began to talk.

"It isn't a big job at present, Gideon," he said. "But, unless I am greatly mistaken, it is going to develop into one of those most stupendous sensations of our time. In a few words, it is connected with the Baron's Court affair. I don't suppose you know much about that."

"Only what I have read in the evening paper, sir," Gideon replied. "A queer case altogether. But then Mr. Bevill was a queer man, wasn't he? Kept a menagerie, and all the rest of it. Murdered by his own ape."

"Nothing of the kind, Gideon," Sir Watney said impatiently. "Didn't I tell you there was a big sensation? At any rate, there will be. Now, here is a list of everybody about Baron's Court at the time of Mr. Bevill's death. When I say everybody. I mean everybody, from the guests in the house down to the scullery maid. If you will glance it over, I daresay you will find that some are familiar to you."

Gideon took the slip of paper and read it.

"Well, sir," he said, "I can say nothing about the servants of course. I know you and your nephew, and this man Frick I have also heard of. The same remark applies to Hatton, the writer. I suppose Mr. de

Barsac is the famous sculptor who has that big house in Park Lane? Great swell he is, knows everybody, and very rich. And—hello—here's my old friend Major Dorn. Doesn't he live somewhere down in that part? A regular bad lot he is, sir. A begging-letter writer, and as cunning as they make 'em. We have never been able to lay him by the heels, but perhaps now—"

"Oh, never mind about that chap," Sir Watney cried. "We are flying at much bigger game, Gideon. Now, what I want you to do is this. You see that name on the list where I put my finger? That's the man I want to know all about. He left Baron's Court nearly a week before Mr. Bevill died and came up to London. He came on business, I think, but that's a detail. I want to know what happened to him from the time he reached London till the hour he left. Everything, mind you. What hotel he stayed at in town, because I happen to know that he didn't go home, and so forth and so on. I don't expect you to find out all at once. When you have traced the first day's doings, let me know. How long will it be?"

"Oh, not very long, sir. With my scouts and one thing and another I can post you by this time to-morrow evening with a diary of a couple of days."

"That will do very nicely," Sir Watney said. "Ring me up to-morrow night about the same time and I will be here to listen. I think that will do."

Faithful to his promise, Gideon rang up on the following evening with quite a budget of information.

"I have done fairly well, Sir Watney," he said. "Your man reached London on Wednesday evening about six o'clock, and put up at a small hotel in Norfolk-street, Strand. Half a minute, and I will give you the name of it."

"Never mind about that," Sir Watney cried. "I am not concerned with with the name of the hotel, merely remarking that it seems a quiet sort of place for a man of that type to stay in."

"I thought so, too, sir," Gideon replied. "At any rate, he went there and he happened to be driven from Paddington by a taxi-man who recognised him. As a matter of fact, he is known to most taxi-drivers in London. Well, he goes to this little hotel off the Embankment, and there takes a bedroom for a few days. What's more, he doesn't give his own name, but calls himself Charlesworth."

"Oh, indeed," Sir Watney said softly. "Oh, indeed. A not unexpected development, Gideon, and one that, on the whole, does not displease me. Well?"

"The next day he stays in the hotel nearly all the time, and on the following morning, at eleven o'clock, he takes a taxi from the rank just outside the Temple Station and drives to Ironmonger Lane, where he spends a couple of hours with a financier called Henderby Lupas. Then he walks back to his hotel, and, after dining there quietly, goes out to the Strand Theatre alone and then he goes to bed. The next morning he goes into Wardour-street, and stays a couple of hours or so in the shop of an old man called Jonas."

"Oh, indeed?" Sir Watney said again, in the same soft tones. "And what does Mr. Jonas do?"

"Just half a minute, sir, while I look at my notes. Ah, here we are. Jonas Jonas, a naturalist and taxidermist. A sort of Roland Ward on a small scale. In fact, I rather think that he was with Roland Ward at one time."

Sir Watney chuckled as he listened. He did not appear to be further interested, but lent his ear more or less casually to the finish.

"And that's as far as I have gone, sir," Gideon said at the conclusion. "I hope I haven't been wasting my time."

"Indeed you haven't," Sir Watney replied. "You have done exceedingly well. I shall be greatly surprised if you haven't told me all I want. Still, you can go on; the more details I have, the more I shall be able to cope with our friend presently. Ring me up again to-morrow night at the same time. For the present, that will do."

It was shortly after breakfast the following morning that Sir Watney left his house and proceeded in the direction of Wardour-street. He found his destination at length, a little dingy shop in that somewhat dingy thoroughfare with the name of Jonas in faded guilt letters over the door. A small man with a long black beard and a pair of piercing eyes came forward and asked Sir Watney's pleasure. When he disclosed his identity, the man behind the counter bowed profusely and expressed the honour he felt in having so distinguished a visitor under his humble roof.

"I came to see you," Sir Watney said, "because I am told you are an exceedingly good workman."

"I hope I am more than that, Sir Watney," Jonas said. "A good friend I met in London can make casts of animals, and stuff them, but I pride myself on the fact that I am a naturalist as well. Sportsmen come to me from all over the world. Now what can I do for you, sir?"

Sir Watney proceeded to put a brown-paper parcel on the counter, and opening it, displayed the bronze cast that had been made for him by de Barsac.

"There," he said. "Now, I think you will admit that that is an extraordinarily fine piece of work, Mr. Jonas. It was made for me by a famous sculptor, and is the exact reproduction of the hand and arm of a chimpanzee. Now, I want you to take that and recreate the arm so to speak, in steel and leather. I want the arm back again, if you understand me, a hollow imitation, but at the same time, so true an imitation that it follows the original in every detail. Make it in the form of a glove so that I can slip it on my hand."

Jonas looked up in surprise.

"That's a funny thing, a very funny thing," he said. "I had a precisely identical commission about nine days ago from a gentleman who brought me in a similar cast."

CHAPTER XXXIII

THE BLACK BOX

A day or two had elapsed at Baron's Court, and, so far as Markham could see, nothing had happened that called for any special vigilance on his part. He had his own suspicions, of course, more especially as regarded the intimacy between Dorn and de Barsac; but, naturally enough, it was impossible for him to follow up his theory in this direction without arousing alarm on the part of the two men whom he had every reason to believe were a pair of particularly choice scoundrels. But, with all his suspicions, Markham could prove nothing, and it was very doubtful as to whether he had any real idea of the facts that had taken Sir Watney in such a great hurry to London.

So, therefore, he hung about the place, pretending to be busy, and keeping his eyes open altogether without result, so that by the end of the week he was both bored and disappointed and longing for companionship. He was free to go over to Lanton Place, of course, and all the more so because Frick and his associates were now busily engaged on the great drama, and day by day Lanton Place presented a picture of the most extraordinary activity.

There were at least a dozen caravans in which the operators were housed, whilst the actors themselves had overflowed into the various farmhouses in the neighbourhood, where they were naturally the source of much interest and curiosity. The weather was still brilliantly fine, and outdoor work was going on apace. For some little time now, Hatton's scene plot had been finished, and thousands of photographs had been taken out there, on the moors. So, therefore, Markham's visits to Lanton Place passed almost unnoticed as far as Dorn and De Barsac were concerned, and, indeed, they were glad enough to have Baron's Court to themselves. Nurse Coterell had vanished directly after Bevill's funeral, and so far as she was concerned they had nothing to fear.

It was Dorn's habit to come over to Baron's Court most days now, and pass most of the time in the studio, discussing certain projects which materially concerned the fortunes of the two men. They would sit there, and talk and smoke, afterwards, lunching and dining in the luxurious fashion that they affected, whilst they idly speculated how much longer this ideal condition of things was going to last, and somewhat uneasily wondering what Henderby Lupas was going to do, and why that unscrupulous financier gave no sign. But though they talked and schemed, they were no nearer to acquiring the money of which they were both desperately in need. They had been too clever, too cunning, and now they were practically at the end of their tether.

Meanwhile, Markham was over at Lanton Place, and seeing as much of Sylvia as was possible. There were occasional breaks in the day's work, when her services were not required, and in these intervals they wandered about the silent and deserted grounds, discussing the future and what it was likely to bring. For most of the day Lanton Place was quiet enough, so that Mrs. Dorn was free to creep about the ruins in the old mysterious way and search for the lost something that was always uppermost in that clouded brain of hers. Markham had been away for a whole day on a little business of his own, and now he was back at Lanton Place and seated in a ruined old summer-house with Sylvia by his side. From where they sat they could occasionally see the pathetic figure of Mrs. Dorn as she went about that ever-ending toil of hers.

"I shall be glad when you can put an end to that," Markham said. "Has it always been going on?"

"Ever since I can remember," Sylvia replied. "And under present conditions, it is sure to go on. I wonder if you have done anything, Lionel."

"In what direction?" Markham asked.

"Well, you remember the letter that my mother gave to you. I mean the charred letter that she found in the ruins."

"From my father. Oh, yes, I have not forgotten. I have not got it with me now, but I have read it over and over again, and every day for some time I had intended going over that cottage of mine to see if I could discover some clue amongst the thousands of odds and ends that were stored there after my father's death. That was what I was doing yesterday."

"Without result, of course," Sylvia said.

"Not altogether. I didn't find anything. You will remember that the box in question was consigned to my father's firm for safe custody. In other words, it was sent to the bank in the usual course. Just a black box, sealed and locked, to be left until it was required. Now, do you happen to remember what sort of a seal it was?"

"Oh, how can I say that?" Sylvia asked. "I could hardly walk at the time. But if it was sealed, and sent by my mother as I understand it was, then probably she would use that peculiar old ring that she wears on her left hand. It is an engraved diamond, a very valuable stone, I believe, and one from which she has never parted. Goodness knows what sentimental value she attaches to it, but there must be some, because she never takes it off night or day. She has never moved it from her finger, as far as I can recollect. I am ashamed to say that my father has tried to force her to give it up on several occasions, but even his refined cruelty has always been without effect. Another of those many mysteries that surround the house, I expect."

"Yes, it's all very mysterious," Markham said. "Does your mother ever write any letters, Sylvia?"

"'Three or four times a year, perhaps," Sylvia said. "Heaven only knows who her correspondents are. She writes secretly and furtively, and then, under cover of the darkness, posts them in the village herself. I have a strong suspicion that they are written to quite imaginary correspondents; I mean that they are dictated by a disordered brain. Anyway, they never come back, and no replies are ever received."

"That's very strange," Markham said thoughtfully. "But what's all that got to do with the engraved diamond?"

"I was going to tell you," Sylvia proceeded. "Whenever my mother writes a letter she always seals the flap of the envelope with green wax. It is a peculiar shade of green wax, and she has had it in her desk ever since I can remember. She doesn't in the least mind writing letters when I am about so long as I don't get too near her, but directly she hears my father anywhere she throws everything back in her desk and locks it. But I was going to tell you that she always impresses the green wax on the envelope with that diamond ring of hers. It makes an impression like a small five pointed star with the letter 'S' in the centre."

An exclamation came from Markham's lips.

"Then in that case, I have found the box," he said. "As a matter of fact, there were three or four black boxes, all of which I opened at once. I could see they had nothing whatever to do with this particular business. But the other box was a small black affair locked and sealed in half a dozen places with a particular shade of green wax. There was nothing on the outside of it to identify it with anybody beyond the addressed label, and as my father's affairs have been wound up so many years, I decided to open it. Before I did so, I noticed the peculiar impression on the wax, which tallies exactly with what you have just told me—a five-pointed star with the initial letter 'S' in the centre. Of course, if I had identified the box with your mother, I should have done nothing of the kind. Well, I opened it."

"And found something?" Sylvia asked eagerly.

"Nothing of the slightest value. Nothing but several packages of tissue paper with some scraps of metal inside. And there is an end of the mystery as far as we are concerned."

"It doesn't matter in the least," Sylvia said. "But it sounds rather disappointing. Can't you see what has happened, Lionel? Can't you understand?"

"I'm afraid I can't," Markham said.

"It is quite plain to me," Sylvia said. "All these years my mother has had one idea fixed in her mind. Probably the only sane idea she has. I have told you more than once that she is under the impression that she has placed somewhere in safety a fortune for me. Her jewels, in fact. I know she had a wonderful collection of stones at one time. And in that queer way of hers she thinks they are safe in some bank; indeed, she has told you so. She is under the impression that your father had them. And so far, she is sane enough. Beyond the shadow of a doubt, she did contrive to pack up her valuables in that box and send them away to your father's bank. And ever since the fire that wrecked her reason, she has been hunting in the ruins to find the receipt. I suppose in her darkened manner she imagined that it would be impossible to get the box back unless she could produce the receipt. She must have done all this for my sake, so that I should be beyond the reach of want after she died. And, of course, she did not tell my father anything about this, because she new perfectly well that he would have robbed her if he had the opportunity, and would squander the money in that selfish way of his. Now, can't you see what happened, Lionel? He knew everything that was going on. He probably drugged my mother; and, when she lay asleep, took the ring from her finger, and, after he had emptied the box, resealed it. Unless, of course, my mother was mad when she sent the box along, and was under the delusion that all the rubbish she put inside represented valuable gems. But I don't believe it. She was much more sane then than she is now, and she could not have displayed all that cunning and caution for the sake of a lot of rubbish. We shall never know the real truth, Lionel, but I feel perfectly certain that I am right. My father took those gems and sold them, and all these years he has known exactly what my mother is looking for. What a shameful confession it is to have to make about one's own father."

"I wouldn't think about that, Sylvia, if I were you," Markham said. "It's no fault of yours, and you can't help having such a father. What I am concerned about is your mother. I am wondering what effect it will have upon her when we tell her all this."

Sylvia was silent for a moment.

"But why should we tell her at all?" she said at length. "Or at any rate, why tell her the truth? Really, she is far happier as she is."

"Perhaps you are right," Markham said. "She knows already what a blackguard of a husband she has."

CHAPTER XXXIV

As Markham spoke, he glanced up in the direction of the pathetic figure groping there amongst the ruin, and as he did so he saw Dorn standing there before him. The latter must have heard what Markham was saying; indeed, he was standing so close by that it was impossible for him not to have done so. And besides, his face was dark and angry, and there was an ugly expression in his eyes.

"What are you doing here?" he demanded. "What right have you got in my grounds? So this is what is going on right under my very nose, is it? You sneak over here in my absence and make love to my daughter without asking my permission. A pretty dishonourable thing to do."

Markham rose calmly to his feet.

"This was bound to happen sooner or later," he said coolly. "Sylvia, would you mind leaving us alone for a few minutes? I think I know how to deal with your father."

Sylvia glanced irresolutely for a moment from one to the other, and then moved in the direction of the house.

"What the devil do you mean by that, sir?" Dorn blazed out. "You know how to deal with me, indeed! Anybody would think you were talking to a criminal."

"They would be quite right," Markham said calmly.

"Go on," Dorn hissed. "I suppose you see this business cannot stop here."

"So I have thought for some little time," Markham went on in the same quiet fashion. "Now, look here, Major Dorn, you and I had better understand one another at once. You implied just now that I was talking to a scoundrel. I am. There, drop that, none of your bluster with me. I know you to be a scoundrel of the worst possible type, and, what's more, the police know it too. They have never laid the king of the begging-letter writers by the heels yet, but I think if I laid certain information that I possess at their disposal, the last of the famous family of Dorn would run a strong chance of finishing his days in gaol. I know all about you, my friend, and I should not have the slightest hesitation in placing the information in proper hands, but for your daughter. The mere fact that I know her and intend to marry her has saved that rascally skin of yours. It seems almost incredible to me that a man of your type could be the father of a girl like Sylvia. But she is as pure and good as she is beautiful, and I love her all the more because she has such a parent. And I tell you frankly that I am going to marry her."

"I don't doubt it for a moment," Dorn sneered. "Whether you would have said the same thing a week or two ago is another question. Astonishing what a difference a few days make."

Markham's lip curled contemptuously.

"Oh, so you have discovered that, have you?" he said. "You have discovered the fact that, thanks to John Bevill's generosity, Sylvia is an heiress in her own right. But your pleasant suggestion lacks point, because Sylvia knew that I loved her long before I came down here. I met her when she was touring in the north of England, and there and then made up my mind that she was the only girl in the world for me. She knows, and has known for some time, that I am only waiting for a promised appointment before offering her a home."

"And what about her mother?" Dorn demanded.

"Oh, I have not forgotten that unhappy wife of yours. I shall be only too pleased to offer her the shelter of my roof. But don't forget this, Major Dorn, I may have only a small income now, but Sir Watney Gibson has made no secret of the fact that some day I shall have all his money. My good sir, your sneers leave me untouched. I know that I am no fortune hunter, and Sylvia knows it, and that being so, the rest of the world can go hang. I don't care two-pence if everybody knows that I have married the daughter of a dissipated old rascal who has spent all his wife's money and robbed her of her jewels besides. I know all about that little black box with the green seals, the little black box filled with scraps of metal instead of diamonds. I know how you drugged your unfortunate wife and removed the ring from her finger before you opened that box and extracted the contents. And I tell you plainly this: If I have any more of your nonsense, I'll put the police on your track if you are ten times Sylvia's father. And if you like you can tell de Barsac I said so. You are a fine pair, you two, but you have overreached yourselves this time. If you hadn't been so infernally clever, the forty thousand pounds John Bevill left to your daughter would have gone to de Barsac, and then he would have been able to pay Henderby Lupas the money he owes him."

The angry flush faded from Dorn's face, and a curious whiteness showed about the corners of his lips. All the fight had gone out of the man now, all his bullying swagger had vanished, and he looked a mean and contemptible coward indeed as he glanced furtively into Markham's calm features.

"I don't know what you mean," he stammered.

"Oh, yes, you do, my friend; oh, yes, you do. It wasn't a bad idea of yours to steal Mr. Bevill's will so that you could show it to Henderby Lupas and convince him of the truth of what you said. But you were in a bit too much of a hurry; you might have waited. Instead of which you stole the will from the safe, and thanks to Frick being about the house, you were very nearly caught. I did not know enough at the moment to denounce you, but I know exactly what happened. You and de Barsac fled through the library window, and, in the confusion, you managed to get up into de Barsac's bedroom with his help. You see, I know all about it. And I was going to keep my counsel, only you challenged me just now, and I felt bound to tell you the truth. I think you and your partner have been sufficiently punished as it is. And perhaps there is worse to come, though I won't say anything about that yet. And now, Major Dorn, I should like to know what you have got to say."

But, apparently, Dorn had nothing to say, for he slunk away a few minutes later in the direction of the house like a dog that has been beaten. Markham followed him with a smile on his face, and then, without waiting to see Sylvia again, went off in the direction of the moor.

He could see several people in the distance, moving about in a sort of orderly confusion, and amongst them Frick giving direction. There were perhaps forty or fifty people altogether dressed in various costumes, and all obviously engaged in connection with the making of pictures. Frick detached himself from the group presently and came over to Markham.

"How are you getting on?" the latter inquired.

"Oh, famously," Frick replied. "We are doing splendidly. Already we have finished most of the main scenes, and if this weather lasts for another fortnight we shall be able to get away from here altogether. It largely depends upon Hatton. He's a rare enthusiast when he gets his heart into his work, and he's always full of ideas. No sooner do we get a series of pictures done for one big scene than some bits of brilliant business occurs to him and he wants it done all over again. He's never wrong, but it's very expensive, though I don't think our people would mind that when they see what fine work we are doing. For instance, yesterday we had completed a grand lot of films when Hatton had an idea introducing a new character that upset the whole scheme. But when it was finished and a lot of fresh photographs taken the whole thing was improved out of all knowledge. Ah, here he comes again. It's any money he's got a new idea in his head. See how excited he is."

Hatton, in his shirt sleeves, with a stump of a cigarette in the corner of his mouth, came flying across the heather in the direction of the spot where Frick was standing.

"Look here," he cried, "I have got a big thing on here."

"More expense," Frick groaned.

"Oh, I like to hear you talking about expenses," Hatton retorted. "You are the biggest spendthrift in England. But listen. About a quarter of an hour ago, I was walking down the little valley yonder behind that waterfall with a view to a background for the scene of the wounded smuggler, and the girl who brings him food, when I ran up against the monkey. You know what I mean—Mr. Bevill's ape. He was sitting there, on the rocks, cleaning himself up, and when he turned and saw me I thought the poor beggar meant mischief. He snarled and showed his teeth and came in my direction, and it looked as if my number was up for a moment. You see, the poor brute has been hunted all over the place with dogs and guns until he is quite desperate. With my heart in my mouth I went towards him and called him by name, and I think he remembered having seen me at Baron's Court, for he began to whimper and cry like a child. It's a very odd thing to me if that beast ever did any mischief to Bevill at all. But that's got nothing to do with it. We were just getting on pretty good terms when a shepherd's dog came prowling about, and directly Vim caught sight of him he shinned up the rocks like lightning and vanished."

"Very strange," Frick said. "But what's all this got to do with this new idea of yours?"

"Everything," Hatton went on. "I am going to bring some wild animals into act four. A dramatic surprise in connection with the menagerie that has broken down in crossing the moors. See, what I mean, Frick, old man?"

"Yes, but where are the pictures to come from," Frick asked. "You have forgotten that."

"I have forgotten nothing," Hatton said impatiently. "Haven't we got a score or more of pictures of animals somewhere or another that we took the few days we were at Baron's Court. You remember, the pictures we took of all the animals in the park. I don't suppose there are many of them any use, but then I don't happen to want many. Half a dozen films will be quite sufficient, I take it, and you can leave it to me to work them in artistically."

"But I don't know where they are," Frick said.

"Oh, there you go," Hatton cried. "What a casual beggar you are, always putting difficulties in the way. Well, as it happens, I know where they are, and I have asked Johnson to dig them out. He's developing the whole blessed lot at the present moment. He'll have them printed in a few minutes, and then I shall know exactly where I am. I shall be greatly disappointed if I don't find at least a dozen pictures that will be suitable for my purpose. I'll just go and see how Johnson's getting on, then I'll come back to you and have a drink and a smoke, which I think I deserve. Perhaps Mr. Markham would like to stay and see how the pictures come out."

CHAPTER XXXV

SUSPENSE

Markham, however, was just a little too exercised in his mind to remain and see the development of those films. In any case, he was not particularly interested; he had wandered out on the moor more to collect his thoughts than anything else, and he wanted to get back to Baron's Court now, for there were letters to write and he was just a little conscious that he was neglecting Sir Watney's interests.

"I am afraid I can't stay," he said. "Of course, it is all very alluring, no doubt, and if I were not so busy I would stay. Perhaps you will come over one of these evenings and show me what you have done."

"Really, we shan't be many minutes," Hatton said. "Oh, well, if you can't stay, there's an end of it."

"We'll come over to-morrow night," Frick said. "We'll both come. I have been working so hard lately that an hour or two in the billiard-room at Baron's Court would be welcome enough."

"All right," Markham said. "I'll regard that as an engagement. And now I must be getting back."

He walked along the road thoughtfully enough, hardly knowing whether to be pleased or disappointed as a result of his interview with Dorn. He certainly had scored off that somewhat elusive individual, and he smiled to himself as he thought of Dorn's face. But, on the other hand, perhaps he had not been discreet in letting the Major know how deeply he had dived into his antecedents. Without anything definite, Markham felt that he stood on the threshold of tragic events, and he was certainly a little uneasy in his mind when he came to realise how his indiscretions might have prejudiced Sir Watney in certain investigations he was making in London.

And, again, he would have to meet both these men at dinner. Sit opposite to these unscrupulous scoundrels whom he had almost gone out of his way to warn. Not that he was in the least afraid of them, but that was not precisely the point. How far would they benefit by what he had said?

But when Markham got back to Baron's Court there was no sign either on the part of Dorn or de Barsac of any enmity. On the contrary, de Barsac seemed to be exerting himself to be agreeable, and Dorn was quite the man of the world. And so the evening passed without friction, so that Markham began to wonder if Dorn had confided anything of what had happened to his confederate. It was just the same at breakfast the next morning, and subsequently luncheon, after which Dorn and de Barsac retired to the studio as usual, leaving Markham wondering what the next movement would be.

But once those two men were alone the smiles vanished from their faces, and they regarded one another with gloomy looks.

"I wonder if we managed to throw dust in that young man's eyes," de Barsac said moodily. "I can't understand where he got his information from."

"I think I can," Dorn said. "I would give a good deal to know what Gibson's up to in London. Can't you see how it is? Gibson left Markham down here to keep his eyes open, and he is doing it."

"I am not much afraid of Gibson," de Barsac said. "He's rather an old ass, isn't he?"

"Now, that's just where you make the mistake," Dorn said. "It's the mistake that every sanguine man makes. He always regards everybody else but himself as a fool. You mustn't forget the other fellow's points of view. You invariably think your plans are perfect, and that there's no flaw in them, and because you think so, you can't understand that the other man has the ghost of a chance. But don't forget that Sir Watney has been mixed up with crimes and criminals all his life."

"Yes—but only in a scientific way. Only after the police have given him all the facts."

"Ah, there you are wrong again," the Major said. "I happen to know that those facts have come quite as often from Gibson as from the police. A great scientist like Gibson isn't particularly anxious to pose as a detective. He would consider it beneath his dignity, but that doesn't prevent him from offering certain theories to the authorities, and getting them to put them forward as their own. Gibson is simple enough to look at, and quite boyishly enthusiastic in his way, but a good bit of a bulldog all the same. But never mind him. What are you going to do about Henderby Lupas?"

De Barsac shrugged his shoulders indifferently.

"Upon my word, I don't know," he said. "It's very certain he won't wait much longer. And I don't like the way in which he is lying low. He knows we are up to something wrong, and he hasn't the slightest intention of identifying himself with it. But he'll have his money, all the same."

"Money you can't possibly pay him?"

"What's the use of pretending that I can? I am right at the end of my tether. I don't know which way to turn. Once Lupas starts to sue me I am done. If he makes up his mind he's going to lose his money he'll prosecute me, and that means five years at the least. By the time I am free again my hands will be ruined. I shall never be able to use a graving tool again. It's a fine prospect."

De Barsac spoke despondently enough now. All the lightness and carelessness seemed to have gone out of him.

"I am not sorry to hear you talk like that," Dorn remarked. "I was beginning to wonder when you would realise the true position of affairs."

"Oh, I always have," de Barsac said. "But what's the use of crying about it? Now, look here, Dorn, there's only one thing to be done. The only way to keep Lupas quiet is for me to marry your daughter."

"Really," Dorn smiled. "That's a happy idea of yours. How do you propose to carry it out?"

"Oh, it's easy enough. She's a young girl, absolutely fancy free, and, without undue vanity, would certainly be flattered by the attention of Victor de Barsac. I don't say that it is because I am de Barsac, any other public man in my position would be the same. I have never met a woman yet who was indifferent to my attentions. My dear fellow, she'd jump at having me. She wouldn't be blind to the advantage of being de Barsac's wife. A fine house and a big position, and all that sort of thing. Motors, and jewels, and holidays on the Continent. That's all the average woman thinks about. Fine idea, isn't it?"

"Oh, there's nothing much the matter with the idea," Dorn said; "but then, with you, an idea is as good as accomplished almost before it is thought about. I suppose it never occurs to you that there are one or two girls in the world who don't care two-pence about those sort of things."

"I have never met one," de Barsac said cynically.

"Oh, no more have I, but they exist. I see what you are driving at. If you could become engaged to Sylvia, or rather her money, then Lupas would wait."

"A crude and brutal way of putting it," de Barsac said. "But perfectly logical. And I don't suppose you would mind, as long as you made a thousand or two out of it."

"Oh, not in the least. I am not likely to touch Sylvia's money in any other way. She wouldn't let me have a penny. She will go away from home and take her mother with her, and decline to have me under the same roof. I don't know anybody who can be more determined than Sylvia if she likes."

De Barsac rose to his feet.

"Then that's settled," he said cheerfully. "On the day that I marry your daughter I agree to pay you five thousand pounds. If I can't pay you in cash, I can, at any rate, turn out something that you can sell. Now, let's get on with it, shall we? I'll come over to your place to-morrow—"

Dorn hesitated for a moment. He could see all the possibilities of this new development, but the more he thought of Sylvia and that amazing determination of hers, the less sanguine he became. As yet he had said nothing to de Barsac as to his encounter with Markham on the day before, except to drop a few hints to the effect that it might be just as well to be civil to the young man who was obviously left behind as a sort of watchdog for Gibson.

"I am afraid it won't do," he said. "You see, unfortunately, Sylvia is engaged already."

"The devil she is," the startled de Barsac said. "Why didn't you tell me that before? What an infernally secretive chap you are! I suppose you have got some game of your own on?"

"I didn't know," Dorn said. "On my honour I didn't know. I swear I didn't."

"Oh well, if you tell me that on your honour, of course I must believe you," de Barsac said.

"That'll do," Dorn said, curtly. "We shall gain nothing by the pot and kettle business. I only knew yesterday afternoon, and that was by accident. I went over to Lanton Place in the afternoon, as you know, and I happened to surprise quite a sentimental little scene in the garden. My daughter with a young man's arm round her waist! It was a bit of a shock, because I hadn't associated Sylvia with that sort of thing. But there is no doubt of the fact that she is desperately in earnest. Those quiet girls always are. But that's not the worst of it. Who do you think the man was?"

"Oh, how should I know," de Barsac said.

"Nobody but Markham. I was never more staggered in my life. It appears that he met Sylvia up in the north of England a year ago when she was on tour, and he fixed it up then. You can imagine how pleased I was. I tried the blustering heavy father business, but that didn't come off. Markham turned upon me and gave me a rare dressing down. To make a long story short, he knows all about my past, and all about yours too, for the matter of that. He spoke freely enough with regard to your dealings with Lupas, and he told me quite plainly that he knew exactly what had happened with regard to the stolen will. He even knew that you helped me in through your bedroom window that night. And he told me that if we hadn't been infernally clever, the money that is now Sylvia's would have been yours. I hadn't a leg to stand on. But he went further than that, De Barsac, he knows something."

Dorn spoke the last words in a hissing whisper. Before de Barsac could reply, the door of the studio opened and Garrass entered with an open telegram in his hand.

"From Sir Watney Gibson," Garrass said. "I am to tell you that he is coming back this evening."

CHAPTER XXXVI

THE PICTURES

During these last few days Sir Watney had not been idle. He had spent a good deal of his time in the dingy little Wardour-street establishment, giving directions to the man Jonas, until the work in hand was finished to his satisfaction. And once that was done he took Jonas on one side and told that startled individual a strange story. When the story was finished certain moneys passed between the two men, and the clever naturalist was bound to secrecy.

"Now, you quite understand," Sir Watney said. "Not one word of this must pass your lips until I give you notice to. It won't be for long, only a few days at the outside, and then you will be free to tell your story to any one. There must be at least a score of journalists in London who will be quite prepared to pay your price for it. But that will not be till afterwards. And when I say that I mean till after you have given your evidence. And, above all things, if anybody comes here asking questions, you have never seen Sir Watney Gibson. We might go a bit further and say you have never heard of him. And if anybody from the police comes here, all you have to do is to tell them to ring up 0056 Gerard, and the person at the other end of the wire will tell them everything. I don't suppose you will be bothered, because I have taken every precaution to prevent such a thing. But still, you never know. And now, one word in conclusion. About that cast. You'll have only made one, remember. Yes, I think that will do. Good morning."

With this Sir Watney turned on his heel and made his way rapidly back to his own house. If de Barsac could have seen his serious face and set features at that moment, he would have been ready enough to reconsider the estimate he had made of the distinguished scientist. There was no longer a smile on his lips, no longer a merry light in those blue eyes of his, nothing but a stern determination of purpose.

For the next hour or two he was closeted with Sergeant Gideon, who came to him with a mass of information in the shape of a daily diary that concerned the doings of an individual who was solely indicated by the letter X. Sir Watney read it through carefully, and nodded his approval.

"You have done very well, Gideon," he said. "Very well indeed. So far as I can see, except when our man was in bed, you seem to have accounted for his movements almost hour by hour. Yes, I think this will serve my purpose. If it does, and I see no reason to doubt it, you may get a telephone message or a telegram from me at any moment after to-morrow, and when this comes, I ask you to act at once. Now listen."

For the best part of half an hour, Sir Watney talked without a break. But he spoke clearly and quietly enough, without heat or passion, but with a terrible and merciless logic that carried absolute conviction to his interested listener. To a mind like that of Gideon, trained to every move of the criminal mind, there was not a single flaw to be detected in Sir Watney's logic. It was all theory, so far, but every thread of it was supported by cold concrete facts. When the recital was finished, Gideon grew enthusiastic.

"You've got it, Sir Watney," he said. "You've got it beyond the shadow of a doubt. I can't see a single weak point in your case. And it's a complicated case enough, goodness knows. I have been mixed up with amazing and ingenious crimes for the last twenty years, but I don't recollect anything so weird as this. It's like one of Edgar Allan Poe's stories. Did you ever read them, sir?"

"Aye, many a time and oft," Sir Watney said. "And you can't tell me how often they have helped me in those criminal investigations of mine. If I had never read them, I should be the poorer mentally, and I flatter myself that Scotland Yard would have missed more than one of its greatest triumphs. And I think that will do, Gideon."

"I should rather think it would, sir," the enthusiastic detective exclaimed. "Good-night, sir, and thank you very much for an object lesson in my own business."

Sir Watney lunched in comfort and ease after a few days of strenuous business, and then spent half an hour or so on a ruminative cigar. He gave a few instructions to his servant and made his way leisurely to Paddington Station. By nine o'clock that evening he was back at Baron's Court, where Garrass had seen that a comfortable dinner awaited him, and after that, he sent for Markham.

Lionel Markham came eagerly enough, anxious to know what had taken place, but he did not speak until he had assured himself that neither Dorn nor de Barsac was within earshot. According to their inevitable custom they had gone off to the studio, and in all probability they would not be seen again till bed-time. To all this Sir Watney listened with the air of one who is not particularly interested.

"Well, my boy," he said, "And how have you been getting on the last few days? As I had no message from you, I concluded that there was no news."

"Very little, sir," Markham replied. "One rather peculiar incident, but that only applied for me personally."

"In that case, I had better have it," Sir Watney said drily. "In affairs like this one never quite knows how one detached incident reacts on another."

In a few words Markham proceeded to tell his uncle of the encounter with Dorn in the garden at Lanton Place, and precisely what followed that none too friendly conversation.

"Ah, that must have been a bit of a blow for Dorn," Sir Watney chuckled. "I suppose I must congratulate you, indeed I do, for Sylvia Dorn is a charming and delightful girl, and as opposite from that rascally father of hers as the poles. It's always nice to hear of a girl of that type getting hold of a good husband, and I'm sure you'll he that, Lionel."

"I am going to try," Markham said quietly.

"Of course you are. Now, let me see how this bears upon what I have been doing. It was very rash of you to let Dorn know how much you had found out. But I suppose on the spur of the moment you couldn't help it. It must have been a bitter disappointment to him, too, for I have not the slightest doubt that he and that other scoundrel de Barsac have some pretty scheme on hand for getting hold of the girl's money. But now that she is engaged to you there will be an end to all that. What's their present attitude to you?"

"Oh, they are civil enough," Markham said. "So far as de Barsac is concerned a good deal too civil."

Sir Watney shook his wise old head sapiently.

"Ah, that sounds bad," he said. "I don't like that a bit. Not that it much matters, because those two fellows have come pretty well to the end of their rope. As far as I can gather, another day or so will finish them entirely. Lionel, I have got to the bottom of the mystery. I am not going to tell you now what the solution is, but you shall hear it before many hours have passed. You shall hear me tell the story as I conceive it in the presence of Dorn and de Barsac. I want you to be there, because you are a pretty active young fellow, and they may be up to mischief. I have worked it all out—worked it out to the last detail. The average man in my position would wash his hands of it now, and turn it all over to the police. But, seeing that I am a student of criminology, I have a natural desire to carry this through myself. It's a most extraordinary story of a most amazing crime carried through in a most amazing way. In all of my complicated experience I have never met anything like it. As I said before, I am not going to unfold the drama until the audience is seated. Now, tell me, have you seen anything of Frick lately?"

"I saw him yesterday," Markham replied. "But I have already told you that. I was out on the moor where they were busy taking pictures, and I saw both Frick and Hatton. The latter had got some wonderful new idea for using some of those animal pictures in connection with the big moorland drama."

Sir Watney started slightly.

"Oh, really," he exclaimed. "Now, I wonder—I wonder—but I needn't go into that now. I had forgotten all about those pictures taken in the park. Do you happen to know whether they were successful or not?"

"So far as I know, they haven't been developed," Markham said. "They did get a few, I know, but Mr. Bevill's unfortunate death put an end to that business altogether, so I believe the films were simply thrown on one side as being quite useless, or, at any rate, useless for the moment. Frick was only too anxious to get away to Lanton Place, and make up for lost time. It was lost time as far as he was concerned, and he was rather afraid that his directors would make a fuss about it. So, therefore, the films were thrown into a box and the whole concern moved on to Lanton Place."

Sir Watney listened intently enough. He seemed to be strangely interested in these details.

"Then I suppose they are still in the box?" he asked. "I mean still undeveloped."

"They were yesterday afternoon," Markham said. "But, as I told you, Hatton had some brilliant idea that they might be worked into his big story, and when I left them they were just starting to develop the films. I was asked to stay, but as I was rather worried about that interview with Dorn, I declined. By the way, I had quite forgotten, Hatton and Frick are coming over this evening for a game of billiards, and they ought to turn up at any moment now. Then you can ask them for yourself."

Almost as Markham spoke, the door of the dining-room opened and Garrass ushered in the expected visitors. It only needed one glance at Frick's face to see that something amazing had happened. He had lost that perennial smile of his, his ruddy cheeks were pale and his hands were unsteady. For once in his life Hatton was silent and distracted, standing behind his comrade in an attitude of doubt and agitation.

"You are just in time, gentlemen," Sir Watney said. "We were just talking about you. Sit down."

Frick crossed to the door, and after satisfying himself that no one was outside, closed it carefully. Then he produced a bulky envelope from his pocket.

"You have found something?" Sir Watney asked.

"Indeed we have, Sir Watney," Frick whispered. "The most damnable thing that ever appeared on a picture."

CHAPTER XXXVII

CLEAR AS DAYLIGHT

Sir Watney Gibson barely moved from his seat. Quite coolly he took a cigar from his case and lighted it, and passed the case along to his visitors. They helped themselves almost mechanically, but stood there without lighting the cigars they had taken and waited for Gibson to speak.

"Well, get on, gentlemen," he said. "You have come here to tell me something, or rather, to show me something, and I am quite curious to see it. Perhaps I may be able to tell you what it is."

Frick pulled himself together.

"I know you are a wonderful man, Sir Watney," he said. "But I don't think you can tell me what's inside the envelope."

Sir Watney waved his hand comprehensively.

"They are pictures," Frick went on. "Pictures we developed a little time ago. Perhaps Mr. Markham has told you what they are."

"He did say something about them," Gibson replied. "Photographs, I presume, taken in the park here. If so, I trust that they are successful."

"So successful that they fairly startled us," Hatton interrupted. "I had hoped to have got an impression or two of some of those wild animals, but I never expected anything like this. Oh, yes, we got one or two good studies, and then suddenly these things came along. Now, Sir Watney, there are the negatives, and there are the prints. They are rather small because we haven't got any enlarging apparatus down here, but they are quite clear, and the figures are unmistakable. They must have been taken just as the sun was setting, with a fine bright light shining through the trees. A magnificent light, in fact. I should like you to take those pictures and look at them through a strong magnifying glass."

Sir Watney Gibson rose and proceeded most carefully to lock the door. There was a small table in the corner of the dining-room on which stood a shaded electric lamp, the light of which he switched on, and then, taking a powerful glass from his pocket he made a long careful examination of the handful of little flimsy pieces of paper that lay before him. Hatton stood and looked over his shoulder.

"You have not got them quite in proper rotation, Sir Watney," he said. "See here is a piece of film, perhaps a dozen photographs altogether, and all taken in a few seconds. Now, let me arrange the pictures one under the other, and then you shall tell me what you make of them."

With this, Hatton proceeded to lay out the pictures in a line one under the other, until at length the sequence was complete. He had been speaking almost in a whisper and evidently under the stress of a great excitement.

"Now, what do you see?" he asked.

"Well, in the first place, my old friend John Bevill, undoubtedly," Sir Watney said, as if speaking to himself. "He is standing in the little open space with something I can't quite make out by his side. Some blurred object. Yes. I see what it is now. It's Vim, just on the very edge of the picture. And then someone else comes along. Perhaps he comes out plainly in the next print. Yes, here he is, and the monkey has vanished. It's de Barsac."

Sir Watney paused for a moment, and very gradually his forefinger trailed down the little line of pictures that lay before him. Gradually his voice sank.

"De Barsac coming out from between the trees," he said. "Glancing about him as if afraid of being seen. He steps quietly behind Bevill, who is utterly unconscious of his presence. He carries something in his hand that looks like a thick but flexible stick. My God, that's it, is it? He strikes Bevill a murderous blow on the back of the head with the stick and thrusts it in his pocket. That is what you call a sandbag, I suppose. The poor old man struggles to his feet, and de Barsac clutches him by the throat. It's only for half a moment, and then he is down on his back with that scoundrel bending over him. He holds on with that murderous grip for a moment and then it is all over. Ah! That is all I needed. I never expected to get it, and I may tell you gentlemen now that I could have done without it. I have enough circumstantial evidence in my hands at the present time to hang de Barsac a dozen times over. But it is only circumstantial evidence, after all, and you never can quite tell what a clever lawyer will do with it. But here we have the whole crime taken by a witness that cannot lie. Small as those pictures are, there is no mistaking the figure of de Barsac, and that of my unfortunate friend John Bevill."

"They are small pictures," Hatton said. "But, at the same time, they are wonderfully clear and accurate, and if we enlarge them, the whole truth will be plain to everybody. And if we throw them on the screen they will be amazing. What a series of pictures! Looking at them from a business point of view, they would fill all the cinema halls in England for months. Just fancy the actual presentment of the murder of Mr. John Bevill! But I beg your pardon, Sir Watney, I ought not to be talking like that. I was carried away for the moment."

"Oh, that's natural enough," Sir Watney said. "I can quite understand your professional feelings. I don't see why those pictures should not be exhibited some of these days. But for the present I shall ask you to leave them in my hands."

"We brought them on purpose," Frick said.

"That's very good of you. I shall pack them up to-night and send them with an explanatory letter to Scotland Yard. They will be an absolute supplement to the information I already have. I suppose you can see what the conspiracy is? If you don't understand, I had better explain. Most people regard de Barsac as a rich man. He ought to be, for he makes a big enough income. But he is reckless and extravagant, and very deeply in debt; indeed, I have every reason to believe that he obtained a large sum of money from a London money-lender by false pretence. If my information on this point is wrong, then it is the fault of Scotland Yard. But I can assure you, gentlemen, Scotland Yard does not make mistakes in these matters. De Barsac owes this money-lender a fortune, and if it is not repaid by a certain date, then he will be prosecuted. Now, unfortunately for my poor friend Bevill, he thought very highly of de Barsac, and meant to leave him forty thousand pounds. I can prove that de Barsac knew this, and I have proved to you that he was in urgent need of the money. And now you see why he anticipated events. He killed my poor friend, and by doing so thought he had made his own future safe. But he was far too clever, as I shall prove to you presently. He went to London, where he remained for a week. Everything he did exactly that week in known to me. Every movement of his was tracked by the police. When he came back here and reappeared in this very room at ten o'clock on the night of the murder he said he had just come down from town. And he had done nothing of the sort. He came down from London the day before on a motor-cycle that he had bought in Oxford-street. He came down in mackintoshes and goggles, and, thus disguised, hung about in the neighbourhood the whole day of the crime. What has become of the motor-cycle we shall find out. And now I come to my part of the tragedy. Everybody thinks that Mr. Bevill was killed by his pet chimpanzee. That was very cunningly worked by de Barsac, rather too cunningly worked, as a matter of fact. Still, it was a very clever piece of strategy, and if my suspicions had not been aroused, it would probably have thrown dust in everybody eyes. But don't forget it came out at the inquest that the real cause of John Bevill's death was a fracture of the skull. It might have been argued that the skull was fractured when the chimpanzee attacked him. It might have been caused by a violent contact with the root of a tree. But these photographs have spoilt that theory. And now I am going a little bit further. We will assume for a moment that the marks made by the chimpanzee on the throat of John Bevill really caused his death. And we will allow that those were the marks of Vim's powerful grip. And, in a way, gentlemen, that is strictly true."

"Then how?" Frick asked. "How on earth—"

"One moment," Sir Watney said, "I must go and fetch something. I won't keep you waiting long, and if anybody comes in the room when I am away, I will ask you to try and look as ordinary as you can under the circumstances."

With this, Sir Watney proceeded to unlock the door and make his way up the stairs to his bedroom. He came back a little later with two objects in his hand. After he had locked the door he proceeded with his story.

"Now, listen," he said. "This heavy object in bronze is an absolutely exact reproduction of Vim's hand and forearm. It is the work of de Barsac, and I should say that he has never done anything finer. He actually did it at my suggestion because I wanted it for a book I am writing. And I have not the slightest doubt that it was this piece of work that put that cunning scheme into de Barsac's head. He went to London, and, from the clay model of that finished bronze, he had a steel and leather glove made in imitation of Vim's paw. Here it is, or at least, here is a duplicate copy of it, made by the same man, a clever naturalist called Jonas who lives in Wardour-street. I found all this out, never mind how. And now, gentlemen, do you begin to see what took place?"

"It's a bit foggy to me," Frick said.

"To me it's as plain as daylight," Hatton cried. "But then, you see, I am a novelist. After de Barsac had cleared the ground, he took the first opportunity of putting his vile project into execution. Of course, he didn't expect to fracture the old gentleman's skull, he only wanted to stun him with that sandbag, which was an unaccustomed weapon in his hands, and, without knowing it, he must have hit his victim a bit too hard. Then, under the impression that he was safe, with that leather and steel glove on his hand, he left those marks on the throat of the man who was his friend. Oh dear yes, it's quite plain to me, Sir Watney. What a cunning plot, what a diabolical scheme that did not implicate any human being, only an unfortunate monkey that everybody is hunting down. I should like to shoot that scoundrel out of hand. May I venture to ask what you are going to do now, Sir Watney?"

CHAPTER XXXVIII

FLIGHT

Meanwhile, Dorn and de Barsac were spending the evening in the studio to which they always repaired after dinner, with a view to discussing the gloomy future. Naturally, they had no idea of the dramatic events which were taking place within a few yards of where they were seated. It was a beautiful night, with a considerable moon, almost a month from the night when John Bevill had met his death. It was warm, too, so that the studio windows were open and the blinds pulled on one side.

For a long time the two scoundrels sat opposite one another, pulling moodily at the choice cigars which had been provided for them by the late kindly host and glancing at one another furtively from under their eyelids, as if each was trying to read the other's thoughts. It was plain enough that they were both ill at ease, especially de Barsac, who started at every sound, and glanced apprehensively through the open window.

"What on earth's the matter with the man?" Dorn exclaimed impatiently. "You are as nervous as a child."

"Ah, it's all very well for you to talk like that," de Barsac said. "But your position is very different to mine."

It was the first time that he had intimated plainly the tragedy which had so long loomed over Baron's Court. It was, in itself, almost an admission of guilt.

"What's the good of talking like that?" Dorn demanded. "You are safe enough. The man is dead and buried, and in a week or two the whole thing will be forgotten. Once those thick-headed farmers have managed to destroy the chimpanzee there will be no more to be said or done."

De Barsac glanced about him moodily.

"Ah, it's all very well for you to talk like that," he said. "But who suggested the idea? Who pointed out to me how comparatively easy the scheme was? Who stood in the background and pulled all the strings whilst I pulled all the chestnuts? And who is going to benefit to the extent of some thousands of pounds? And who would have benefited if that sentimental old idiot hadn't changed his mind? Look here, Dorn, I killed John Bevill, and you know it. And if the rope is ever put round my neck, I'll take damned good care it's round yours too. I'll not die by myself."

A light of terror leapt into Dorn's eyes.

"Are you mad?" he cried hoarsely. "Oh, you must be, and the windows open and all."

"I don't care," de Barsac said recklessly. "I don't—good Heavens, what's that?"

There was a sound of something moving outside amongst the leaves, and a moment later a queer face looked in through the open window. Then there was a chatter of rage, and the great brown shape of Vim came into the room. De Barsac jumped to his feet and, like a flash, drew a revolver from his pocket. He would have fired, but Dorn restrained him.

"Don't shoot," he whispered hoarsely. "We shall have the whole household round us if you do."

There was no occasion, however, for, at the first sight of the shining muzzle, the sagacious chimpanzee leapt like a cat through the open window and vanished. Vim had learnt to his cost what a firearm meant. Trembling from head to foot, de Barsac dropped into his seat again.

"That devil meant to kill me," he said hoarsely. "He knows, he knows perfectly well. He must have been very near at hand when I—when his master died. And he'll get me some of these days. How it is those farmers can't manage to shoot him I don't understand. And this is the second time he has been after me lately. I can't stand it much longer, Dorn. This business has shaken my nerves more than I can tell you. I am going to clear out; I am going to America. You must do the best you can. I have done."

Dorn listened uneasily enough. De Barsac was in a state now to confess everything. What he would do on the other side of the water Dorn neither knew nor cared. The great plot had failed; there was no longer any chance of raising a penny-piece so far as Baron's Court was concerned. And this being the case, the sooner de Barsac was gone, the better. They had hardly settled down to discuss the details of this new idea before another face looked in at the window, and there, in the moonlight, they could see the sinister features of Henderby Lupas.

"Ay, my Adonis," de Barsac said, with some attempt at swagger. "To what are we indebted for this late visit? But come inside, come inside."

"Only for a moment then," Lupas said, as he climbed into the studio. "You are neither of you worth it, but I have come to warn you. The game is up. The whole story is known."

"What are you talking about?" Dorn asked uneasily.

"Oh, don't try and fool me. I'll just ask de Barsac one question. Did you ever hear of a man called Jonas, a man who keeps a naturalist's shop in Wardour-street?"

A queer cry came from de Barsac's lips.

"You don't mean to say—" he stammered.

"I do. Jonas happens to be one of my clients. I have got hundreds of them in London who owe me money. But Jonas is honest enough, but he is a dreamer and a poor man of business, and that's how he comes to be in my debt. He was with me a few days ago, asking for further time to pay off an instalment, and, as an inducement, told me that he had secured an important new customer who had promised him a good deal of work. Now, I like all sorts of information, and I pressed him to tell me who this customer was. He didn't want to tell me, but as I refused to give him more time unless he did so, he very unwillingly consented. Then I found it all out. The man he spoke of is no less than Sir Watney Gibson."

De Barsac, with a pale face and lips that he strove in vain to keep steady, glanced across at Dorn, whose features were, if possible, more pallid than his own.

"Go on," he said hoarsely. "Go on."

"Is there any real necessity?" Lupas asked. "I don't want to say too much, and indeed, I have already told you more than is prudent. I don't want to get myself into trouble, and, at the same time, I don't want to lose my money. I have got a little scheme on hand which I will tell you presently, if de Barsac is ever lucky enough to reach a place of safety. I very much doubt it, but I am fond of my money, and I have taken the risk of being mixed up in a crime by coming down here."

"For Heaven's sake, get on," de Barsac said with dry lips.

"Oh, very well, if you will have it. Sir Watney Gibson went to Jonas, and left with him a bronze cast of a monkey's paw. That was your work, de Barsac, though Jonas didn't know it, and there is no occasion for me to say what particular ape that cast was taken from."

De Barsac rocked backwards and forwards in his chair and groaned. It was plain to him now how the shadows were closing in on all sides, and how Gibson, with that amazing instinct of his for putting his finger on the right spot, had gone straight to the heart of the conspiracy. And as this came home to de Barsac, he glanced across at Dorn with an expression in his eyes that was absolutely murderous.

"You devil!" he said. "You devil! Why did you tempt me to do this thing?"

"Here, that will do," Lupas said uneasily. "You can keep these mutual recriminations till you are alone together. I have my suspicions, of course, but I don't want to sit quietly down here and listen to a confession of murder. Good Lord, fancy me being in the witness-box, and having it dragged out of me that I heard that remark."

"You are quite right," Dorn said soothingly. "We shall have to go, both of us will have to go. But go on, Lupas; tell us the worst."

"There's very little left to tell," Lupas went on. "Sir Watney Gibson wanted that hand reproduced in leather and steel. Here, hold up, de Barsac."

For de Barsac had fallen forward and lay half fainting in his chair. Then he pulled himself together and looked at the other two with wild, haggard eyes.

"Well, isn't it enough?" Lupas demanded. "I can tell you a little more, if you like. When I had heard all this I looked up a broken-down police detective who does certain touting work and watching for me, and I got him to make inquiries. As a result of those inquiries, I discovered that de Barsac's movements all last week and the week before were successfully traced from the time he left here till the hour of his return. You were watched the whole time, de Barsac. They know all about that motor-cycle you bought in Oxford-street—but what's the good of going on? Now, have you got any money?"

"Not five pounds in the world," de Barsac groaned.

"And I am no better off," Dorn said. "Perhaps I could put my hand upon forty pounds. But what's the good of that?"

"Well, it'll take you both to Falmouth, anyway," Lupas said. "You had better get there as soon as possible and write to me in London. You will know how to write, and you can adopt any nom-de-plume you like. You can leave me to make all the other arrangements. And now I'm off."

He disappeared abruptly, leaving the other two facing one another, until at length Dorn rose and moved towards the door.

"I am going to get the little car out," he said. "We will drive across the moors and get to Falmouth that way. I'll take the car down to the end of the avenue, and you can join me in ten minutes."

A little later on the car slid down the avenue through the open gates into the road where Dorn picked up his companion, and together they sped along in the moonlight. They did not see the brown shadow that rose from the hedge and the pair of red, vengeful eyes that followed them as they tore along the road in the direction of the open country.

"Here, rouse yourself," Dorn said. "That ghastly face of yours would give you away anywhere. You would be arrested on suspicion by the first policeman you came past. We'll go round this way and make a wide detour and strike the moor road again by the other side of the waterfall. It's rather a dangerous road at this time at night, but we must risk that."

They circled wide, going far out of their way at first, and as they turned inland again the brown shadow of Vim moved along in the moonlight with a grim determination of purpose and a resolution that had in it something human.

CHAPTER XXXIX

WIPED OUT

The little car scouted round the edge of the park and from thence by the winding road on to the moor. This was a matter of a mile or two, and the road finally turned almost to the edge of the park again, so that anyone crossing it could have been in a position to cut the car off before it left the precincts of the house. But once this was done the long wide thoroughfare stretched away in the moonlight for miles and miles towards the south-west. It was a somewhat narrow track, by no means good for motor traffic, but then, on the other hand, it was a lonely road with no hedge on either side, and little chance of encountering traffic. Then the road wound again in serpentine fashion, so that the best part of an hour elapsed with Dorn and de Barsac barely ten miles on their way.

For a long time they hardly spoke to one another, each apparently wrapped in his own gloomy thoughts. They were close together, and yet entirely far apart, each wondering what the other was thinking, and each full of suspicion and mistrust. It was de Barsac who spoke at length. He had the wheel in his hand, and Dorn was huddled down by his side.

"Well, what do you think of it?" he asked.

"I don't know what to think," Dorn said. "I am still wondering if we have done the right thing. And if I am not wrong, it isn't too late yet."

"What, to go back?" de Barsac asked.

"Well, why not? Nothing is known, nothing can possibly be known. You have only got—"

"Ah, it's all very well for you," de Barsac growled. "You are all right, or at least you think so. But not if I like to speak. I am not going to shoulder it all."

Dorn was silent for a little while. He was carefully weighing up his chances. So far as he could see, there was no case against him. He knew all about that black tragedy; he had known all about it from the first. It was he, with his superior cunning, who had suggested the whole thing to de Barsac. He remembered vividly enough how he had led up to it, and how the scheme had occurred to him that night at dinner when de Barsac had proudly produced the bronze cast of the monkey's paw. He recollected how pleased he had been when the idea first occurred to him, and how, by slow degrees, he had unfolded the whole diabolical conspiracy to his companion. De Barsac had demurred at first; he had placed a hundred difficulties in the way; but gradually, as the desperate condition of his affairs had been painted by Dorn in gloomy colours, he had come round the the plan, and finally accepted it with something like enthusiasm. And he had done every bit himself, Dorn had seen to that. He had gone to town, where he had had that cast made, or rather, reproduced in steel and leather, he had seen to every detail without so much as Dorn moving a hand. And finally, in the park, in strict solitude, as he thought, he had dealt John Bevill the fatal blow that was to mean freedom for himself.

No, the more Dorn thought it over, the more sure he felt that no blame could be attached to him. He was bitterly contemptuous of the cowardice which had caused him to turn his back on Baron's Court and fly like a criminal. He saw now that he had been carried away by Lupas' dramatic disclosure, and he began to see that it would have been better had he remained. De Barsac, watching him furtively from time to time, seemed to see what was passing in his companion's mind.

"You want to leave me, do you?" he asked.

"What makes you think that?" Dorn asked.

"Oh, I don't know. I—I feel it. Well, you can please yourself. But don't forget that I can reach you wherever I am. If anything happens to me, I shall tell the truth, the whole truth, and nothing but the truth. I shall tell them that the scheme was yours. It will be useless for you to deny it. Now, what are you going to do?"

Dorn moved uneasily in his seat.

"Let's talk it over," he said. "We can go on to Falmouth just the same. If we stay there a day or two, no one will ask us any questions. Now, what have you got to be afraid of? Where's the evidence?"

"Oh, well, that's all right from your point of view. But you heard what Lupas said. Every movement I made in London is known to the police, and, of course, to Gibson. He put them on to me. He guessed how those marks came on Bevill's throat. Heaven only knows how, but you may depend upon it he saw through our scheme, and set to work on his theory. It was a bit of sheer bad luck for me when Gibson found out that I had been to Jonas. And you may be absolutely certain that Jonas told him all about the commission he was carrying out for me. Of course he did. And, once that was done, Gibson would be quite clear in his mind. Oh, there's no way out."

"Wait a minute," Dorn said. "You can deny it. They can't prove anything. Surely we can invent some plausible reason why you went to Jonas. You are a sculptor, and you might have wanted that model for any purpose. Leave it to me, I will think of something ingenious. And then all you've got to do is to brazen the whole thing out."

"Oh, you mean well enough," de Barsac muttered; "but you are not looking facts in the face. Of course, no one can prove I was in the park that night, that fact never will be proved. It isn't enough, Dorn, it isn't enough. What am I going to say about my movements in London? What excuse can I offer for putting up in a little public-house on the Thames? And how about that motor-cycle I bought, which is now at the bottom of the lake in the middle of the park, together with my goggles and mackintosh. Why should I want to sneak from London in that way and then turn from Baron's Court in the night of Bevill's death and tell everybody I have just come back by train? Your scheme was too clever. I ought to have gone back to town again by the way I came. My game was to say I had read all about Bevill's death in the papers. But it's no use crying over spilt milk. It's done now. And again, there's all that business of the missing will under which I was to benefit to a big extent. The police will investigate my affairs, and it won't take them many days to discover how desperately in need of money I am. And yet it looks so plain, so easy to place the deed on the shoulders of the chimpanzee, especially after he had attacked his master twice. No, we must go on, Dorn, we must go on. You play the game with me, and I'll play it with you. Stick to me as long as there is any necessity, and I won't let you down."

"Oh, I am going to do that," Dorn said. "But, in spite of all you say, I still think that you have everything to gain by facing it out. How do you expect to get away? It's all very well for Lupas to promise all sorts of things, but he can't carry them out, and if he sees the slightest danger to himself he won't hesitate to throw us to the dogs. If what you say is correct, all England will ring with this business in a few hours. No, you take my advice. Lie up for a day or two in Falmouth and then we can come back."

"Thinking about yourself," de Barsac sneered. "Thinking about yourself, so you can stand by and pretend that you knew nothing at all about it. And when I am dead and gone, you can whine and snivel to everybody you meet and tell them how sorry you are that you ever met Victor de Barsac. And all the while this never would have happened if I hadn't listened to you. It was your scheme from first to last, you dirty dog, and well you know it. Besides, they may have found out other things."

De Barsac scarcely knew how true this was. As yet, the story of the pictures was not known to those two men pushing their way across the country in the moonlight, two fugitives from justice with the bloodhounds of the Law already upon their track had they only known it. And so they pursued their way for some minutes in silence, until they came to a spot eight or ten miles from Baron's Court where the road narrowed between two high banks that formed a cliff on either side which gave a little farther on until it shelved down to a little bridge over a stream that ran in the valley some sixty feet below. It was no more than a shining silver thread now, for the hot summer had dried up the stream so that it trickled over its rocky bed whispering as it went. The bridge was barely wide enough to admit the passing of the car, and the parapet on the left side was barely a foot in height. It was by no means a safe passage in the dark—in fact, a highly dangerous one—but it was easy enough in the moonlight with a certain amount of care, so that de Barsac slowed up slightly as the car began to climb the slight incline to the crown of the bridge.

Just as it reached the crest, a shadow seemed to move slowly down the rocky bank on the right, a shadow that grew nearer and nearer until it seemed to rise sheer of the rock and come down heavily right into the car. It was a heavy body, heavy indeed, but the impact was singularly light. De Barsac was conscious of a warm brown, hairy body clinging about his neck and shoulders; he saw two long hairy arms reaching down to the steering wheel.

Then, as he realised what had happened, a strangled cry broke from his lips.

"Here, Dorn," he cried. "Pull that brute off my shoulders. By heavens, it's that infernal monkey."

De Barsac spoke truly enough. With an effort he got the wheel in his hand again and tried to steer the swaying car close against the wall of rock. Then the long brown hand over his own gasped the wheel again and tugged at it viciously. Almost unconsciously, de Barsac had put his foot upon the accelerator so that the car shoved forward and, at the same time, turned sharply to the left. It crashed against the low stone parapet, and a second later fell hideously down those sixty feet to the dry bed of the river below. It was all over in less time than it takes to tell. The two men dropped out of the car like flies, crashing on the rocks below with the overturned car upon them. As it went down over the parapet, Vim made a big leap for safety, and swung clear on the branch of an overhanging tree. Then, presently, as there was no sound from below he made his way down to where those two bodies were lying stark and white in the moonlight. His teeth chattered and he showed them in a horrible grin. Then he turned away and swiftly crossed the moors; smiling to himself as if at a good deed well done.

CHAPTER XL

ALL SAID AND DONE

It was Sir Watney who first discovered that there was something wrong. He had been seated for an hour or more in the dining-room at Baron's Court, working out the problem to its last details and making up his mind what to do next. His first impulse was to call up Scotland Yard on the telephone, but he reflected that the telephone at Baron's Court was in a public place, and therefore it would be perhaps imprudent to discuss these startling details in the hearing of anyone. He would go over to the studio and see what he could do with the two men who were closeted there. Not that he expected much from this course, but he might see some signs of guilt on the part of these two scoundrels. And, besides, Gibson had no doubt in his mind that Dorn was as deep in the business as de Barsac. He hoped not for the sake of Sylvia and Markham, but whatever happened as far as these two were concerned, it seemed to Sir Watney that his duty lay plainly before him.

"Stay here a moment," he said, "I'll just go over to the studio and ask Mr. de Barsac and Major Dorn to join us. They may possibly be interested."

Sir Watney came back in a few moments with the information that the studio was empty, and a little later Garrass appeared with the statement that the small car was missing and that Dorn and de Barsac had gone off in a great hurry, telling the head chauffeur that they had been called to Falmouth on business. Sir Watney listened gravely enough till Garrass had gone.

"The birds have flown, gentlemen," he said. "Either they must have been listening outside and heard what we were saying, or some kind friend has given them a warning. At any rate, they have gone, and, for the moment, there's nothing more to be done or said. We must wait till the morning. Now, I trust you gentlemen will say nothing of this."

Frick and Hatton went off a few minutes later with a promise to say nothing of what they had heard until the police approached them, and once the servants had retired and the house was quiet, Sir Watney got London on the telephone. It took some little time on a particularly bad line to explain what had happened, but it was finished at length, and Sir Watney was free to return to the dining-room, where Markham awaited him.

"Well, were you successful?" Markham asked.

"Oh, yes, I managed to make them understand. One of the big men from the Yard will be here to-morrow. Of course, Lionel, you realise what all this means?"

"I think so," Markham said gravely. "Those two rascals have found out that we know everything and they have flown. It is a terrible thing altogether, and what I am to say to Sylvia I don't know. What can I say?"

"We must hope for the best," Sir Watney replied. "We will try and spare the poor girl as much scandal as possible. But, you see, Dorn having gone off with de Barsac, practically admits his guilt. There's not the slightest doubt that those two men were in it together, and, in all probability, the scheme was Dorn's. He's far the more cunning rascal of the two. Let's hope that they try and get away. And if, perchance, some accident overtakes them, as it might—"

Markham shook his head hopelessly. There was nothing for it now but to go to bed and wait events on the morrow. It was late before Markham and Sir Watney were down, and when they came it was only to find a white-faced farmer and his shepherd in the dining-room with startling news.

It was soon told. At dawn the shepherd, crossing the moor in search of some lost sheep with his dog, had come across a broken motor-car lying in the bottom of the gully on the Falmouth road. It was plain to him that the car had run off the track and had collapsed at the bottom of the ravine. It was the dog who had first called the shepherd's attention to the fact that there was something under the car, and, after a good deal of trouble, the shepherd had managed to remove the chassis and, to his horror, had discovered two bodies underneath. They were quite dead, and so far as the scared labourer could judge they had been dead for many hours. Sir Watney listened with a grave face, but with something like hope in his eyes.

"This is very disturbing," he said. "But why do you come here? What's it got to do with Baron's Court?"

"Well, sir," the farmer said, "it was Mr. Bevill's car. I have seen it a score of times. And I happen to know that those two gentlemen who were killed were staying here. One of them was a foreigner, but I forget his name."

"Was it de Barsac?" Sir Watney asked.

"That's it, sir—de Barsac. And the other gentleman is known by everybody in these parts. Better known than trusted, if I may be allowed to say so. It's Major Dorn, who lives over at Lanton Place."

In spite of himself, Sir Watney breathed a little more easily. It was quite clear that what he had hoped for had come about, and he began to see his way clear to keep Sylvia's name out of the scandal. The truth about de Barsac would have to be told, of course, but there was no evidence against the other man, nor was there likely to be now.

"What have you done with the bodies?" Gibson asked.

"We brought them along here in a cart," the farmer explained. "One of the servants told us to put them in what he calls the studio. So we can't tell you any more than we have, sir. And if you don't mind now, we'll get back. I suppose, we shall have to come over for the inquest?"

The inquest was held late that evening, and the usual verdict was brought in. No one knew how the accident happened, and no one could guess except that the car had probably skidded on the bridge and had gone over the low parapet. Two leading officials of Scotland Yard sat gravely by when the evidence was being given, but no comment came from them, neither did they speak until the proceedings had terminated and they were alone in the library with Sir Watney.

He told them all that he had discovered, link by link, and chain by chain until his case was complete. There was not the semblance of a weak spot in it anywhere, so far as the detectives could see and when Sir Watney had finished they congratulated him warmly on what he had done.

"And that's about the end of it, sir," the chief detective said. "The most extraordinary case that ever came under my notice. They were probably both in it, though naturally we can't be sure as far as Major Dorn was concerned. Of course, Sir Watney, you won't mind if we tell all this to the press—in fact, we've got to do it. We must clear the thing up properly. We can't leave anybody to be the victim of local gossip. And it seems to me that you have cleared everybody, including that monkey. I'd like to see him."

It was indeed a strange case, vividly told, that filled hundreds of columns in the newspapers on the following day. The story excited a widespread interest from one end of the country to the other and before another twenty-four hours had elapsed large sums of money were being offered for Vim from various music-hall entertainers. But Vim, who strangely enough had come back home early in the morning following the death of de Barsac and Dorn, and was now seated quietly enough in his accustomed spot, was not destined to create sensation on any music-hall stage, for Frick and Hatton had put in a first claim and had already arranged for that most intelligent ape to be transferred to the cinematograph company.

"He has taken a great fancy to me," Frick said. "He will follow me anywhere. As you know, Sir Watney, it was I who found him in the park and brought him home. He came up to me like a child, and he has been following me about ever since. I believe he knows that justice has to been done."

And indeed, it seemed like it, for Vim sat at Frick's feet chattering and smiling, and obviously pleased to find himself at peace with the world again.

There was much to be done during the next few days, amongst other things John Bevill's bequests to be attended to. He had left Baron's Court and the greater portion of his fortune to fund a sort of practical natural history university. There were big legacies to his niece and servants, and, of course the money left to Sylvia besides. The best part of a fortnight had elapsed before Sir Watney felt himself free to leave Baron's Court and return to London.

"You had better stay and clear up the odds and ends," he said to Markham. "And, by the way, how are the people at Lanton Place? I am sorry to say, I had almost forgotten them. What arrangements have you and Sylvia made?"

"I have hardly seen her since the day of her father's funeral," Markham explained. "She was very much distressed, of course, but it would be mere hypocrisy to say that she had any great sorrow. But we have made no arrangements. She is quite rich now, and I am correspondingly poor, and that being so I shall have to wait."

"There is no occasion to do anything of the sort," Sir Watney said. "Why should you wait? Some of these days you will be comparatively rich yourself. You'll have all my money, anyhow. And that being the case, I don't see why you shouldn't have some of it now. Go and tell her so."

It was a pleasant meeting for Sylvia and Markham, and none the less pleasant because it was quiet and restrained.

"There is really nothing to wait for now," Markham said. "You must get rid of this dreary old place. Those cinematograph people are prepared to buy it, I know, and it will be a fine opportunity for your mother to get away from here. She must come with us of course; she must live with us as long as she lives. Does she understand things at all? Did you make her understand, for instance, that the black box was empty?"

"I did," Sylvia said. "I made her comprehend that she had been robbed, and since she has got that into her mind, she has been quite different. She never goes near the ruins now. And since my father's death she has begun to rest. I believe if we can get her away from here she will be quite normal again."

"Then there's nothing to stop us," Markham said. "The sooner we get away from here the better I shall be pleased. And you won't keep me waiting long, Sylvia, will you?"

She placed her hands upon his shoulders and raised those clear eyes of hers to his. And as he bent and kissed her all the shadows vanished and all the world seemed full of light.

FRED M WHITE – A CONCISE BIBLIOGRAPHY

NOVELS (A-Z)

Ambition's Slave (1916)
The Argus Eye (1919)
Blackmail (1902)
The Blue Daffodil (1934)
The Brand Of Silence (1911)
A Broken Memory (1929)
The Bubble Reputation (1908)
By Order Of The League (1886)
The Cardinal Moth aka The Accused Orchid (1903)
The Case For the Crown (1918)
Claxton's Mill (1912)
A Clue In Wax (1930)
The Corner House (1905)
The Councillors of Falconhoe (1922)
Craven Fortune (1904)
A Crime On Canvas (1909)
The Crimson Blind (US title: The Mystery Of The Crimson Blind) (1905)
A Daughter Of Israel (1892)
The Day: Or The Passing Of A Throne (1914)
A Deal In Letters (1923)
The Devil's Advocate (1924)
Dropped From The Fast Express, or A Daughter's Sacrifice (1911)
The Edge Of The Sword (1907)
The Ends Of Justice (1906)

A Fatal Dose (aka Behind the Mask) (1907)
The Fight For The Child (1925)
The Five Knots (1907)
"Found Dead" (1930)
The Four Fingers (US title: The Mystery Of The Four Fingers) (1907)
A Front Of Brass (1910)
The Garden O' Dreams (1909)
A Golden Argosy (1886)
The Golden Bat (1924)
The Golden Rose (1909)
The Green Bungalow (1923)
The Grey Woman (aka Sinister House) (1928)
The Happy Exile (1920)
A Harbour Of Refuge (1918)
Hard Pressed (1910)
The Honour Of His House (1920)
The House Of Mammon (1913)
A House Of Sorrows (1911)
The House Of The Schemers (1906)
The House On The River (1925)
In Trust (1892)
Jim Crowshaw's Mary (1911)
The King Diamond (1927)
Lady Clara (1913)
Lady Edna's Awakening (1920)
The Lady In Blue (1915)
The Law Of The Land (1906)
The Leopard's Spots (1920)
The Lonely Bride (aka The White Bride) (1907)
The Lord Of The Manor (1907)
Love, The Foe (1910)
A Maker of Millions (1909)
The Man Called Gilray (1911)
The Man Who Found Christmas (a novelette) (1915)
The Man Who Knew (1932)
The Man Who Was Two (1921)
The Man With The Vandyk Beard (1925)
The Midnight Guest: A Detective Story (1907)
A Mummer's Throne (1910)
My Lady Bountiful (1905)
The Mystery Of Crocksands (1923)
The Mystery Of The Ravenspurs (aka The Black Valley) (1911)
The Mystery Of Room 75 (1922)
Naboth's Vineyard (1889)
The Nether Millstone (1906)
Netta, The Story Of Sin (1909)
New Century Calendar Clue (1948)
Number Thirteen (1914)

The Old Secretaire: A Christmas Story (novelette) (1887)
On The Night Express (1930)
The Open Door (1907)
Paul Quentin (1908)
Paul, The Sage (1910)
The Phantom Car (1929)
Powers Of Darkness (1912)
The Price Of Silence (1925)
The Psalm Stone (1905)
Queen Of Hearts (1930)
A Queen Of The Stage (1908)
The Riddle Of The Rail (1926)
The Robe Of Lucifer (1896)
A Royal Wrong (1913)
The Salt Of The Earth (1918)
The Scales Of Justice (1908)
Secret Of The River (1934)
The Secret Of The Sands (1911)
A Secret Service (1913)
The Seed Of Empire (1916)
The Sentence Of The Court (1913)
A Shadowed Love (1905)
The Shadow Of The Dead Hand (1926)
The Silver Stream (novelette)
The Slave Of Silence (1906)
A Society Jezebel (1917)
The Sundial (1908)
Tregarthen's Wife: A Cornish Story (1901)
The Turn Of The Tide (1923)
The Weight Of The Crown (1904)
The White Battalions (1900)
The White Bride (aka The Lonely Bride) (1910)
The White Glove (1910)
The Wings Of Victory (1919)
The Yellow Face (1906)

SHORT FICTION SERIES

THE MASTER CRIMINAL (1897-1898)

A series of 12 short stories featuring Felix Gryde, who describes himself as "a really clever soldier of fortune."

The Head Of The Caesars
At Windsor
The Silverpool Cup
The "Morrison Raid" Indemnity

Cleopatra's Robe
The Rosy Cross
The Death Of The President
The Cradlestone Oil Mills
Redburn Castle
"Crysoline Limited"
The Loss Of The "Eastern Empress"
General Marcos

THE LAST OF THE BORGIAS (1898)

A series of stories featuring Professor Victor Colonna, a vigilante physician who murders undesirable people with undetectable poisons.

The Scrip of Death
The Crimson Streak
The Holy Rose
The Saving Of Serena
The Varteg Necklace
The Three Carnations

DRENTON DENN - SPECIAL COMMISSIONER

Drenton Denn is a tough newspaper reporter on the payroll of The New York Post. His hallmarks are a straw hat, a Norfolk jacket, a perennial cigar, and a terrier by the name of "Prince."

The Yellow Moth
The Red Speck
Dust
The Fire Bugs
The Great White Moth

THE ROMANCE OF THE SECRET SERVICE FUND (1900)

This series features Newton Moore, the top agent at The Secret Service Fund.

By Woman's Wit
The Mazaroff Rifle
In The Express
The Almedi Concession
The Other Side Of The Chess Board
Three Of Them

THE DOOM OF LONDON

This sci-fi series of six stories describes a variety of catastrophes which ravage London.

The Four White Days
The Four Days' Night
The Dust Of Death
A Bubble Burst
The Invisible Force
The River Of Death

THE SAGE OF TYBURN (1905-1906)

Each of these stories was preceded by the header The Sage Of Tyburn.

No. 1 - The Chronicle Of The Yellow Girl
No. 2 - The Chronicle Of The Blue-Eyed Syndicate
No. 3 - The Chronicle Of The Inconsequent Princess
No. 4 - The Chronicle Of The Elderly Adonis
No. 5 - The Chronicle Of The Libelled Velasquez

THE DRAGON-FLY (1909)

Six stories about an impecunious but brilliant amateur criminologist, entomologist and ornithologist by the name of Horace Daimler. Each of the stories was preceded by the header The Dragon-Fly.

No. 1 - How Horace Daimler Got His Name
No. 2 - The Three Red Rats
No. 3 - [title unknown]
No. 4 - [title unknown]
No. 5 - A [illegible] Crime
No. 6 - The Mirror Over The Fireplace

REAL DRAMA (1909)

A series of stories published under the subtitle "Being Some Leaves From The Notebook Of A Late Theatrical Agent."

His Second Self
An Extra Turn
"Not In The Bill"
The Plagiarist
The Man In Possession
A Pair Of Handcuffs

THE TELEPHONE STAR (1912)

A series of stories about Keith Marrit, a star journalist working for a fictitious newspaper called The Telephone.

No. 1 - The Case Of El Hamid, The Seer
No. 2 - The Case Of The Genuine Counterfeit
No. 3 - The Case Of The Yellow Car
No. 4 - The Case Of Lord Wintercotte
No. 5 - The Case Of The Rusty Nail
No. 6 - The Case Of The One-Eyed Chauffeur

GIPSY TALES (1903-1916)

A series of stories describing the adventures of a wily British navvy with Romany roots, who is known only as "Gipsy." In his fantasies Gipsy portrays himself as a playwright, and tries to stage-manage the dramatis personae and the situations that feature in the stories.

A Matter Of Kindness
A Liberal Education
A Stranger In Bohemia
Drops Of Water
The Unpremeditated Curtain
Mere Details
Out Of Season

THE DIARY OF A LONELY SOUL (1915)

The Diary Of A Lonely Soul - Story 1 [title unknown]
The Diary Of A Lonely Soul - Story 2 [title unknown]
The Diary Of A Lonely Soul - Story 3 [title unknown]
The Diary Of A Lonely Soul - Story 4 [title unknown]
The Diary Of A Lonely Soul - Story 5 [title unknown]

AN A-Z OF OTHER SHORT FICTION

According To The Statute
The Ace Of Hearts
Adventure (aka A Trick of Fate)
After Reynolds
Alias "James Jones"
An Ally

And This Is Fame
Anonymous
The Apple-Green Plate
Applied Mechanics
The Arms Of Chance
Art Critics
At Short Notice
Aunt Mary
Autumn Manoeuvres
The Azoff Diamonds
A Bad Cold
The Balance Of Nature
The Barrister At Bay
Below Zero
The Better Way
Big Fish
The Big Thing
Billy's Xmas
A Bit Of Egypt
The Black Admiral
The Black Cat
The Black Narcissus
The Black Prince
Blind
Blind Chance
The Blindworm
A Block Of Marble
A Bootless Errand
Brayton's Secret
The Broken Lute
A Broken Sceptre
The Broken Trail
The Buff Gauntlet
Burglar Bill's Pupil
By Grace Of His Majesty
By Wireless
A Call On The Phone
A Captious Critic
The Case For The Prisoner
The Charlatan
A Christmas Bride
A Christmas Deputy
Christmas Cards
The Christmas Carol
A Christmas in Peril
A Christmas Star
The Clock Struck Twelve
The Colonel's Christmas Pudding

Compounding A Felony
The Convict
Coralie And The Pearls
A Corner In Elephants
The Courage Of Despair
Crossed Swords
The Dancing Shadow
The Daughters Of The Moon
A Daughter Of Nature
The Dawnstar
A Deal In Diamonds
Denny
A Derelict In Clover
The Desert Ship
A Dog's Life
The Doll's House
The Dormer Window
A Dose Of Quinine
The Doubting D, or, A Cranky Cryptogram
A Draught Of Life
Early Closing Day
An Eastern Princess
The Eavesdropper
The Ebbing Tide
The Egg Of The Little Auk
The Emsdam Dispatches
The Empty House
An Error Of Judgment
The Evidence For The Prisoner
Excess Profits
An Eye For An Eye
The Eye Of The Camera
The First Stone
The Foil
Forget-Me-Not
For Love's Sake
For Once In A Way
For Value Received
A Foster-Father
Found!
The Fourth Man
Free Labour
A Friendly Call
From Information Received
Full Fathoms Deep
Gabrielle
A Gamble In Love
A Game Of Draughts

A Garden Of Pearls
Gentlemen Of The Jury
The Gates Of Ramshi
The Grey Bat
The Grey Raider
The Guiding Star
The Half-Crown Princess
The Hand Invisible
Hardy's Big Coup
The Heart Of The Anarchist
Heavy Metal
The Heels Of The Dawn
Her Christmas Dawn
His Christmas Gift
His Majesty's Mails
A Hole In The Net
The Hospitallers
Ice In June: A Playwright's Story
Icky Of Oluk Lake
Imperial Preference
In Black And White
In Rosemary Lane
In The Dark
In The Fog
In The Pit
Introducing Mr. Pentsymon
The Joinville Tunnel
Judgment Reserved
Karma
Kindergarten
The Kingmaker's Token
Lady Mary's Bulldog
The Language Of Flowers
The Last Drive
The Law Of The Jungle: A Tale Of Mean Streets
The Leather-Pushin' Private
The Left Hand
The Lesson The Ants Taught
The Livery Of Death
The Lonely Furrow
The Long Arm Of Bronze
Love In Aether
The Luck Of The Game
Made In England
The Man Himself
The Man Who Got Through
The Man Who Rang The Bell
The Man With The Eyeglass

A Masked Battery
The Master's Voice
A Matter Of Habit
'Merica
A Message from the Flood
The Midnight Call
The Missing Blade
The Missing Note
The Mistletoe Bough
Moray The Traitor
More Than Coronets
The Morning Glory
Music Hath Charms
A Musical Treat
The Mystery Of Room Five
Natural Selection
Nerves
The Night Express: The Story Of A Bank Robbery
The Northern Light
Not On The Records
An Object Lesson
The Odds On Zero
One Day With A Working Ant
One Foggy Night
One Of The Old Guard
On Peace Night
The Onus Of The Charge
The Orpheusia
Ostentation
The Other Man's Story
The Pardon
A Parrot Cry
The Path Of Progress
The Pawn And The Rook
Pearls Of Price
Photo By Lesterre
Pictures In The Snow (a Christmas story)
A Place In The Sun
The Platinum Chain
A Popular Novelist
Poste Restante
A Prize Crop
Proof Positive
The Purple Terror
A Queen In Hiding
A Question Of Money
Rachel's Seventh Year
Rawhide Science

The Real Dramatic Touch
A Record Round
Red Petals
Rob Peter—Pay Paul
A Rope Of Snow
Rose Of The Desert
A Royal Bag
The Royal Train
The Salmon Poachers
Santa Anna
A Satisfactory Reference
Saviour From The North
The Second Chapter
Second In The Field
The Shebeeners
A Single Hair
Sir Jeremiah's Big Shoot
Sister Louise
The Sixteenth Chapter
A Sleeping Partner
Sleeping Partner
A Sound In The Night
"Special" To The Telephone
A Stolen Interview
The Straight Game
The Stranger Within The Gate
Sub Rosa
The Substitute
The Superman
The Supreme Test
The Sword Of Justice
A Table Tragedy
The Thirty-Seventh Month
This Little World
A Thrilling Exit
The Throat Of The Wolf
The Ticket
To Be Let Furnished
Treasures Three
The Two Bon-Bons
Two Of Them
The Unbelieving Eye
Unbidden Guests
The Unexpected
An Unrecorded Crime
The Vital Spark
The Vital Spot
War Ribbons

The Waterwitch
The Western Way
When The Moon Set
The White Geranium
The White Spot
White Wings (1922)
The Wings Of Chance (1922)
The Witness (1920)
The World Next Door (1916)